FRIENDSHIP
and
DEVOTION,
or
THREE
MONTHS
in
LOUISIANA

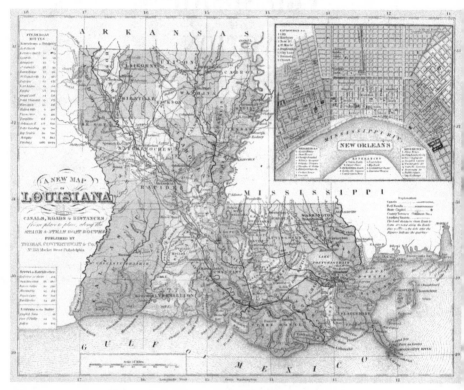

Figure 1. *A New Map of Louisiana, with Its Canals, Roads & Distances from Place to Place, Along the Stage & Steam Boat Routes* (Philadelphia: Thomas Cowperthwait & Co., 1850).

FRIENDSHIP
and
DEVOTION,
or
THREE MONTHS
in
LOUISIANA

CAMILLE LEBRUN

Translated with introduction and annotation by
E. Joe Johnson and Robin Anita White

University Press of Mississippi / Jackson

BANNER BOOKS SERIES

The University Press of Mississippi is the scholarly publishing agency of
the Mississippi Institutions of Higher Learning: Alcorn State University,
Delta State University, Jackson State University, Mississippi State University,
Mississippi University for Women, Mississippi Valley State University,
University of Mississippi, and University of Southern Mississippi.

www.upress.state.ms.us

The University Press of Mississippi is a member
of the Association of University Presses.

Originally published in 1845 by Pornin as
Amitié et dévouement, ou Trois mois à la Louisiane

First printing 2021
∞

Library of Congress Cataloging-in-Publication Data

Names: Lebrun, Camille, 1805–1886, author. | Johnson, E. Joe (Edward Joe),
translator. | White, Robin Anita, translator.
Title: Friendship and devotion, or Three months in Louisiana / Camille
Lebrun ; translated with an introduction and annotation by E. Joe
Johnson and Robin Anita White.
Other titles: Amitié et dévouement, ou trois mois à la Louisiane.
English | Three months in Louisiana
Description: Jackson : University Press of Mississippi, 2021. | Series:
Banner books series | "Originally published in 1845 by Pornin as Amitié
et dévouement, ou Trois mois à la Louisiane"—Title page verso. |
Includes bibliographical references. | Summary: "After a short preface
meant to educate young readers about the geography, culture, and history
of the southern reaches of the Louisiana Purchase, the novel tells the
tale of two teenaged, orphaned Americans, Hortense Melvil and Valentine
Arnold. The two young women, who characterize one another as "sisters,"
have spent the majority of their lives in a Parisian boarding school and
return to Louisiana to begin their adult lives. Almost immediately upon
arrival in New Orleans, their close friendship faces existential
threats: grave illness in the form of yellow fever, the prospect of
marriage separating the two, and powerful discrimination in the form of
racial prejudice and segregation"— Provided by publisher.
Identifiers: LCCN 2021021066 (print) | LCCN 2021021067 (ebook) | ISBN
9781496836380 (hardback) | ISBN 9781496836397 (trade paperback) | ISBN
9781496836403 (epub) | ISBN 9781496836410 (epub) | ISBN 9781496836427
(pdf) | ISBN 9781496836434 (pdf)
Subjects: LCGFT: Novels.
Classification: LCC PQ2330.L785 A4513 2021 (print) | LCC PQ2330.L785
(ebook) | DDC 843/.7—dc23
LC record available at https://lccn.loc.gov/2021021066
LC ebook record available at https://lccn.loc.gov/2021021067

British Library Cataloging-in-Publication Data available

Aux écrivaines d'antan

CONTENTS

· ·

ACKNOWLEDGMENTS

We have been very fortunate to enjoy the generous assistance of community groups, colleagues, friends, and loved ones at various stages in this effort, whether in reading proposal drafts, tracking down information for endnotes, or poring over drafts of the translation. These stalwarts include John Fitzpatrick, Joe White, James Fries, Adam Tate, David Gilbert, Barbara Goodman, Gwen and Tom Barnett, LaJuan Simpson-Wilkey, Ruth Caillouet and Barbara Holland, Shayla Mitchell, Chad Youngblood, Eduardo Febles, Daphne McConnell, Barbara Blatchley, Susan Rashid Horn, Brian Ferguson-Avery, Becky Godlasky, Scott Fish, Bill Edmiston, Kay Doig, Martha Bowden, and Greg Brown. For their institutional support in this venture, we would also like to thank Clayton State University and Nicholls State University. Lastly, we would like to thank the anonymous reviewers of our manuscript for their suggestions in improving the introduction to this volume. At the University Press of Mississippi, we would like to thank Katie Keene, Mary Heath, Todd Lape, and the careful attention of Lynn Whittaker.

While we undertook this translation in order to make a lesser-known French novel accessible to English readers, we do wish to acknowledge that modern-day Louisiana is and, we hope, will remain a home to Francophone peoples. French is not a foreign language in Louisiana, where a linguistic minority still read, write, and speak the language. Not only is Louisiana's Centenary College home to *La Bibliothèque Tintamarre*—the only French-language publishing house in the United States—but there has been more than three hundred years of literature written in French by authors calling the area their home.

INTRODUCTION TO
THIS TRANSLATION

Although sometimes publishing under the initials of "P.G." and the pseudonyms of "Laure Dartigue" and "Fabien de Saint-Léger" and once under her actual name, "Mme Camille Lebrun" was the preferred *nom de plume* of Pauline Guyot (1805–1886), a choice that we will respect in this volume. After her mother's financial ruin, this unmarried Parisian supported her mother and herself first by giving piano and voice lessons, next by teaching French, English, and Italian, and finally through prolific writing.[1] Lebrun penned many book-length volumes. Some of them ran to multiple editions and appeared in publication until the end of the nineteenth century. Her works include novels, a travelogue, translations, and collections of tales. She also published a wide variety of articles and stories in French magazines and even began her own educational magazine in 1849, titled *Miroir de la France: Revue pour tous* (*A Mirror of France: A Magazine for All*).[2]

Representative of Virginia Woolf's lament about the invisibility of women writers in literary history and comparable to other successful, prolific peers such as Catherine Woillez (1781–1859) and Julie Delafaye-Bréhier (1785–1850), Lebrun's works remain largely obscure to modern literary critics in the United States and France, a circumstance this translation aspires to help rectify.[3] This neglect arises, in part, from the fact that many of Lebrun's texts have long been out of print, but more especially that they were not of the sort to have gained literary prestige in their era. Many of Lebrun's works were openly educational in nature, generally marketed to adolescent

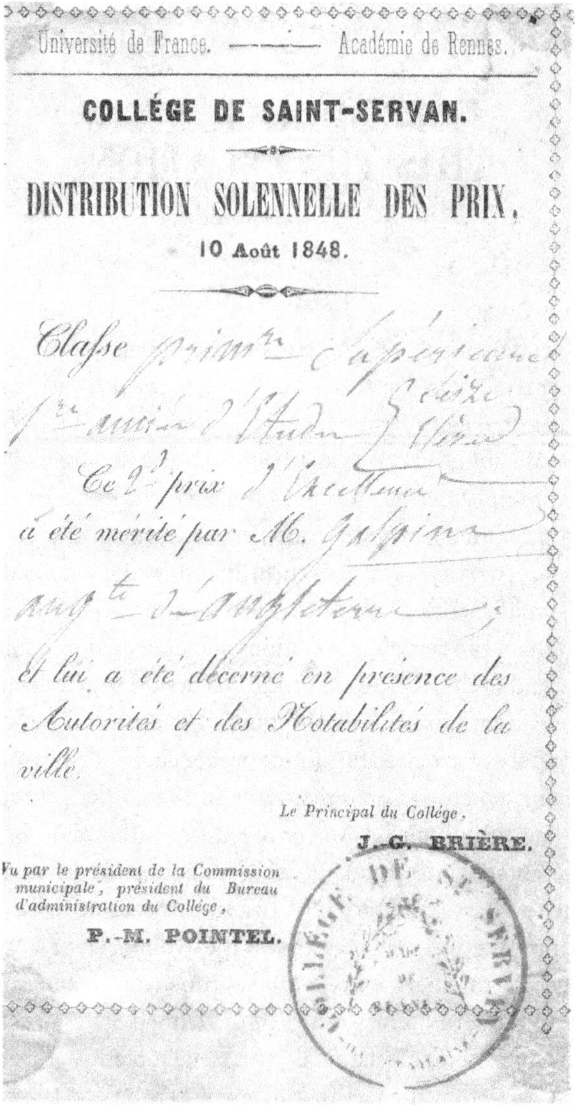

Université de France. — Académie de Rennes.

COLLÉGE DE SAINT-SERVAN.

DISTRIBUTION SOLENNELLE DES PRIX,

10 Août 1848.

Classe primaire supérieure
1re année d'Étude
Ce 2d prix d'Excellence
a été mérité par M. Galpine
[illegible] d'Angleterre;
et lui a été décerné en présence des Autorités et des Notabilités de la ville.

Le Principal du Collège,
J.-G. BRIÈRE.

Vu par le président de la Commission municipale, président du Bureau d'administration du Collège,
P.-M. POINTEL.

Figure 2. In the bookplate on the left, from an 1846 edition of Lebrun's novel, young Monsieur Galpine, a student at the Collège de Saint-Servan (a secondary school in Brittany), received this book as Second Prize for Excellence on August 10, 1848, in the presence of municipal authorities and notables. On the right, on September 10, 1852, Mademoiselle Hambidge, a student at Mademoiselle Collier's boarding school in Saint-Pierre-lès-Calais (now a neighborhood of the city of Calais), earned distinction for her verb conjugations, application, math, and English (reading and grammar) and was awarded a copy of the 1850 edition of the novel.

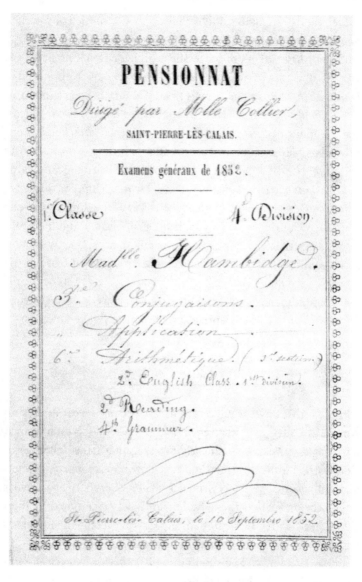

PENSIONNAT

Dirigé par Mlle Collier,

SAINT-PIERRE-LÈS-CALAIS.

Examens généraux de 1852.

1. Classe   4. Division

Mad.lle Hambidge.

3.e Conjugaisons.
  „ Application.
6.e Arithmétique. (1.e section.)
    2.e English Class. 1.re division.
    2.d Reading.
    4th Grammar.

St.-Pierre-lès-Calais, le 10 Septembre 1852.

readers, and brought to print by French presses specializing in such publications, such as Pornin, Mame, Mégard, and Amyot.

One of Lebrun's more successful works for teenaged audiences was the illustrated novel *Amitié et dévouement, ou Trois mois à la Louisiane* or, as this translation is titled, *Friendship and Devotion, or Three Months in Louisiana.* Pornin published the first two of at least eight editions of the novel, with the remaining, corrected editions printed by Mame between 1845 and 1861. At least as early as the 1857 edition, either the publishers or the author shortened the novel's title to *Trois mois à la Louisiane.*[4] Like similar works of the era, this novel appears in a series vetted by representatives of the Roman Catholic Church, with printed testaments from local bishops and their representatives as to the work's rectitude and quality; this translation includes those ecclesiastical *bona fides.*[5] As we can also see in the images of two bookplates, such books would serve as gifts or awards for young students; teachers and school officials deemed Lebrun's novel worthy to serve as a prize at their honors day ceremonies.

An Old Book for Our Times

Although this novel would seem to have been of clear interest to American readers of yore, given both its setting and success in France, it was never translated into English for publication in the United States. Contrast that with other travel and adventure novels containing American settings and characters written by male authors born two decades after Lebrun, such as those by Lucien Biart (1826–1897) or Jules Verne (1828–1905). While both of those writers condemned slavery and prejudice without fundamentally challenging white supremacy, their works doing so appeared in English *after* the American Civil War.[6] *Amitié et dévouement*'s printings, however, occurred exactly during the era of mounting hostility in the United States between slaveholders and abolitionists, which culminated in what the French would style as the "War of Secession." The lack of a contemporary

English translation may have been due to timing, but only in part. It also is because the novel would have been controversial.

In the antebellum South, Lebrun's novel would have raised hackles because it is overtly critical of racial prejudice, linking that attitude to a sin of pride, whereas many churches invested in maintaining the existing social order. Various points in Lebrun's novel question the validity of white supremacy, envision the abolition of slavery, and sympathize with enslaved runaways. The book openly establishes the worthiness of multiracial, Black, and indigenous peoples. The plantation-owning Francis Melvil, a sympathetic character, publicly espouses an orderly emancipation of enslaved persons, although he never actually frees his own in the novel. When Melvil expresses his condemnation of slavery and promotes wage earning for those to be freed, a similarly positioned relative launches into a clichéd and patently self-interested defense of slavery voiced by many enslavers of the era. The cousin predicts the ruin of France's former colony in the event of emancipation, but we infer that he simply means the ruin of a Louisiana that puts him atop the social order.

The novel also addresses gross abuses enabled by this system of white supremacy. It evokes the notorious example of Marie Delphine (née Macarty) LaLaurie or "Madame LaLaurie" (c. 1780–1849), a contemporaneous New Orleans socialite who tortured and allegedly murdered her enslaved persons. Under threat of mob justice, she fled to Paris, yet ultimately suffered no other consequence than the inconvenience of exile from her French Quarter mansion on Royal Street in New Orleans. The novel parallels this historical figure with a similarly harsh woman who owns a plantation adjacent to Melvil's. In the novel's penultimate chapter, those whom she has enslaved and abused, set fire to her home and crops, causing the woman's financial ruin and nearly killing her. This event, which the novel's narrative voice does not condemn, would have undoubtedly angered and frightened slaveholders throughout the American South, fearful as they were of figures like Denmark Vesey and Nat Turner, or, for people in the French Caribbean, of events like the successful rebellion in Haiti. Yet other elements would likely have disturbed many American readers of the time, whether north or south of the Mason–Dixon Line. They include the novel's criticism of pew segregation in churches, its sympathetic depiction of mixed-race characters, and a "happily ever after" ending of miscegenation wherein Francis Melvil rejects American prejudice and society by marrying his sister's friend, shortly before the trio's definitive departure from America to France.

While Lebrun is critical of racial prejudice and does give voice to abolitionist sentiments in this story, we should keep in mind what she does *not* do. Like many other French writers before and after her, Lebrun is guilty of what Christopher L. Miller characterizes as "eliding the Atlantic slave trade [and] French participation in that trade" (75), the latter of which resulted in the transportation of nearly one and a half million enslaved Africans to the French Atlantic of Haiti, Guadeloupe, Martinique, and Louisiana.[7] In Lebrun's brief, prefatory history of France's colonies in North America, she acknowledges neither the French enslavement of Native Americans in the areas near Mobile and New Orleans nor the introduction of enslaved Africans to the area. Rather, she connects the presence of people of African descent to the continued existence of slavery in the southern United States. American readers must remain aware, however, that slavery still existed in French colonies at the time of this novel's first publication. Although slavery had been abolished in France's colonies during the Revolution in 1794—*after* Haitian revolutionaries had emancipated themselves—Napoleon reinstated it in the remaining French colonies in 1802. France continued to transport enslaved Africans long after the British and Americans had stopped doing so in 1807 and 1808, respectively. The second (and final) abolition of slavery in French colonies did not occur until 1848, three years after the publication of this short novel.[8]

The elements that would have made the novel controversial in the United States in 1845 are exactly what make it of interest for twenty-first-century readers grappling with the legacies of slavery and systemic racism in our society in which the assertion that "Black Lives

Matter" is, for some, fraught with contention. In the period leading up to and during the Civil War, various texts in English appeared relating to women of color in Louisiana and their subjugation. The novel *The Quadroon; a Lover's Adventure in Louisiana* (1856) by Captain Mayne Read, an Irish American author, was adapted by Irish playwright Dion Boucicault who named the play *The Octoroon* (1859), which ran in New York to great success. *The Octoroon: or, The Lily of Louisiana* (1861–1862) by British author Mary Elizabeth Braddon appeared as an antislavery work of fiction about America. *Louisa Picquet, the Octoroon: or Inside Views of Southern Domestic Life* (1861) by Picquet is an American narrative about a woman of African heritage who was born into slavery, as the daughter of a white man who was also her mother's master. In these later works written in English, the focus is on Louisianan women of color who were concubines due to slavery. Lebrun, however, fictionalizes young and free women who are as pious as they are well educated. Decidedly, this novel is not a lurid recounting of tales of sexual slavery; instead, it fleshes out whether an interracial friendship can flourish in Louisiana in the nineteenth century. Critic Shannon Dawdy posits that the nineteenth and twentieth centuries' Anglo–American Louisianans obsessed over questions of race (108). The above English titles reflect an imaginary racial arithmetic (quadroons and octoroons being a quarter or an eighth Black), and these equations could not be further from Lebrun's title focusing on devoted friends spending time together in Louisiana. The adolescent protagonists, who share youth, gender, background as orphans, language, and education, transcend Anglo–American distinctions of race or caste.

Lebrun does not seek to portray the quotidian brutality of American plantation slavery. Nor does she exaggerate the institution's almost unimaginable cruelty and trickery. As this novel was being written in France, Solomon Northup, a New Yorker who had lived his life as a free African American until 1841, was suffering a cruel fate on a plantation in Louisiana's Avoyelles Parish. Kidnapped by slave traders in Washington, DC, Northup lived in bondage in Louisiana from 1841 to 1853. His *Twelve Years a Slave* (1853), adapted as a feature-length film in 2013, is a rare first-person written account of his enslavement. As it happens, the Red River region located in Avoyelles Parish is precisely where Lebrun's fictive plantation La Cyprière is located. *Friendship and Devotion* is certainly a lighter and more romantic tale than Northup's and has a happy end, but the book nonetheless shows readers the anxiety and trepidation that a free woman of color suffers as she is shunned by white plantation society in Louisiana.

Much more can be said, beyond the scope of this introduction, about the slaveholding culture of New Orleans, the sugarcane and plantation culture in Louisiana, and the many contradictions concerning racial matters, as traveling and immigrating Europeans encountered and adapted to life in the one-time French colony. We encourage reading of related texts such as George Washington Cable's novels and stories about Creole life and translations of the works of the Louisianan French writers Alfred Mercier and Sidonie de La Houssaye. Useful scholarly works include Ned Sublette's *The World That Made New Orleans: From Spanish Silver to Congo Square* (2008), Dianne Guenin-Lelle's *The Story of French New Orleans: History of a Creole City* (2016), and Donna McGee Onebane's *The House That Sugarcane Built: The Louisiana Burguières* (2017).

A Blending of Genres

Like some of Lebrun's other works, *Friendship and Devotion* embodies three genres at once: a travelogue, a moralizing novel, and a friendship tale. The novel is, nevertheless, a travelogue only of sorts. There is no indication Lebrun ever traveled to Louisiana; she seems to have derived her knowledge of the area through research into other accounts.[9] Given those facts, one must sometimes make allowances as to the accuracy of her claims about the state, but she clearly did make an effort to give a faithful rendering. As we can perceive from the subtitle of Lebrun's 1848 account *Le Dauphiné* (a one-time province in southeastern France that she visited in the company of friends), travelogues of the era were educational. They usually contained history, picturesque descriptions, accounts of antiquities, moral scenes, famous people, natural curiosities, castles and ruins, anecdotes, monuments, public buildings, and local customs.[10] Those features are exactly the sorts of things *Friendship and Devotion* provides.

The novel begins with a brief history and geography of France's former possessions in this portion of North America, especially the southern reaches of the Louisiana Purchase. In various chapters, the narrator describes the area's flora and fauna of particular interest to Europeans and includes some of the dietary particularities of Louisiana. The novel also has various characters giving encyclopedic, even pedantic, explanations in fantastically long, detailed sentences in the original French. As a travelogue would do, this volume depicts the customs and mores of the region's inhabitants as well. According to the novel's narrator, one of the most striking things about the area is its unusual mixture of races and customs, which she figures as being both multinational and triracial, notwithstanding the occasional appearance of Native Americans:

> The character of its inhabitants is a strange combination of the frivolity of the French, of the nonchalance of Creoles, of the mercantile spirit of Anglo-Americans, and the vainglory of the Spanish hidalgo. Moreover, as slavery hasn't been abolished in the southern states of the American Union, a great number of blacks can be found there and, consequently, of mulattos: the two groups detest one another and both find themselves to be the object of scorn from whites. (4)

Friendship and Devotion, as we might expect from the series in which it first appeared, and typical of almost all such books meant for the young of the era, also has a strong moralistic bent. To its credit, it does so without the oft-tiresome insistence on piety and prayer present in works by contemporary writers such as Mme Woillez.[11] While Lebrun does have her protagonists attend Mass in the novel's opening chapters in order to thank the deity for their safe passage across the Atlantic, we quickly find the church to be a setting of racial segregation, which the narrative condemns. Later, once the protagonists are at the Melvil plantation, they continue to attend Mass at their local parish, but go there on palanquins borne by enslaved persons. Churchgoing in antebellum Louisianan society, therefore, is fully enmeshed in the racial dynamics of the era.

A test of morality is at the center of the story, too. The protagonist, Valentine, already described as having a character marked by a "blend of sensitivity and vanity" (7), all too quickly begins to adopt American prejudices with regard to white supremacy. The sin of pride, which the novel characterizes as "the most unforgiving of all faults" (12), holds other dangers, as the narrator notes: "Often, one of the saddest consequences of despotism—that is to say, authority exerted without control—is to lead the most generous hearts and minds so far astray they gradually come to regard those in submission to them as beings of too inferior an order in creation for them to have to be concerned about their lot" (30). Like Valentine, other Europeans arriving in Louisiana also start to adopt or, at least, give way to local customs and mores. For example, the Deschamps, the French family that chaperones the two friends to the New World, fail to protect Valentine from the racial animus of other guests during a party that they host. Such is also the case with the prideful Doctor Henríquez, who asserts in a conversation with Hortense: "As a foreigner—I was born in Spain, as you know—I must, more than another perhaps, respect that which you call prejudice" (77).[12] The irony of Valentine's situation, as we shall see, is that she, too, becomes a victim of racial prejudice, leading her to wonder at one point: "Oh, my God! Have I been humiliated enough?" (71).

Children's Friendship Tales

The consequences of this victimization are at the heart of *Friendship and Devotion*'s tale of the exemplary friendship of Hortense Melvil and Valentine Arnold. Friendship was a subject upon which Lebrun wrote specifically at least three times: in her first publication containing two novellas, the 1841 *Le bracelet, ou l'étourdie corrigée; suivi de Théodore et Constantin, ou les amis de collège* [The Bracelet, or the Scatterbrained Girl Corrected; followed by Theodore and Constantin, or the Schoolboy Friends]; her first novel, the 1843 *Une amitié de femme, roman de mœurs* [A Woman's Friendship, a Moral Novel]; and the 1845 *Friendship and Devotion*. The long, misogynistic tradition of such depictions prior to the latter part of the eighteenth century was that "true" friendship was not possible between women due to temperament, competition in love, the demands of maternity and marriage, and so on.[13] Lebrun herself used the stereotypically false friendship of women as a plot motivator in *Une amitié de femme*. In it, the female protagonist, Lucile, is horrified to learn she is the victim of the evil plots of her erstwhile best female friend, opining: "It's awful, [. . .] it's awful, isn't it, seeing oneself the victim of such despicable machinations? That's where this friendship of women has led me!" (309).[14] Interestingly, Lebrun effects a neat gender reversal in her Louisiana novel, in which the failed friendship will prove to be that of two men.

Unlike her earlier novel, *Friendship and Devotion* is part of a pattern of new articulations in French literature concerning age-old themes of idealized friendship. This evolution occurs along with the great expansion of literacy and schooling in France in the post-revolutionary years and with the explosive growth in publication of books meant for younger readers. Venerable friendship themes (an exemplary pair having similar moral character, the sharing of resources and confidences) are combined with new tropes that are more readily understood by younger readers.[15] In these newer kinds of stories in which friendships can form across social class lines, lifelong friendships often start in an educational setting. Heroic deeds that begin or give proof of a devoted relationship are of a more down-to-earth nature, like nursing a friend through illness, rescuing a friend from abuse, or facing a challenge together. Ultimately, a successful friendship has a transformative effect on the surrounding community or creates a new community. *Friendship and Devotion* has almost all of these elements.

Hortense and Valentine first met as children in a Parisian boarding school. After they return to Louisiana, one must nurse the other during an epidemic, despite the fear of fatal contagion. The crisis occurs after Valentine learns of her mixed-race parentage, when her sense of lost social standing prompts a rash decision that threatens her friendship with Hortense. Hortense, too, must face her own tests of devotion to the friendship. Repeatedly, throughout the novel, her white peers physically separate from her friend: at church, in conversations, in walks, and at balls. As do so many other European immigrants in the novel, will she, readers wonder, succumb to the prevailing racial prejudices of a segregated America? Will she seek to maintain her social standing with an advantageous marriage, fall prey to the laziness of her temperament, or remain true to her friendship? In the end, the power of the two young women's friendship ultimately hints at a possible response to the area's dynamics of racial policing. From initial instances of free people of color calling attention to the color lines in New Orleans and expressing astonishment that the two friends might call one another sister, we come to observe instances in which Black characters actively resist white supremacy by aiding Valentine when the stakes are high. And what of Robert and Hortense Melvil? How will their obligations to Valentine transform them? And what of Valentine? What will her transformation be? What will she do for the good people of New Orleans of all colors? Read on, dear readers, to find out . . .

A Few Words about This Translation and Language Use

For the vast majority of this novel, Lebrun uses a standard French for all characters who are educated, while mentioning the occasional use of English by various characters. Although there are very modest efforts at representing a Louisiana Creole dialect as spoken by Native Americans and others, she makes no major attempt to represent the local color à la the French-educated, Louisianan author Alfred Mercier (1816–1894) in his 1881 *L'Habitation Saint-Ybars* or by Sidonie de La Houssaye (1820–1894) in her posthumous tetralogy, *Les Quarteronnes de la Nouvelle Orléans* (both works also involve miscegenation). Our translation, therefore, largely uses standard American English, rather than a Creole-inflected English in the style of George Washington Cable, and makes a mindful attempt to represent the effect that Lebrun seeks in a similar English.

Given the era and the novel's subject matter, readers should also expect that, in matters concerning race, Lebrun's language is fraught. Whereas white supremacy in the rest of the United States was propped upon a strictly biracial categorization that assumed the displacement or elimination of Native Americans, Lebrun is attempting to depict accurately the triracial culture of Louisiana at the time, which categorized people as Black, mixed race, or white (and she acknowledges a similar displacement of Native Americans). Her efforts, therefore, lead her to use the word *mulâtre* [mulatto] to describe the second of the three groups, a potentially offensive word in English in our times, which this translation repeats. Furthermore, she uses the words *Peaux-Rouges* and *sauvages* to describe Native Americans, expressions that are pejorative in both modern French and English. Because we feel it is important to reveal Lebrun's own instances of cultural insensitivity, we have translated that expression into the similarly offensive "redskins." Whenever it is clear that *nègre* or *noir* refers specifically to enslaved people, we have used the word "slave," while generally using the word "black" for Black people who are free—retaining the lowercase "b" as consistent with nineteenth-century usage. We acknowledge that "enslaved person" (as used in this introduction) is the currently preferred term rather than "slave," but that expression would be anachronistic in this nineteenth-century novel.

This translation is based on the original 1845 Pornin edition of the novel, but also includes corrections made for the Mame editions that began with the novel's third printing. This translation relies heavily on three dictionaries, which are included in the references: the two-volume, 1875 bilingual dictionary by E. Thunot and C. E. Clifton, *Nouveau dictionnaire anglais-français et français-anglais abrégé de Boyer* (Paris: Baudry, 1875), the *Glossary of Mississippi Valley French, 1673–1850* by John Francis McDermott (London: Forgotten Books, 2017), and the Albert Valdman and Kevin J. Rottet-edited *Dictionary of Louisiana French: As Spoken in Cajun, Creole, and American Indian Communities* (Jackson: University Press of Mississippi, 2010). We were delighted to confirm that Camille Lebrun employs appropriate Louisiana words such as *piastre* for "dollar" or *congo* for "water moccasin." Unless otherwise indicated, all translations of French text in the endnotes are our own.

Selected Chronological List of Major Works by Camille Lebrun

Le bracelet, ou l'étourdie corrigée; suivi de Théodore et Constantin, ou les amis de collège. Paris: Pesron, 1841.

Une amitié de femme, roman de mœurs. Paris: Amyot, 1843.

Histoire d'un mobilier, scène de mœurs. Paris: Amyot, 1843.

Julien Morel, ou l'aîné de la famille. Tours: Pornin, 1844.

Petites histoires vraies racontées aux enfants. Paris: Marcilly, 1844.

Le royaume des nains. Paris: Marcilly, 1845.

Les vacances à Fontainebleau. Tours: Pornin, 1845.

Amitié et dévouement, ou Trois mois à la Louisiane. Tours: Pornin, 1845.

Madeleine, ou la jeune montagnarde. Limoges: Barbou, 1846.

La famille Raimond. Paris: Marcilly, 1846.

Entretiens sur les sacrements de baptême et l'eucharistie. Le Mans: Sagnier et Bray, 1847.

L'improvisatore, ou la vie en Italie. Traduit du danois. By Hans Christian Andersen. Paris: Amyot, 1847.

Le Dauphiné. Histoire, descriptions pittoresques, antiquités, scènes de mœurs, personnages célèbres, curiosités naturelles, châteaux et ruines, anecdotes, monuments et édifices publics, coutumes locales. Paris: Amyot, 1848.

Contes moraux. Rouen: Mégard, 1857.

Les récréations. Rouen: Mégard, 1859.

La famille Aubry. Rouen: Mégard, 1863.

La jeune meunière. Tours: Mame, 1867.

Une noble famille. Rouen: Mégard, 1868.

La chasse aux papillons. Rouen: Mégard, 1875.

Les enfants bienfaisants. Rouen: Mégard, 1875.

Histoire d'un caniche blanc. Paris: Librairie Nationale d'Education et de Récréation, n.d.

Selected Travel Accounts, Histories, and Other Works Concerning Louisiana

Allain, Mathé, Barry J. Ancelet, Tamara Lindner, and May Rush Gwin Waggoner. *Anthologie de la littérature louisianaise d'expression française, de 1682 à nos jours.* Lafayette: University of Louisiana at Lafayette Press, 2017.

Andry, Mme Laure. *Histoire de la Louisiane racontée aux enfants louisianais.* Nouvelle-Orléans: Imprimerie Franco-Américaine, 1882.

Barbé-Marbois, François. *Histoire de la Louisiane et de la cession de cette colonie par la France aux Etats-Unis de l'Amérique Septentrionale.* Paris: Firmin Didot, 1829.

Baudry Des Lozières, Louis Narcisse. *Voyage à la Louisiane et sur le continent de l'Amérique septentrionale fait dans les années 1794 à 1798; contenant un tableau historique de la Louisiane, des observations sur son climat, ses riches productions, le caractère et le nom des Sauvages; des remarques importantes sur la navigation; des principes d'administration, de législation et de gouvernement propres à cette Colonie, etc.* Paris: Dentu, 1802.

Boucicault, Dion. *The Octoroon, a Play in Four Acts.* London: The De Witt Publishing House, 1859. https://archive.org/details/octoroonplayinfooobouciala.

Brandon, M. E. *The Octoroon.* New York: George Munro's Sons, [1895?]. https://babel.hathitrust.org/cgi/pt?id=njp.32101035230927&view=1up&seq=2.

Caillot, Marc-Antoine. *A Company Man: The Remarkable French-Atlantic Voyage of a Clerk for the Company of the Indies. (Relation du Voyage de la Louisianne ou Nouvelle France fait par Sr. Caillot en l'Année 1729).* Edited by Erin M. Greenwald. New Orleans: New Orleans Historic Collection, 2013.

Chateaubriand, François-René de. *Atala, ou les amours de deux sauvages dans le désert.* Paris: Migneret & Librairie Dupont, 1801.

Chateaubriand, François-René de. *Les Natchez.* Bruxelles: A. Weissenbruch, 1827.

De La Houssaye, Sidonie. *Les Quarteronnes de la Nouvelle-Orléans.* Shreveport, LA: Éditions Tintamarre, 2006.

Gayarré, Charles. *Histoire de la Louisiane.* 2 vols. Nouvelle-Orléans: Magne & Weiss, 1846.

Guenin-Lelle, Dianne. *The Story of French New Orleans: History of a Creole City.* Jackson: University Press of Mississippi, 2016.

Hennepin, R. P. Louis. *Description de la Louisiane, nouvellement découverte au Sud-Ouest de la Nouvelle France.* Paris: Chez la Veuve Sébastien, 1683.

Herz, Henri. *Mes voyages en Amérique.* Paris: Achille Faure, 1866.

Le Page du Pratz, Antoine Simon. *Histoire de la Louisiane contenant la découverte de ce vaste pays.* 3 vols. Paris: Bure, Delaguette et Lambert, 1758.

Mercier, Alfred. *L'Habitation Saint-Ybars, ou, Maîtres et esclaves en Louisiane.* Shreveport, LA: Éditions Tintamarre, 2003.

Mercier, Alfred. *Saint-Ybars: Masters and Slaves in Creole Louisiana*. Translated by Elizabeth A. Julian. Shreveport, LA: Éditions Tintamarre, 2015.

Northup, Solomon. *Twelve Years a Slave*. Auburn, NY: Derby and Miller, 1853.

Onebane, Donna McGee. *The House That Sugarcane Built: The Louisiana Burguières*. Jackson: University Press of Mississippi, 2017.

Picquet, Louisa, and Hiram Mattison. *Louisa Picquet, the Octoroon: or Inside Views of Southern Domestic Life*. New York, 1861. https://docsouth.unc.edu/neh/picquet/picquet.html.

Reid, Captain Mayne. *The Quadroon: or, A Lover's Adventures in Louisiana*. New York: Robert M. De Witt, 1856. http://www2.latech.edu/~bmagee/louisiana_anthology/texts/reid/reid--quadroon.html.

Robin, César Charles. *Voyages dans l'intérieur de la Louisiane et de la Floride Occidentale, et dans les isles de la Martinique et de Saint-Domingue, pendant les années 1802, 1803, 1804, 1805 et 1806, contenant les nouvelles observations sur l'histoire naturelle, la géographie, les mœurs, l'agriculture, le commerce, l'industrie et les maladies de ces contrées, particulièrement sur la fièvre jaune, et les moyens de la prévenir. En outre, contenant ce qui s'est passé de plus intéressant, relativement à l'établissement des Anglo-Américains à la Louisiane. Suivis de la flore louisianaise*. Paris: F. Buisson, 1807.

Sublette, Ned. *The World That Made New Orleans: From Spanish Silver to Congo Square*. Chicago: Lawrence Hill Books, 2008.

Tocqueville, Alexis de. *De la démocratie en Amérique*. 4 vols. Paris: Pagnerre, 1848.

BIBLIOGRAPHY

Abrams, Eve, and Katy Reckdahl. "Which Came First the Mockingbird or the Musician?" May 30, 2014. https://www.wwno.org/post/which-came-first-mockingbird-or-musician.

Andry, Mme Laure. *Histoire de la Louisiane racontée aux enfants louisianais.* Nouvelle-Orléans: Imprimerie Franco-Américaine, 1882. https://archive.org/details/histoiredelalou00andrgoog/page/n9/mode/2up.

Allain, Mathé, Barry Jean Ancelet, Tamara Lindner, and May Rush Gwin Waggoner. *Anthologie de la littérature louisianaise d'expression française de 1682 à nos jours.* Lafayette: University of Louisiana at Lafayette Press, 2017.

Barbé-Marbois, François. *Histoire de la Louisiane et de la cession de cette colonie par la France aux Etats-Unis de l'Amérique Septentrionale.* Paris: Firmin Didot, 1829.

Baudier, Roger. *The Catholic Church in Louisiana.* New Orleans: A. W. Hyatt, 1939.

Bescherelle, Louis-Nicolas. *Dictionnaire classique et élémentaire de la langue française.* Paris: Têtu et Cie, 1844.

Biart, Lucien. *A travers l'Amérique: Nouvelles et récits.* Paris: A. Hennuyer, n.d. [1876].

Buffon, Georges-Louis Leclerc, and Philippe Guéneau de Montbeillard. *Histoire naturelle des oiseaux.* 9 vols. Paris: De l'Imprimerie royale, 1770–1783.

"The Cabildo: Two Centuries of Louisiana History. Antebellum Louisiana I: Disease, Death, and Mourning." https://www.crt.state.la.us/louisiana-state-museum/online-exhibits/the-cabildo/antebellum-louisiana-disease-death-and-mourning/index. July 24, 2019.

Campanella, Richard. *Bienville's Dilemma: A Historical Geography of New Orleans.* Lafayette: Center for Louisiana Studies, University of Louisiana at Lafayette, 2008.

Campanella, Richard. "Long Before Hurricane Katrina, There Was Sauve's Crevasse, One of the Worst Floods in New Orleans History." June 11, 2014. https://www.nola.com/entertainment_life/home_garden/article_ea927b6b-d1ab-5462-9756-ccb1acdf092e.html.

Carrigan, Jo Ann. "Privilege, Prejudice, and the Strangers' Disease in Nineteenth-Century New Orleans." *Journal of Southern History* 36, no. 4 (Nov. 1970): 568–78.

Carter, Maria. "Is Myrtles Plantation the Most Haunted Home in America?" *Country Living*, October 11, 2017. https://www.countryliving.com/life/a45181/myrtles-plantation-louisiana-haunted/.

Chevallier, Emile. *Les salaires au XIXè siècle*. Paris: Librairie Nouvelle de Droit et de Jurisprudence, 1887. https://gallica.bnf.fr/ark:/12148/bpt6k863346/f5.image.

Cocks, R. S. "A List of the Shrubs of Louisiana." *Journal of the Arnold Arboretum* 3, no. 4 (April 1922): 173–82. http://botanicus.org/item/31753003541742.

Cookery for English Households: By a French Lady. London: Macmillan and Co., 1864.

Diop, David. "'Battre et nourrir': le singe, le 'nègre' et l'esclavage aux XVIIe et XVIIIe siècles." In *Le Singe aux XVIIe et XVIIIe siècles: Figure de l'art, personnage littéraire et curiosité scientifique*, edited by Florence Boulerie and Katalin Bartha-Kovács, 81–90. Paris: Hermann, 2019.

Domínguez, Virginia. *White by Definition: Social Classification in Creole Louisiana*. New Brunswick: Rutgers University Press, 1986.

Favors, Jelani M. *Shelter in a Time of Storm: How Black Colleges Fostered Generations of Leadership and Activism*. Chapel Hill: University of North Carolina Press, 2019.

Félice, Fortunato Bartolomeo de. *Encyclopédie, ou dictionnaire raisonné des connoissances humaines: N—Oehr*. Vol. 30. Yverdon, 1774.

Galloway, Colin C. *First Peoples: A Documentary Survey of American Indian History*. 4th ed. Boston: Bedford/St. Martin's, 2012.

"German Settlers in Louisiana and New Orleans." https://www.hnoc.org/research/german-settlers-louisiana-and-new-orleans. July 24, 2019.

Gore, Laura Locoul. *Memories of the Old Plantation Home & A Creole Family Album*. Vacherie, LA: Zoë Company, 2007.

"Guyot (Mlle Pauline)." In Vol. 4 of *La littérature française contemporaine, 1827–1844: Continuation de la France littéraire*, edited by Charles Louard and Félix Bourquelot, 235–36. Paris: Daguin, 1848.

Hall, Gwendolyn Midlo. *Africans in Colonial Louisiana: The Development of Afro-Creole Culture in the Eighteenth Century*. Baton Rouge: Louisiana State University Press, 1992.

Hémard, Ned. "Up on the *Azotea*." In *New Orleans Nostalgia: Remembering New Orleans History, Culture and Traditions*. 2012. https://www.neworleansbar.org/uploads/files/UpOnTheAzoteaArticle.7-11.pdf.

Herz, Henri. *Mes Voyages en Amérique*. Paris: Achille Faure, 1866.

Hume, Justin. *Extinct Birds*. London: T & AD Poyser, 2012.

Johnson, E. Joe. "Can Women and Men Be Friends? Writings on Friendship in France's *Ancien Régime* and C. B. Fagan's Comedy *L'Amitié rivale de l'amour*." *1650–1850: Ideas, Aesthetics, and Inquiries in the Early Modern Era* 17 (2008): 109–132.

Johnson, E. Joe. *Once There Were Two True Friends: Idealized Male Friendship in French Narrative from the Middle Ages through the Enlightenment*. Birmingham, AL: Summa Publications, 2003.

Kelley, Laura D. "Yellow Fever." In *Encyclopedia of Louisiana*, edited by David Johnson. New Orleans: Louisiana Endowment for the Humanities, 2011. https://64parishes.org.

Koeppel, Dan. *Banana: The Fate of the Fruit That Changed the World*. New York: Plume, 2009.

La Bonte, Donald R., and Tara P. Smith. "Sweet Potato: Louisiana's Most Popular Vegetable." https://www.lsuagcenter.com/portals/communications/publica tions/agmag/archive/2012/spring/sweet-potato-louisianas-most-popular-vege table. September 13, 2019.

La Chesnaye-Desbois, François-Alexandre Aubert de. *Le dictionnaire raisonné et universel des animaux*. Paris: chez Claude-Jean-Baptiste Bauche, 1759. https://books.google.com/books?id=y3YiAQAAMAAJ&pg=PA312&lpg=PA312&dq=Louisiane+reptile+m%C3%A9d%C3%A9cin+contre+les+piq%C3%BBres+de+serpent+18e&source=bl&ots=dAk2Lh9Krl&sig=ACfU3UoDIG2shaky D9AZqClUVjLeZaGJ7A&hl=en&sa=X&ved=2ahUKEwj86-_OoPbiAhUDO qoKHaADDeIQ6AEwBXoECAkQAQ#v=snippet&q=morsure%20Louisiane&f =false.

Larousse, Pierre. "Lebrun (Pauline Guyot, connue sous le pseudonyme de Camille)." In Vol. 10 of *Grand dictionnaire universel du XIXe siècle*, 294. Paris: Larousse & Boyer, 1877. https://books.google.com/books?id=Sx1QLl-PGYIC&dq=LE BRUN+(Pauline+Guyot,+connue+sous+le+pseudonyme+de+Camille)& source=gbs_navlinks_s.

Latham, John. *A General Synopsis of Birds*. 3 vols. London: Printed for Benj. White, 1781–1785. https://www.biodiversitylibrary.org/item/105229#page/7/ mode/1up

Lebrun, Camille [Pauline Guyot]. "Colonies françaises, 2me étude: La Martinique." In *Le Miroir de la France*, 291–307. Paris: Bureau de la Direction du Miroir de la France, 1850.

Lebrun, Camille [Pauline Guyot]. *Une amitié de femme, roman de mœurs*. Paris: Amyot, 1843.

Lebrun, Camille [Pauline Guyot]. *Le Dauphiné. Histoire, descriptions pittoresques, antiquités, scènes de mœurs, personnages célèbres, curiosités naturelles, châteaux et ruines, anecdotes, monuments et édifices publics, coutumes locales*. Paris: Amyot, 1848.

Lebrun, Camille [Pauline Guyot]. *Histoire d'un caniche blanc*. Limoges: Eugène Ardant, n.d.

Lebrun, Camille [Pauline Guyot]. "Le poney de Cardigan." In *Les enfants bienfai-sants*, 51–72. Rouen: Mégard et Cie, 1875.

Lebrun, Camille [Pauline Guyot]. "Le vieux Noir et le jeune Blanc." In *Contes moraux*, 37–106. Rouen: Mégard et Cie, n.d.

"Lebrun (Mme *Camille*)." In Vol. 30 of *Nouvelle biographie générale*, edited by Jean-Chrétien-Ferdinand Hoefer, 170–71. Paris: Firmin-Didot, 1862.

"Lebrun (Pauline Guyot, connue sous le pseudonyme de Camille)." In Vol. 10 of *Grand dictionnaire universel du XIXè siècle*, edited by Pierre Larousse, 294. Paris: Administration du Grand Dictionnaire Universel, 1873.

Le Conte, René. "Les Allemands à la Louisiane au XVIIIe siècle." *Journal de la société des américanistes* 16 (1924): 1–17.

Lelièvre, J. F. *Nouveau jardinier de la Louisiane, contenant les instructions nécessaires aux personnes qui s'occupent du jardinage.* Nouvelle-Orléans: Chez J. F. Lelièvre, Libraire, 1838.

McDermott, John Francis. *A Glossary of Mississippi Valley French, 1673–1850.* London: Forgotten Books, 2017.

Merriam, Alan P., and Fradley H. Garner. "Jazz: The Word," *Ethnomusicology* 12, no. 3 (September 1968): 373–96.

Miller, Christopher L. *The French Atlantic Triangle: Literature and Culture of the Slave Trade.* Durham: Duke University Press, 2008.

"Mississippi River Facts." https://www.nps.gov/miss/riverfacts.htm.

Monaghan, Frank. *French Travellers in the United States, 1765–1932. A Bibliography by Frank Monaghan, Department of History, New York University, with Supplement by Samuel J. Marino, Head Librarian, McNeese State College, La.* New York: Antiquarian Press Ltd., 1961. https://libsysdigi.library.illinois.edu/OCA/Books2012-08/frenchtravellersoomona/frenchtravellersoomona.pdf?fbclid=IwAR0Vm2IkDk-luIpyXo9RLWBucr7fNXqJ_B3z1CjI2c2aoZNKfJgsWN oMMgs.

Monicat, Bénédicte. *Devoirs d'écriture: modèles d'histoires pour filles et littérature féminine au XIXe siècle.* Lyon: Presses Universitaires de Lyon, 2006.

Palmer, Jennifer L. *Intimate Bonds: Family and Slavery in the French Atlantic.* Philadelphia: University of Pennsylvania Press, 2016.

Peabody, Sue. *"There Are No Slaves in France": The Political Culture of Race and Slavery in the Ancien Régime.* New York: Oxford University Press, 1996.

Plyer, Allison, and Lamar Gardere. *The New Orleans Prosperity Index: Tricentennial Edition.* April 11, 2018. https://www.datacenterresearch.org/reports_analysis/prosperity-index/.

Robin, César Charles. *Voyages dans l'intérieur de la Louisiane et de la Floride Occidentale, et dans les isles de la Martinique et de Saint-Domingue, pendant les années 1802, 1803, 1804, 1805 et 1806, contenant les nouvelles observations sur l'histoire naturelle, la géographie, les mœurs, l'agriculture, le commerce, l'industrie et les maladies de ces contrées, particulièrement sur la fièvre jaune, et les moyens de la prévenir. En outre, contenant ce qui s'est passé de plus intéressant, relativement à l'établissement des Anglo-Américains à la Louisiane. Suivis de la flore louisianaise.* 3 vols. Paris: F. Buisson, 1807.

Scharf, J. Thomas. *History of Saint Louis City and Country, from the Earliest Periods to the Present Day.* Philadelphia: L. H. Everts, 1883.

Slawson, Douglas C. M. "Segregated Catholicism: The Origin of Saint Katharine's Parish, New Orleans." *Vincentian Heritage Journal* 17, no. 3 (1996): 141–84.

Spear, Jennifer M. *Race, Sex, and Social Order in Early New Orleans*. Baltimore: Johns Hopkins University Press, 2009.

Stern, Walter C. *Race and Education in New Orleans: Creating the Segregated City, 1764–1960*. Baton Rouge: Louisiana State University Press, 2018.

Tate, Adam L. *Catholics' Lost Cause: South Carolina Catholics and the American South, 1820–1861*. Notre Dame: University of Notre Dame Press, 2018.

Thorpe, T. B. "Sugar and the Sugar Region in Louisiana." *Harper's New Monthly Magazine*, July–November 1853, 746–67.

Thunot, Eugène, and Ebenezer Clifton. *Nouveau dictionnaire anglais-français et français-anglais abrégé de Boyer*. Paris: Baudry, 1875.

Valdman, Albert, and Kevin J. Rottet. *Dictionary of Louisiana French: As Spoken in Cajun, Creole, and American Indian Communities*. Jackson: University Press of Mississippi, 2010.

Vapereau, Gustave. "Lebrun (Pauline Guyot connue sous le nom de *Camille*)." In Vol. 2 of *Dictionnaire universel des contemporains*, 1052. Paris: Hachette, 1861. https://books.google.com/books?id=VW9UAAAAYAAJ&printsec=frontco ver&source=gbs_ge_summary_r&cad=0#v=onepage&q&f=false.

Villiers, Marc de. "Extrait d'un journal de voyage en Louisiane du père Paul du Ru (1700)." *Journal de la Société des Américanistes de Paris* 17 (1925): 119–35.

White, Robin, and Michèle Autheman. "Mais qui donc asteur parle le français en Louisiane." *L'année francophone internationale: Voyages en francophonie* 27 (2019): 109–120.

Wyss, Johann David. *The Swiss Family Robinson*. New York: Sterling Publishing, 2006.

Figure 3. Caption, translated, is "Bless you, my child, for your pious works."
Title page illustration of the 1845 edition of *Amitié et dévoument, ou trois mois à la Louisiane.*

FRIENDSHIP
and
DEVOTION,
or
THREE
MONTHS
in
LOUISIANA

CAMILLE LEBRUN

Translated with introduction and annotation by
E. Joe Johnson and Robin Anita White

Monsignor Graveran, Bishop of Quimper, to M. l'abbé Musy.

Quimper, March 4, 1845

My dear Monsieur Musy,

I can only approve of the zeal you bring to reviewing the MORAL GYMNASIUM series: your editing work will be a guarantee to parents and schoolteachers who wish to put these books into the hands of their children and pupils.

It will not be possible for me to review your efforts, for I would need to read all of these works and do not have enough time to do so. I rely, moreover, on your prudence and judgment so that nothing slips therein, which is contrary to Religion or dangerous for hearts.

† Jh. M. Bishop of Quimper.

BREST, MAY 27, 1845

MESSIEURS R. PORNIN AND CO, À TOURS.

I have read with infinite pleasure the work titled *Friendship and Devotion,* which is a worthy addition to the MORAL GYMNASIUM OF EDUCATION series. One could not undertake a more agreeable and more morally useful trip into the fields of the ideal, and the depiction of the sites and customs of Louisiana seemed to me to be traced by a master's hand.

Most sincerely, etc.

C. MUSY,

Chaplain of the Royal Navy.

PREFACE

Of all the provinces of which the vast states of the American Union are currently composed, Louisiana is perhaps the most curious to explore from the triple perspective of its variety of appearance, richness of vegetation, and diversity of human types.[1]

Indeed, bathed on its seaboard by the ocean's waves, its inlands watered by rivers of immense extent and span, bounded on the west by Mexico, on the east by Florida, Carolina, and Kentucky, this region without limits to the north, changes vistas, climes, and productions, depending on the direction taken by the traveler.[2]

The portion bordering the Gulf of Mexico and the mouth of the Mississippi, silt-filled and insalubrious like all alluvial soils, is—due to its commercially favorable location and despite the pestilential maladies that periodically come to assail it—infinitely more populated than the magnificent land stretching between the Mississippi, the Arkansas, and the Red River.

It is upon the plain encircled by these three rivers that one encounters the most beautiful plantations. Their owners engage especially in the cultivation of sugarcane, rice, and cotton. In neighboring forests can be found different kinds of flowering trees, such as the catalpa, magnolia, and tulip tree, and myriads of birds, some of which join the charm of a melodious song to the brilliance of a multihued plumage of the most vivid colors.

Formerly, different tribes of Indians inhabited this plain, including the Choctaw, Natchez, Creek, and Cherokee. The latter two also were spread over the northern United States and Canada.[3] But now, the majority of these savages, stalked by a civilization more threatening to them than war, has taken refuge upon the northwestern savannas, incommensurable solitudes that adventurous settlers have nonetheless begun to invade. The fierce battles that the indigenous tribes wage against one another also contribute to diminishing their numbers, and it likely won't be long before the race of redskins becomes entirely extinct.[4]

Above the confluence of the Mississippi and Missouri stretch vast prairies where pasture grasses reach the height of the flowering shrubs dotting them. There, the air is pure and invigorating, the land graciously undulating, the streams crisscrossing it perfectly limpid, but the lack of shade keeps settlers from making homes there. One can walk for days on end there without spotting a single tree; all that's to be found, therefore, are herds of buffalo and, sometimes, a few Indian hunters.

As for the area around the Platte River, it is nothing but sandy plains as deserted as those of Africa. It has been calculated that their extent must include at least a hundred leagues, and several geologists are of the opinion that, in an epoch long before our own, the ocean occupied this basin, which ends at the foot of the Rocky Mountains.

Now that we've succinctly described the geographical circumstances of Louisiana,[5] we will summarize in a few lines the historical details concerning the founding of this beautiful colony, as well as the various dominions under which it has passed in succession over the course of less than two centuries.

We know that—over a short span of years and based on vague information supplied by Indians—hardy explorers set out from the city of Quebec in order to find a way through those lands to the Gulf of Mexico. Back then, Canada belonged to France, which ceded it to England in 1768. Breton fishermen cast upon that coast by a violent tempest were the first to make its discovery in 1504, but it was not until twenty-one years later that a Florentine navigator[6] took possession of Canada in the name of Francis I, despite the opposition of the natives who, for the most part, were cannibals. The new colony promptly grew and prospered.

The first Canadian explorers venturing to cross the hitherto-unknown lands of the interior of North America to journey to the shores of the Gulf of Mexico stopped at the place where the Arkansas River joins the Mississippi. This expedition took place in 1673.[7]

Six years later, La Salle, a governor of Canada, requested and obtained authorization to undertake this voyage himself.[8] He made it as far as the Illinois River. In 1682, the same governor, a man of an energetic mind and active nature, took sixty men with him and headed down the Mississippi to the land of the Chickasaw. He built a fort at that location, after which he continued to follow the river's course and reached the Gulf. Delighted by the beauty of the surrounding land, he named it Louisiana.[9] Following his advice, Louis XIV, in 1699, sent the Chevalier d'Iberville to establish a permanent colony there and govern it.[10]

Biloxi and Mobile were the first settlements established by the French there. The construction of the city of New Orleans didn't begin until the regency of the Duke of Orléans, whose name was bestowed upon it.[11]

In 1764, France ceded Louisiana to Spain, which had the wisdom to leave a French governor in place there for four years and, in 1800, after the Third Treaty of San Ildefonso, returned it to our government.[12]

Napoleon did not think it was relevant to proclaim this retrocession, for he intended to cede the colony to the United States, which he did in 1803.[13]

The result of these successive changes is that Louisiana offers the bizarre mixture of lifestyles[14] and customs peculiar to each of the three countries whose laws have reigned over it in succession. The character of its inhabitants is a strange combination of the frivolity of the French, the nonchalance of Creoles,[15] the mercantile spirit of Anglo-Americans, and the vainglory of the Spanish hidalgo. Moreover, as slavery hasn't been abolished in Louisiana nor in the other southern states of the American Union, a great number of blacks can be found there and, consequently, mulattos: the two groups detest one another, and both find themselves to be the object of scorn from whites.

TROIS MOIS A LA LOUISIANE.

Figure 4. An illustration of early encounters of the French
with Native Americans in the 1859 edition of *Trois mois à
la Louisiane*, an edition that no longer contained mention
of friendship or devotion in its title.

We would like to hope that this short sketch—which we deemed
appropriate to corroborate all of the events the following story will
present with a scrupulous exactitude—will not be unfavorably welcomed by our readers whose habitual disdain for prefaces had, for a
short while, made us hesitate to write this one.

CHAPTER ONE

· ·

The Arrival

One lovely June evening, the *Jeune-Nantaise*,[1] a merchant ship from France, dropped anchor in the Gulf of Mexico at the mouth of the Mississippi. Also anchored there were six or so recently arrived ships, some from the northern states, others from Cuba or England. All of them were waiting for the Louisianan steamships that would tow them to New Orleans.

The ships soon appeared before the impatient gaze of the passengers and seamen. They watched them come with an almost amazing swiftness down the river the primitive tribes of America had once known by the name of *Namesi-si-pou*[2]—the River of Fishes—and which some among them had so superbly and eloquently nicknamed the "Father of Waters."

Over its course of some twelve hundred leagues,[3] the Mississippi collects a great number of large tributaries, including the Missouri, the Arkansas, and the Red River. Its immense width at the place where it empties into the Gulf of Mexico might, therefore, cause one to mistake it for a deep bay rather than an estuary, if the grayish color of its muddy waters didn't reveal its origin beforehand when contrasted with the green tint of the sea waves.

Such are the precision and promptness generally accompanying all maritime activity that the tugboats, after a few minutes' stop, began to return up the Mississippi, dragging behind them the various aforementioned ships. They did so less swiftly, it's true, than when

9

venturing down. Afterwards, a complete inactivity reigned among the ships' crews, who had no further maneuvers to execute.

The weather was magnificent. No haze dulled the clearness of the sky, and the wafting breeze ceaselessly freshened an atmosphere that had been blazing hot during the day. With its dying rays, the setting sun gilded the distant treetops, while the approaching night, spreading its shadows over the Gulf, already kept one from distinguishing the regular oscillation of the waves.

The darkness enveloping the sea like a veil, the ruddy light to the west, which seemed to enflame the sky and illuminated the land with its reflections, the calm, finally, and the solemn silence of Nature at rest—all of it contributed to impress upon this tableau that imposing appearance that lifts the soul and inclines it to meditation.[4]

The few passengers strolling the deck of the *Jeune-Nantaise* at that moment suddenly stopped, as though in common accord, and interrupted their conversations almost involuntarily to devote their entire attention to the spectacle appearing before their eyes.

Two young women in particular seemed to be enjoying this display with a gentle emotion—it's because, for them, Louisiana possessed the magnetic charm of the homeland. In their earliest childhood, they'd been taken to European soil, which might have become their second motherland had they lived there along with their families; but their sojourn in France had been nothing but one long seclusion. Thus, despite their education and Parisian ways, Hortense and Valentine greeted the American shores of their birth with that enthusiasm which is one of the distinctive feelings of youth and which presented Louisiana to them as the most delightful destination in all the universe.

They were both orphans and called one another "sisters," even though they weren't.

Hortense was a charming young woman whose slender figure, fine features, and childlike appearance made her look no more than fifteen, although she was then close to eighteen. Her blond hair, rosy complexion, and blue eyes were indicative of an English heritage, whereas her simultaneously indolent, capricious, and indecisive disposition, as well as the nonchalance of her movements, gaze, and speech, revealed the French Creole in her.[5] Indeed, Mr. Melvil, Hortense's father and the younger son of one of the noblest families in the kingdom of Great Britain, had married the daughter of a plantation owner in Martinique prior to settling in New Orleans.

Valentine Arnold, although younger than her friend by a year, seemed to be her elder. A true example of American beauty, she drew attention for the elegance of her perfectly proportioned, average frame, the olive-complexioned whiteness of her skin, and the regularity of the lines of her face, which was framed by two ample bands of black hair. Her brown eyes' gentle expression and her mouth's slightly disdainful one, the one at odds with the other, betrayed the blend of sensitivity and vanity forming the basis of her character, the result of which being that this young woman was, by turns, gracious and haughty, indulgent and short-tempered, devoted and tyrannical, depending on whether this precious quality or that dangerous failing held sway over her soul.

No doubt, the wise advice and gentle rebuke of a mother would have shielded Mademoiselle Arnold against an exaggerated opinion of her own merit, which almost all those privileged by nature or fortune are apt to conceive. However, due to some odd resolution whose motive remained unknown to Valentine, her parents, rich merchants in Mobile—one of Louisiana's chief trading ports and located at the estuary of the similarly named river—had sent her, scarcely out of the crib, to Paris, where they were investing their yearly profits in government-backed annuities.[6]

Naturally, this latter circumstance gave cause to suppose they'd planned to rejoin their only child in France eventually. Be that as it may, because yellow fever—that fearsome epidemic that claims so many lives in the New World[7]—had struck down Mr. and Mrs. Arnold during a stay in Natchez while the scourge was running rampant there, a mystery still shrouded their true intentions and the motives inducing them to separate their daughter from them at an age when mothering would have been so essential to her.

Hortense, too, had been brought to France in her infancy by her brother, who was both twelve years her senior and her sole remaining protector. Quite wisely, Francis Melvil thought education in Europe was both less costly and more thorough than in America.[8] As it was, their father, bankrupted by risky investments, had died, leaving behind no assets for either sibling.[9]

Luckily for them both, Francis, who thereafter determined to take up the profession of a lawyer one day, was endowed with that persistence and love for work without which the highest intellectual abilities are but a meager resource in times of adversity. Owing more, perhaps, to that strength of will—which almost infallibly attains its goal when inspired and sustained by praiseworthy intentions—than to his oratorical talents, the young man had gained a rich and considerable clientele in Louisianan society.

In the majority of the states in the Union of which Louisiana is now part, attorneys as well as physicians, artists, and craftsmen in general are amply remunerated. This generosity arises from the ease and rapidity with which people gain, lose, and regain their fortunes in this extremely business-oriented country. The prospect of getting rich quickly thrusts into all sorts of business ventures three quarters of a population that, moreover, has a greater liking for commerce than for the so-called liberal professions.[10]

It should come, therefore, as no surprise that Francis Melvil, pursuing his chosen career without, however, ever deviating from the most scrupulous trustworthiness, had succeeded over the course of ten years in amassing sufficient savings to buy a beautiful plantation named the Cyprière,[11] located some forty leagues from New Orleans, on the western bank of the Red River, a bit above its confluence with the Mississippi.[12]

The income from this plantation managed by a mulatto[13] of proven ability and probity varied from three to four thousand piasters,[14] or fifteen to twenty thousand francs, depending on whether the harvests of sugarcane, cotton, and rice were good and whether the price of these various products held in the markets.

With the exception of one of the Melvils' elderly relatives, who'd been living in retirement at the plantation ever since Francis had bought it, of Maurice the mulatto manager, and a little white boy named Augustin, the Cyprière was inhabited only by black slaves of either sex.

Mr. Melvil had also deposited in the Banque de France,[15] which he regarded as being sounder than American banks, a considerable sum destined to serve as his sister's dowry once it was time to marry her off and she herself had chosen among the many suitors who, he foresaw, would come flocking after her return to Louisiana. For not only was Hortense rich and pretty, she could be reproached for scarcely any other fault than that excessive indolence which—rendering her incapable of taking the initiative to make any decision whether great or small—had the dual disadvantage of keeping her both from always acting according to the noble and generous inclinations frequently arising from her soul and of leaving her defenseless to the suggestions of those around her.

To counter as much as possible the disagreeable consequences of this moral and physical sloth whose existence Francis had had more than one occasion to recognize during his trips to Paris and which the schoolmistress of the boarding school in which Mademoiselle Melvil had been raised had striven in vain to overcome, the excellent brother desired to give to her as a husband a man whose firm character and sound judgment could counterbalance the young woman's lack of energy and variability of ideas.

Mr. Melvil counted among his friends a Spaniard who, having studied medicine in Montpellier,[16] had come to establish his practice in New Orleans. Although he was barely twenty-six years old, thanks to several brilliant cures, Doctor Henríquez had already acquired a veritable fame in Louisiana.

Naturally solemn like most of his compatriots, he possessed to the highest degree that even temper, that judicious frame of mind, and that strength of willpower that Francis wished to find in the man who would become his sister's husband. Moreover, since Hortense benefited from a good reputation, because she was lovely and her manners refined, Mr. Melvil thought with good reason that, were Hortense and the young physician to one another's liking, their union would be a perfect match in every respect.

Mademoiselle Melvil had no knowledge of her brother's plans. The latter was likewise unaware she'd persuaded Valentine to leave France for Louisiana, because, at the moment for farewells, Mademoiselle Arnold, affected more deeply by the chagrin this separation was causing her dear friend than by her own very profound feelings, had suddenly resolved to depart.

Although still a minor, Valentine enjoyed great independence, receiving advice only from the elderly legal advisor charged with her tutelage and from the schoolmistress who, for the last twelve years, had played a motherly role for both her and Mademoiselle Melvil. That lady, although she was quite attached to these charming orphan girls, hadn't sought to keep either of them in her home any longer. She entrusted both of them to a Parisian family with whom she'd been intimately connected for many years and who were being summoned to Louisiana for the first time to collect a splendid inheritance.

And now that we've introduced to our readers the main characters who will play a role in this story, let's return to the *Jeune-Nantaise* whose long crossing hadn't been affected by any damage or slowed by any storm.

It was getting late, and Madame Deschamps, the French lady in charge of bringing Mesdemoiselles Arnold and Melvil to New Orleans, came and roused the young women from their gentle reverie.

Seated on the same cushion, their arms intertwined and holding hands, they vainly endeavored to revive memories too distant and too muddled to take a settled form. Everything was to be new for them in their native land! Such was the reflection each of them mentally made as they stood to follow Madame Deschamps, whose husband and children had already retired for the evening.

Scarcely, however, had the morning twilight's feeble glimmer begun to appear when the two friends returned to the spot they'd occupied a few hours earlier, accompanied by Mademoiselle Ridué, a Parisian lady's maid persuaded by generous wages to follow the Deschamps family to America.

Now, contrary to what had occurred the night before, it was the eastern horizon turning purple with the dazzling fires of the sun, unleashing them upon the ocean, whereas to the west, the earth remained as though shrouded in darkness. Little by little, however, the sun spread its beams over all of nature, and New Orleans soon took distinct shape before the eyes of our young Louisianans.

The city's orderly layout, its houses' uniformity, its streets' perfect alignment give it a very particular mark of elegance and symmetry that attracted the attention of those passengers on the *Jeune-Nantaise* who were coming to Louisiana for the first time.[17] By the time they disembarked at the city's wharf, an early crowd composed of whites, mulattos, and blacks was already rushing about.

That day, the lackadaisical habits of this population, among which so many diverse races mingle without intermixing, had given way among a few individuals to the influence of curiosity, among others to that of affectionate sentiments or to the obligation of fulfilling a duty.

Just by looking at these faces of such varied expressions, one could immediately guess that those people were awaiting a friend, others a master, several a stranger, the majority any news.

And the disembarked passengers from the six to eight boats we mentioned at the beginning of this chapter were likewise looking all about. Then people found one another, exclaimed, and embraced, for Louisiana's Creoles, for the most part, have preserved the expansive character of the French, the founders of this lovely colony, which was ceded in 1764 by the motherland to Spain, which returned it to her in 1800. But France didn't keep it long. Napoleon's sale of the entirety of Louisiana to the United States took place in 1803.

"So where's Francis?" said Mademoiselle Melvil, looking anxiously around the multitude from which no one was advancing towards her to welcome her.

"My brother must be ill!" she continued after a few minutes of silent waiting.

"Come along, young ladies," said Madame Deschamps, who'd been met by Mr. Hervey, a New Orleans notary and custodian of the papers concerning the estate that lady had been summoned to inherit.

Mademoiselle Arnold then took her friend by the arm and led her along in the path of Monsieur and Madame Deschamps, who, completely occupied with their children, were heading towards a hotel where Mr. Hervey, forewarned of their arrival, had taken care to reserve an apartment for them.

"Oh! My goodness, my dear, what's wrong?" exclaimed Madame Deschamps when, looking back to assure herself Valentine and Hortense had caught up, she saw the latter's face covered in tears.

"She's taken aback and alarmed by Mr. Melvil's absence," explained Mademoiselle Arnold. "I'm telling her it won't be long till we see him arrive. It's very early. Perhaps he didn't think the *Jeune-Nantaise* would get here so early in the morn."

"Are you waiting for Mr. Francis Melvil, ladies?" asked the notary who, having heard Valentine's answer, interrupted his conversation with Monsieur Deschamps to address this question to the young women.

"Yes, monsieur," they both said together.

"Do you know my brother?" added Hortense.

"Who in New Orleans doesn't know of that famous lawyer, the glory of the Louisiana Bar?" answered Mr. Hervey, courteously greeting the young lady.

"Please, monsieur, do tell me where he is, what he's doing, how his health has been?" continued Mademoiselle Melvil eagerly.

The intensity of her worry had momentarily vanquished her habitual indolence—Francis had always been for her such an affectionate relative!

"I recently received news of your brother," said Mr. Hervey, "and—"

"—Is he away from this city, then?" Hortense asked again.

"He left New Orleans about three weeks ago."

"To go visit his Cyprière plantation, no doubt?"

"I don't think so. According to what I heard, Mr. Melvil was summoned to Washington by a rich merchant whose entire fortune depends on the outcome of a serious lawsuit."

"What a vexing mishap!" exclaimed a discouraged Hortense.

Indeed, the last letter written by the young woman to her brother—to let him know the French family with whom she was making the transatlantic crossing was embarking from Nantes two weeks earlier than first planned—couldn't have reached him. This letter had preceded the two friends' arrival in New Orleans by only one week, and Mr. Melvil had departed a month before.

This circumstance made Hortense and Valentine's situation rather awkward. Monsieur and Madame Deschamps were prevented from stopping over in New Orleans for very important reasons, the explanation for which would seem tedious to our readers. The same reasons that had obliged them to hasten their departure from France were forcing them to go, without delay, to take possession of the cotton and sugar plantations they'd just inherited and which were scattered inland at great distances from one another.

Our young Creoles couldn't accompany them in their far-flung peregrinations. It was equally impossible for them to take up residence in Mr. Melvil's house. Still unmarried, he'd turned half of his apartment, which was too vast for himself alone, over to Doctor Henríquez, himself a bachelor, as we already know, and whose close proximity, as a consequence, wouldn't have been very seemly for the two orphans.

This final observation was made by Mr. Hervey, who, being a widower, couldn't offer his home as a shelter for the young ladies either. As for the two of them, not only were they unaware of the bonds of intimate friendship uniting Francis and Henríquez, but of the Spanish doctor's very existence.

Despite or rather, perhaps, because of his secret wedding plans concerning his friend, Mr. Melvil hadn't wanted to extol the young doctor to his sister or to announce to the latter the imminent arrival

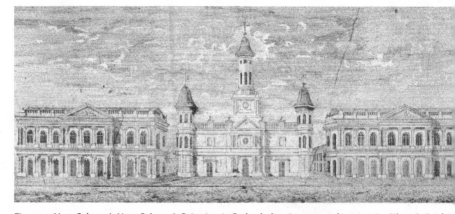

Figure 5. New Orleans's New Orleans's Saint Louis Cathedral, as it appeared in 1838, in *Gibson's Guide and Directory of the State of Louisiana, and the Cities of New Orleans & Lafayette* (New Orleans: Gibson, 1838), 305. Reprinted by permission of the Historic New Orleans Collection, acc. No. 87-085-RL.

of Hortense. He'd likely done so to keep any bias from influencing the judgment Henríquez and Hortense would form concerning one another once they met for the first time.

Under such circumstances, Mesdemoiselles Arnold and Melvil had no other option but to remain at the hotel where the notary had reserved an apartment for Monsieur and Madame Deschamps and to wait there patiently for the return of Francis, to whom Hortense hurried to write a few lines to apprise him of her stranded situation.

For her part, Madame Deschamps, who couldn't continue much longer as the two friends' protectress, decided to leave with them her new lady's maid, Mademoiselle Ridué, whose perfect rectitude was beyond dispute.

Thus were matters settled over lunch at the Hôtel de l'Europe of which, per Mr. Hervey's assurance and to Madame Deschamps's great satisfaction, the proprietress was a very kind, highly respectable woman.

Getting up from the table, the ladies embraced and bid one another farewell, for the steamboat upon which the Deschamps were to travel up the Mississippi to one of their new properties located on that river's shores was ready to depart.

Immediately after this separation, Mesdemoiselles Arnold and Melvil went to New Orleans's Saint Louis Cathedral, with the pious intention of thanking God for their safe crossing.

CHAPTER TWO

The Saint Louis Cathedral

It being a Sunday and precisely the time for the High Mass, the city's Catholic populace was flocking into the church.[1] By the time Valentine and Hortense came in, accompanied by Mademoiselle Ridué, the nave was already so full of people the young women had to abandon all thought of finding a spot there.

Mademoiselle Arnold, noticing an unoccupied pew inside a sort of enclosure formed by a balustrade, quickly slipped into it.[2] Once there, she first knelt to offer her prayer of thanksgiving to God, and it wasn't until she stood up that she realized her companion hadn't followed her. After setting her handkerchief and prayer book on the pew to mark a spot for herself and Hortense, Valentine took a few steps away. With repeated waves, she encouraged her friend, who'd remained with the Parisian housekeeper among the crowd mobbing the church's entrance, to come join her.

Mademoiselle Arnold then noticed, not without surprise, that all the women around her were of mixed race.[3] A bit farther away, she saw another enclosure where a large number of black women were squeezing in. Nowhere else in the church was there even one of them to be seen! The eccentric and sumptuous clothing of several of the latter, however, sufficed to show they weren't slaves.[4]

Raised in France and kept by her life in the boarding school in a state of semi-ignorance concerning the various prejudices exerting such great influence over the whole world, Mademoiselle

Arnold at first felt an astonishment mixed with a sort of generous indignation upon seeing creatures—whom religion teaches us to regard as our equals before God—being cooped up, so to speak, in the Lord's temple. But this reaction was almost immediately quelled by an idea emanating from pride, the most unforgiving of all faults.[5]

Really, thought Valentine, *don't those races differ from our own both morally and physically? And isn't the supremacy that white people here assume for themselves over blacks and mulattos a right they'd be wrong to renounce?*

"Could you please pick up that missal?"[6] a woman with an olive complexion and kinky hair asked Mademoiselle Arnold. She was holding the hand of a charming young girl with white, rosy skin, whose silky hair hung down in light ringlets over her forehead and neck.

"If this seat is yours, I'll give it up," answered Valentine, as she picked up her missal. "I was saving it for that young lady," she added, while pointing out Mademoiselle Melvil to the mulatress.

"But," responded the latter, "white women never come in here."

"Oh!" said Mademoiselle Arnold, who felt a twinge of regret at having entered this box pew.

Indeed, and as though to give further weight to the words the mulatress had just spoken, a young man stopped the passing Hortense, who was trying to make her way to her friend, and led her into the nave where he managed to find her a seat.

"Should I leave then?" murmured Mademoiselle Arnold.

"Why?" asked her neighbor with an astonished look.

"I fear I'm not wanted here," she answered with a bit of embarrassment.

At that response, a smile, whose expression seemed undefinable to Valentine, flickered on the mulatress's lips.

"And besides, I'd like to rejoin the person I was pointing out just now," added the young woman.

"As for that, you mustn't think of doing so," the other woman responded curtly.

"It's true they're even more jammed in the nave than in the rest of the church," Valentine continued. "I'm very upset Hortense allowed herself to be led to that place. The heat there must be even more stifling than in this box pew."

"Probably. We have an open window overhead—"

"I absolutely must go get her. Nothing could be more harmful to her health than stuffiness," said Mademoiselle Arnold, in a whisper, talking to herself.

Nevertheless, the mulatress heard her.

"So, you weren't born in America?" she asked.

"Louisiana is my homeland, but I was brought up in France."

"Then I'm no longer amazed at your profound ignorance of our customs. You must learn, therefore, that a white woman here *must* not, *cannot* take a seat among women of color."

"There are exceptions, however—"

"The rule setting an impassable barrier between each of the principal races of which our population is comprised never varies."

"But this child," insisted Valentine, "and myself?"

"This child!" repeated the mulatress, who seemed to have heard only the first part of the question addressed to her. "This child, my dear, sweet student, isn't white either!"

While saying this, the governess affectionately gazed upon the little girl pressing against her.

Mademoiselle Arnold made a gesture of disbelief.

"You haven't noticed she lacks two degrees for that?" said the mulatress.[7]

"I'd have never suspected," responded Valentine.

At that instant, the bishop of New Orleans, who was presiding that Sunday, appeared clad in his pontifical vestments.[8] Upon seeing him climbing the steps leading to the altar, everyone in attendance bowed. Until the end of the mass, Mademoiselle Arnold kept a religious silence.

When the moment for leaving the church came, she turned to acknowledge the neighbor with whom she'd talked for several minutes before the religious service and saw that the mulatress had already left the pew to go join a group of women of color who were awaiting her nearby. After exchanging a few words with each other, those women simultaneously turned their gaze towards Mademoiselle Arnold and stared at her until the moment when the young woman rejoined Hortense, who'd just exited the nave. They then examined the two friends with a curiosity mixed with astonishment, after which they drifted apart.

In the meantime, Valentine and Hortense headed towards the church's doorway.

"It's so hot!" Mademoiselle Melvil was saying.

"You'd have been better off with me," Valentine answered her. "We were less packed in and had a bit of air."

"I tried to follow you," continued Hortense, "but a young man dressed in black kept me from doing so—"

"I saw that," Valentine interrupted her.

"I thought," added Mademoiselle Melvil, "he was one of the church's vergers and in charge of finding seats for attendees."[9]

"That's possible. Still, I'm more inclined to imagine, based on his state of inactivity after showing you into the nave, that, as far as he was concerned, his hurry to find you a seat was an act of politeness he felt obliged to perform on behalf of a foreign woman."[10]

"How do you figure people guess we've just arrived?"

"Ha! Just from seeing you on the verge of entering the box pew where the women of color gather and which, in my ignorance of Louisianan customs, I'd rashly slipped into."

"Ah!" said Hortense languidly.

"Whatever the case," continued Valentine, "I'm hardly grateful to that courteous fellow for an excess of thoughtfulness that separated you from me."

"Heavens! How my head aches," said Mademoiselle Melvil, placing her hand on her forehead and hurrying to reach the church's doorway. "The air's so crisp and cold!" she next exclaimed, taking a step back and tightening her muslin scarf against her chest, as though she were suddenly freezing.

Figure 6. Lithograph of Jules Lion's 1842 daguerreotype of the St. Louis Cathedral.
Courtesy of the Collections of the Louisiana State Museum.

In fact, during the two hours the High Mass had lasted, the air temperature had suddenly changed. This unexpected transition from roasting heat to a penetrating cold is, unfortunately, all too common in Louisiana, where the north wind can abruptly gust with a violence whose results are extremely dangerous for frail, ailing people.[11]

"Mademoiselle Ridué!" Mademoiselle Arnold hastened to call out, upon seeing the Parisian maid in the middle of the parvis.[12] She had just exited the cathedral through a door closer to the forecourt than was the entrance to the small chapel where Valentine had remained during the Mass.[13]

"Have a hackney coach come for us," added Valentine once Mademoiselle Ridué had gotten nearer to her.

"Where will I find one?" murmured the maid, who was rather annoyed about performing the task Valentine had just given her.

"*Me* bring one to *you* right away,"[14] said a young, ten- or twelve-year-old black child who was selling pomegranates and oranges on the square.

And without awaiting a response to his helpful and, perhaps, self-serving offer, he handed over his stand to his little sister, who was crouching beside him. He then ran to a neighboring street where hackneys were parked.

In the meantime, Mademoiselle Arnold had taken Hortense's arm and made her go back inside the now almost-deserted church. The faintness that Mademoiselle Melvil felt was growing by the moment. Valentine worriedly observed its progress.

"Sister," she said to her companion with a tender solicitude, "sit down on this pew."

At these words, two black women who were nearby began looking at the pair of young women inquisitively.

"Mistress," said one in a half-voice and with an accent of profound surprise, "mistress, did you hear that? They call one another 'sisters'!"

"They really do!" cried out the other one in a higher tone.

"They really do," repeated the former of the two speakers.

"They've probably just arrived from Europe," they added together, after a pause of a few seconds spent curiously examining their neighbors.

Mesdemoiselles Melvil and Arnold, towards whom the black women were thereby attracting attention, had heard this short discussion. The elder of the latter two, no doubt wealthy and free, was wearing a green taffeta dress bestrewn with violet, pink, and yellow flowers. Bracelets, chains, rings of gold with gems showed her desire to display her wealth and independence. She was wearing a poppy-red crepe hat adorned with white feathers and, over her shoulders, a cashmere harlequin shawl—irrefutable proof of black women's taste for garishness no less than their indifference to the most ardent heat.

As for the younger one, she'd covered her head simply with a red scarf and was dressed in white percale. She wore no other jewels but for enormous, coral drop earrings that hung to her shoulders and a gilded chain from which was suspended a silver timepiece.

Clearly, she was the other woman's attendant.[15]

"What were those women saying?" Hortense asked her friend plaintively.

"They're astonished we call each other sisters," Valentine answered with a smile.

"We really don't look alike," remarked Mademoiselle Melvil, whose condition of suffering and exhaustion was becoming increasingly visible.

"Mistress," continued the young black woman, whose gaze was still tactlessly fixed upon the friends, "that young white girl's getting horribly pale—Looks like she's going to faint—"

"Have her inhale this," said the elder one, pulling from her bag a crystal flask capped by a chiseled vermillion stopper.

While the companion attended to the errand with which her mistress had just charged her, the former, noticing the bishop crossing through the church in order to return to his residence, approached him.

"Your Excellency," she said to him in the most reverential tone, "I was unable to attend the sermon this morning, which was followed by a special collection by the *demoiselles de la Providence*[16] for their girls' orphanage of which you're the protector. Here are five hundred piasters I've saved up for them. May I dare ask you to have them accept my offering?"

Saying this, the black woman handed the bishop a purse that he took, answering: "Bless you, my child, for your pious works. We won't forget you in our prayers."

The venerable prelate then drew away.[17]

At that time, Mademoiselle Melvil, whose strength had been briefly revived by inhaling the smelling salts the young black woman had presented on her mistress's behalf, stepped towards the latter; and, returning her flask to her, said a few words of thanks, which Valentine seconded with a kindly nod.

"Assuredly," she thought, "this race which, in so many respects, is visibly inferior to our own, could sometimes teach us lessons of philanthropy and generosity!"

It was easy, in these reflections apparently suggested by a sentiment of equity, to recognize the quick progress that American prejudice had already made upon the otherwise elevated heart of the young woman. An hour before, she'd wondered doubtfully whether whites had any real right to supremacy over blacks and mulattos—and already she was considering this right to be incontestable. Perhaps if she were to return the next day to attend the holy sacrifice of the Mass in the cathedral, she might well remain outside the church, rather than take a seat in the box pew reserved for women of color.

And yet, we'll repeat, Mademoiselle Arnold had an exceptional heart and mind—but her overly proud character led her to adopt willingly any opinion that confirmed her preconceptions concerning her own superiority. She was a bit taken aback, therefore, by the air of indifference evinced by the old black woman in response to the salutation with which Valentine had honored her. In any event, the impression this slight incident made on her mind quickly faded due to the concern caused by the state of physical and emotional weakness into which her friend soon fell again.

Valentine signaled Mademoiselle Ridué, who'd opportunely come to announce the arrival of a hackney in front of the church entrance, to take one of Mademoiselle Melvil's arms, while Valentine held her up by the other. Without this combined support, the poor young woman would have had great difficulty reaching the cab into which it was also necessary to help her climb. To the strange lassitude and violent headache of which she'd previously complained was added a very sharp pain in her right side and lower back.

The hotel where the young Creoles[18] were to stay while awaiting Mr. Melvil wasn't far from the cathedral. All the same, during this short ride, the young woman's suffering increased even more.

"My God!" she was murmuring. "Must I die, then, without ever seeing my brother again?"

"Why are you talking about dying," exclaimed Valentine, "when you have a friend—what am I saying? A sister, whose duty it is to sit at your bedside, to care for you, to watch over you!"

While speaking thus, Mademoiselle Arnold pressed Hortense against her bosom.

"Be careful, mademoiselle," the prudent Parisian maid said in a low voice in Valentine's ear, "be careful. Your friend's illness might well be a contagious fever and—"

"—All illnesses are accompanied by a fever," answered Mademoiselle Arnold, in an assured manner that didn't encourage Mademoiselle Ridué to complete her interrupted sentence.

She understood Valentine was of one of those courageous and devoted natures that never retreat from any danger once they deem it their duty to expose themselves to it. Far, however, from allowing this noble example to influence her, Mademoiselle Ridué leapt from the cab as soon as the coachman had stopped his horses in front of the Hôtel de l'Europe. She hurried inside the hotel and was so alarmed that the proprietress, upon seeing her, went towards her, to ask her about the cause of the extreme agitation to which she appeared to have fallen prey.

. . . .

CHAPTER THREE

Yellow Fever

Once Mademoiselle Ridué had explained to the proprietress the condition of extreme suffering that had suddenly beset Mademoiselle Melvil, the good woman answered:

"Truth be told, if we were in the month of August or July, I'd imagine, from the details you've given me, that your young mistress has just come down with yellow fever."[1]

"Good heavens!" cried out the maid, clasping her hands and letting herself collapse onto a chair in the dining room where she had entered first. "Yellow fever! Some sort of plague, from what I heard on the ship!"

"You don't know about that sickness in Europe?" asked the slave who performed the cooking duties in the hotel and who'd come running to the Frenchwoman whose exclamations he'd heard from the nearby pantry.

As for the proprietress, once she'd learned of the alarming situation of one of the young women entrusted to her, she hurried to go look after Mademoiselle Melvil.

"Certainly not," answered Mademoiselle Ridué.[2]

"Since you don't know about it, how come you're so frightened of it?" continued the cook, whose natural penchant for chitchat had been singularly heightened by the facility with which, contrary to the majority of black slaves, he expressed himself in both French and English, an ease he owed to the circumstance of having spent his entire life in New Orleans residential hotels where he was around foreign servants daily.

"What fine reasoning!" the maid retorted. "So you figure you had to have had an illness to fear it?"

"Not really, for there are some, especially among what people call 'epidemics,' that attack you just once. If they don't get you the first time around, they don't strike again. Besides, you must know that, too, since you've seen cholera. That one's been to every country in the world."

"And it's precisely because I've witnessed its ravages that I tremble every time I hear the word 'epidemic' uttered."

"Yellow fever takes after cholera like a sister does her brother, that's for sure," replied the slave, taking a mischievous delight in stoking the Frenchwoman's fears, all the while pretending to try to calm them.

"Luckily," said Mademoiselle Ridué, vainly striving to repress a trembling voice that belied the apparent confidence of her words, "luckily, for the moment, we don't have to fear the onset of either of those two scourges. Cholera has disappeared from the entire face of the globe, for forever, so we must hope, at least—and yellow fever never flares up—your mistress just affirmed to me—before the month of August."[3]

"Or July," added the cook.

"July!—after all, what does it matter, since we're only at the beginning of June?" remarked the maid, who was trying to combat the fear increasingly tormenting her imagination.

"There's no doubt," murmured the slave, "that June and July make two, but they're so close to one another that, goodness me, I wouldn't be at all surprised some day, if the scourge—that's how you qualified the epidemic, I believe—mistook what month it was."

"Quiet, you ill-omened bird," shouted Mademoiselle Ridué, "you're making my soul run cold!"

"Hey, chef!" shouted a child from the back of the kitchen, which was connected to the dining room by a hallway.

But the cook who, like the majority of black slaves, hated all white servants in general because of the scorn the latter openly display towards them, the cook, shall we say, was having way too much fun with the poor Parisian woman's perpetual reversals of ideas to abandon the game so quickly. He therefore turned a deaf ear to his young assistant's call and started addressing the maid again:

"Since, in your opinion, it can't be yellow fever that your mistress has—"

"Mademoiselle Hortense isn't my mistress," Mademoiselle Ridué interrupted right away.

"Oh! So you're serving the other one?"

"I'm in no one's service here," the maid responded sourly.

"What! You don't receive any wages?" insisted the cook.

"For an average salary of eight hundred francs[4] per year, I decided to follow Madame Deschamps to America, as her head dressmaker and for fashion of all kinds," replied Mademoiselle Ridué with a stung tone. "As for the young people with whom I consented to remain temporarily as a companion—"

"Hey, chef!" came again the same child's voice heard earlier.

Simultaneously, a young twelve- or thirteen-year-old mulatto appeared at the threshold of the hallway door.

"The cassava cakes have been molded," he said.[5]

"That's good," answered the cook.

"And the pecans have been shelled," continued the other.

"Good."

"If you wait too long, the syrup you told me to put on the fire will turn to caramel."

"That's fine. I want to make pralines with it."

"Pralines!"[6] repeated Mademoiselle Ridué, who was rather gluttonous and who'd decided to move abroad because of the prospect of sucking on sugarcane all day long and eating pineapple, oranges, and citrons.

"Yes, mademoiselle, and pecan pralines, too!" answered the little kitchen helper, taking the place of the cook who, meanwhile, figured it was time to go take a look at the pan of syrup.

While saying so, the child opened his apron, which was full of little nuts or almonds of an oblong shape, which he offered to the French woman.[7] The latter, having tasted them and found them to her liking, didn't have to be asked twice to fill her handbag with them.

"We ate breakfast so quickly this morning," she then said to the young mulatto, "I just can't wait till dinner.[8] Couldn't you serve me up something?"

"Anything you'd like," answered the kitchen boy with a tone of importance. "We're able to satisfy whatever you desire. I defy you to find a larder better supplied than ours throughout the city. The Hôtel de l'Europe is so renowned! I'm sure we'll have more than sixty foreigners for dinner today—luckily our chef never lets himself be caught by surprise. From the first light of day, there are six of us under his command. If you want some rice or tapioca soup, a snipe or pheasant salmis, some fried topinambour or fried sweet potatoes, some stewed guava or fried bananas, you just say the word."[9]

At this enumeration of different dishes, among which she simply had to choose, Mademoiselle Ridué felt her appetite redoubling.

"Give me whatever you like," she answered, "so long as you don't make me wait, because I feel like I'm about to faint."

"In that case, I'll bring you everything cold," said the child.

And he ran into the pantry from which he brought out in succession two roasted quails or small woodcocks, some ash-roasted sweet potatoes, some rice-flour cookies, and a half-dozen oranges.

The sight of this improvised meal chased away the somber ideas that Hortense's sudden indisposition had inspired in Mademoiselle Ridué. She no longer dwelt on the fearsome yellow fever except to tell herself that, by the time the scourge ordinarily devastated the city, she'd be long gone, for Mr. Melvil could hardly delay more than one or two weeks before coming to join his sister, and immediately after his arrival, the Parisian maid was to go await the Deschamps family at a plantation some sixty miles from New Orleans. As is known in Louisiana, the epidemic doesn't extend its ravages beyond the limits of the cities located near the seashore or great rivers.[10]

With regard to poor Hortense's situation, Mademoiselle Ridué likewise found a way of reassuring herself by this judicious reasoning: namely, that the symptoms of all serious illnesses, of whatever nature they might be, share a great similarity, and that headache, those aches in her limbs, that profound prostration of which the young woman complained, were the ordinary prelude to typhoid, scarlet fever, et cetera—all quite dangerous, it's true, but being well known in Europe, seemed less frightening to her than did yellow fever.[11]

It was while giving herself over to these reflections that Mademoiselle Ridué brought her chair closer to one of the edges of the large table where her place setting was and got ready to do justice to the dishes the young mulatto had just placed there. But right when the latter was setting before her one of those porous, earthen jugs that have the invaluable advantage of conveying a great coolness to the water or liqueurs they contain, the young woman paled. Drops of cold sweat pearled on her forehead. The knife and fork she was about to use on the quail already served on her plate fell from her hands.

The following words uttered in the vestibule adjoining the dining room had dolefully sounded to her ear:

"That young lady has yellow fever—"

"Did you hear that?" stammered the Frenchwoman, fixing her haggard gaze on the young kitchen boy.

"Yes," answered the child nonchalantly, for whom the epidemic's premature invasion could scarcely cause any emotion since he'd have to endure its onslaught sooner or later.

As a slave in a hotel, he couldn't dream of leaving the city come the time when New Orleans's wealthy and free inhabitants took refuge in the countryside to escape the scourge. What's more, the black, mulatto, and mestizo races have much less to fear from the ravages of this pestilential illness than do Creoles[12] and especially Europeans who are not yet acclimated.

"They said—I think—yellow—fever?" continued Mademoiselle Ridué, who uttered the last words with an expression of terror.

The young boy nodded in affirmation.

"But perhaps the person who said so is mistaken," ventured the maid, to whom her young companion's insouciant air had given a little hope.

"Oh! That man's never wrong, no! I recognized his voice, which is quite well known to me. Doctor Henríquez—who was probably summoned for one of the foreign ladies who arrived this morning and who cured me last year of pleurisy—is an able physician. Whenever yellow fever crops up in a house and especially in a hotel full of Europeans, it doesn't stop its march for very long. I'll bet you a hundred to one we'll have more than twenty sick people here by day's end. Luckily for them, Doctor Henríquez is the house doctor and is quite capable of getting all of them through it."

Mademoiselle Ridué didn't hear this comforting conclusion. At the threatening phrase that had preceded it: "we'll have more than twenty sick people here," the maid, frozen with terror, had fainted. Seeing this, the young kitchen boy ran to look for one of the slave women responsible for personal service to the women lodged in the hotel, but when they returned together to the room, the Frenchwoman had disappeared.

Now, let's get back to Mademoiselle Melvil, whose condition had seemed of sufficient concern to the hotelkeeper that she immediately sent for Dr. Henríquez in whom she had great confidence. Furthermore, since this good woman, while addressing the young Spaniard in the presence of the two young ladies, limited herself to calling him "Doctor," and not having had the occasion to name Mademoiselle Melvil, neither the latter nor the physician had any suspicion that, for her part, the man of science upon whom her return to health was greatly dependent was intimately connected to her brother or, for his part, that the pretty patient confided to his care was his friend's sister.

Fearing to upset the young woman dangerously by abruptly informing her of which malady she was feeling the first symptoms, the doctor, after examining Hortense, silently wrote down his diagnosis, which he then handed to Valentine.

"Oh! I beg you, sir," said Mademoiselle Arnold, who, having guessed the motive for this silence, led Henríquez into the vestibule, in order to question him freely, "do come back as quickly as you can!"

"I'll come back this evening—sooner even, if I can," responded Henríquez. "But I foresee that, by a few hours from now, my colleagues and I will have many patients to visit."

Upon finishing these words, the doctor took a few steps away.

"Doctor," continued Valentine, "won't you tell me the name of my sister's illness?"

"Your sister?" repeated the Spaniard, looking fixedly at the young woman.

"It's a title of friendship we give to one another," she explained.

"Ah!" said Henríquez, with a peculiar emphasis Mademoiselle Arnold was too preoccupied to notice.

"Well, sir!" she added with a pleading tone, "won't you answer me? It's essential, however, that I—"

"That's right," interrupted the doctor, who mistook Valentine's motive for insisting, "that's right. If you haven't had yellow fever yet—"

"I understand!" murmured Mademoiselle Arnold.

Henríquez continued:

"You'd be prudent to withdraw immediately to the countryside, for this terrible illness is both contagious and epidemic."

A disdainful smile was the young woman's sole response to this advice she took as an insult.

Well now! she thought to herself, while climbing the stairs to return to Hortense's room. So, there are hearts insensitive and selfish enough to suppose that personal fears are enough to smother the sweet sentiment of friendship? That I would abandon my dear companion, my chosen sister, when illness has confined her to a bed of suffering, her, the poor child, so weak, so quick to get discouraged, to become frightened! In any case, God protects those who put their trust in Him, and don't I have that trust that He'll grant me the strength to save my friend, or the grace to die with her!

By thus expressing the wish that her own existence not extend beyond the term fixed by Providence for that of her friend, Mademoiselle Arnold wouldn't be exaggerating the grandeur of affection she'd vowed to Mademoiselle Melvil. Although a bit younger than the latter, she loved her with that tender, exclusive, and devoted affection that is akin to maternal sentiment. Furthermore, her conduct throughout the duration of Hortense's illness bore witness to the sincerity of her thoughts—we say *her thoughts* because many people lie to themselves. Some people are prompted to do so by that impulse of self-regard predisposing us to judge ourselves favorably. Others find themselves pushed to it by the need to dull the reproaches of their conscience. One must have a noble and courageous soul to dare search into its most hidden folds and render an exact account of its oft-selfish sensations.

But we already know that neither courage nor moral nobility was lacking in the rich character of Valentine for whom a tinge of pride alone sometimes darkened her angelic goodness.

Pride is an aberration of the human mind in addition to constituting an offense against the Creator, from a religious point of view. Indeed, who, among us inhabitants of the earthly world, can set himself as the judge of his own merit and of that of his fellows? Someone who, to us, seems ill favored by nature from physical and intellectual perspectives possesses deep in his or her heart infinite treasures of true charity and holy resignation, which place them above those whose apparent superiority and false virtues attract our admiration and respect. Moreover, according to the teachings of Christianity, if man were a creature capable of attaining perfection, he'd have cause to thank God for it and not to take glory in it.

Let us add, too, that no one, in our current state of civilization, could rest assured of maintaining his intrinsic value amid the different, more or less liberally constituted societies among which chance or his own will might lead him.

And stopping here this little digression that is linked, more than our readers might think, to the various events that this book will unfold before their eyes, we shall resume in the following chapter our momentarily interrupted narration.

CHAPTER FOUR

Sundry Events

Scarcely had Mr. Melvil received the letter in which his sister apprised him of her arrival before he departed hurriedly, leaving a lawyer in Washington in charge of his client's lawsuit.

It was via the newspapers, while he was traveling, that the terrible news of the sudden outbreak of yellow fever in New Orleans reached Francis.

When he entered the city, he was painfully struck by the profound sadness prevailing there. During the week that had just passed, the epidemic had progressed all the more rapidly because it had caught Louisianans by surprise that year. Rarely, or rather never, had it struck New Orleans before the month of July, and it was only the middle of June! The periodic emigrations that city's inhabitants make to the countryside hadn't begun yet; thus, the plague's victims were numerous.

By the first day—as per Doctor Henríquez's distressing prediction—a third of the recently arrived Europeans were stricken with yellow fever. Twenty-four hours later, all of New Orleans's hotels resembled hospitals. Caretakers for the ill were no longer to be found; the Grey Nuns[1] then, as they always do everywhere, for that matter, gave admirable proof of courage and abnegation; the physicians likewise showed themselves to be full of zeal and devotion. Doctor Henríquez, among others, seemed tireless; many people owed him their lives.

Among the latter, we would cite Mademoiselle Melvil if, by the young Spaniard's own admission, the restoration of her health hadn't resulted more from the ceaseless efforts of friendship than the prescriptions of science. There was no doubt that, without Mademoiselle Arnold, Hortense would have succumbed from the dual burden of her suffering and isolation.

Indeed, her brother was absent, and Madame Deschamps had departed. Mademoiselle Ridué, giving into an unconquerable reaction of panic, had fled. Mr. Hervey, the notary, had embarked on the same steamship as his new clients to go spend a few days with one of his sisters, who possessed a plantation along the Mississippi. In addition, the good mistress of the Hôtel de l'Europe saw her four daughters, whom she'd not had time to send to the countryside as she had in prior years before the invasion of yellow fever, all simultaneously afflicted by that terrible malady. As for Valentine, she addressed fervent prayers to heaven that the epidemic not affect her while her chosen sister was in danger.

A week after the young ladies' arrival in New Orleans, when Mr. Melvil, forewarned of his sister's situation, entered the latter's room with an indescribable feeling of anxiety, the already convalescing Hortense said to him, pointing at Valentine sitting at the bedside:

"Thank her first, brother, because she's the one who saved me."

"Mademoiselle Arnold here!" exclaimed Francis.

He already knew this young woman whom Hortense had indicated to him to be her dearest companion; he'd seen her several times at Hortense's boarding school. What's more, he remembered his father had had business dealings with Valentine's father.

Although, in the letter she had recently written to her brother, Mademoiselle Melvil had forgotten to mention Mademoiselle Arnold's arrival in Louisiana, she nonetheless was briefly taken aback by the exclamation of Francis, whose tone expressed regret more than satisfaction.

She hastened to detail to Mr. Melvil the infinite care that loving and courageous friend had lavished upon her, and the young lawyer showed his gratitude to Valentine in such a way as to efface the impression that words dictated by an initial reaction of surprise might have had on her.

Embarrassed by this praise and thanks, Mademoiselle pretended to need to prepare for the patient an infusion ordered by the doctor and withdrew into another room.

Francis followed her with his eyes while she went out, but it was only after she'd shut the door that he murmured with a tone of compassion:

"Poor child! Why did she come to Louisiana?"

"Are you afraid she'll fall victim to the epidemic?" asked Hortense.

"I certainly hope not," he responded. "Since she's resisted the harmful influence of the pestilent air around you so far, we can presume she'll escape it entirely."

"In that case, why do you regret that she accompanied me? You're not unaware of the loving affection that has bound us to one another since our childhood."

"No, assuredly, but I couldn't foresee—"

"—That we wouldn't want to be separated?" Hortense cut him off. "Yet there's nothing more natural. We were raised together. We're about the same age. We were both born in this country. Truth be told, Francis, I don't understand your astonishment!"

"You don't understand," said Mr. Melvil, "because you don't know. Well," he continued, talking to himself, "the damage is done. We'll have to try and remedy it."

"I beg you, brother," exclaimed Hortense, "explain yourself more clearly. What danger threatens Valentine here?"

"It's not precisely a danger, but a family secret of which your friend is likely uninformed. Otherwise, she wouldn't have left Europe where it was clearly her parents' wish that her life take its course."

"If it's a secret, brother, I won't ask you to divulge it to me, but, for mercy's sake, tell me what the consequence of it will be. Will my chosen sister be forced to return to France? Must I prepare myself to hear her farewells soon and to embrace her for the last time perhaps?"

While Hortense was saying this, her eyes filled with tears.

"Good heavens, sister, I couldn't so instantaneously resolve this important matter to which all of Mademoiselle Arnold's future hopes are linked. But look how emotional you are! Calm down. We'll speak of all this again later. In the meantime, don't repeat a word of our conversation to your friend. It would disturb her peace of mind needlessly. The most urgent thing at this moment is for you to get better and to protect that interesting young lady from the ravages of an epidemic that's less to be feared, it's true, for her constitution than your own, but from which, all the same, she might well not escape.[2] I'll write to Maurice so he can have everything prepared to welcome you. Once you've regained enough strength to undertake the trip, we'll leave for our plantation where you'll spend the rest of the summer with Mademoiselle Arnold and Madame Launay. The latter's company won't be very pleasant for you, I fear. Her disposition has been embittered by a series of domestic chagrins and reversals of fortune. She has, moreover, for some time now, almost completely lost her sight, and her obsessions and demanding nature increase, it would appear, by the year. But you're not someone, my good sister, who needs reminding that misfortune and suffering must always be respected."

Mademoiselle Melvil answered Francis with a nod of her head and reached out a hand to him, which he gripped gently in his own.

The joy this excellent brother felt upon seeing Hortense in a state of convalescence advanced enough to relieve him of all fear concerning her recovery was tempered by the worry he felt for the future of the devoted friend who'd saved his sister.

This concern was founded mainly upon the knowledge Francis believed, not without reason, that he'd acquired as much by her own remarks as by those of Hortense concerning Mademoiselle Arnold's eminently proud spirit. He told himself that impressionable temperaments, such as that of Valentine, almost always lack the necessary moral strength to bear the shock of those unforeseen events that, in a single blow, upend the most brilliant positions.

The likely fate of this beautiful and noble person therefore awoke in him a mixed sentiment of interest and pity, even though the abstraction in which these thoughts cast him gave him, at that moment, an air of indifference, which Mademoiselle Melvil didn't notice, for that matter. She, too, was preoccupied by the vague words uttered by Francis concerning Valentine's arrival. She also had faith in her brother's perfect goodness, and this faith wouldn't be shaken by simple appearances of coldness to which she was accustomed in any case.

One might have already noticed that Francis spoke formally to his sister, deviating in this respect from the informal customs of French and Spanish Creoles, and conforming to those of the English, who are never casual with their most intimate friends or closest relatives.[3]

Mr. Melvil had inherited his father's indisputably British nature. A great firmness of principles, an exterior calmness that was unfailing except in exceptional circumstances, a naïve sensibility he tried to conceal with as much care as others do to conceal a fault—such were the instinctual traits of his character.

To complete this sketch of the young lawyer, we will add that he had a high brow, ash blond hair, a Saxon nose, and pale blue eyes and that he had a high waist, his bearing was a bit stiff, and his gestures were rare. As for his physiognomy, upon which he almost never let his secret emotions appear, it nonetheless revealed that mark of rectitude and sincerity of which all his actions bore the trace.

Francis, meanwhile, concerned about tiring his still rather weakened sister with an overly prolonged conversation, arose and left Hortense's apartment to go to the one prepared for him. The house where he lived ordinarily was located on a street too distant from the Hôtel de l'Europe for him to want to stay there now.

Scarcely had he left the young woman's room than the latter saw him reappear, holding Dr. Henríquez by the hand. The two men had just run into one another in the corridor.

"Sister," said Mr. Melvil, "I'm too happy to put off naming to you the skilled physician who cared for you during your illness and whom I've known for a long time now. Señor Henríquez—Mademoiselle

Melvil,"[4] he next said, with an air of ceremonious formality and in accordance with American-style introductions.

There was a silence then. The Spanish doctor, charmed by his unknown patient's transformation into his best friend's sister, mentally congratulated himself for the zeal with which he had cared for her. For her part, Hortense was surprised she hadn't guessed that this physician, whose grave countenance, expressive yet serious physiognomy, and guttural accent betrayed his Spanish origin, was the same Dr. Henríquez mentioned by the notary Hervey.

Mr. Melvil was the one who started speaking again first:

"How long will it be, do you think," he asked Henríquez, "before my sister can bear the fatigue of a trip of forty leagues?"[5]

"Why," answered the doctor, "I couldn't say just yet . . . Still, mademoiselle is so young, and the person who looked after her during the course of her illness seems to me to be such a careful and intelligent caretaker, that it might be possible before the end of the week."

"That's a long time!" Hortense interjected.

"You're impatient!" continued a smiling Henríquez. "I, on the contrary, find this delay to be rather short for a recovery as recent as yours. Some people, especially Europeans—"

"I'm Louisianan!" Mademoiselle Melvil hastened to say.

"Flowers transplanted to foreign lands are affected to some extent by the influence of the climate and soil where they were cultivated," replied the doctor, with a peculiarly Spanish gallantry. "As I was saying," he carried on, "Europeans who've been afflicted with yellow fever, for a long while after, their whole lives even, will feel effects from this illness which, furthermore, has a more violent effect on robust temperaments than those of delicate constitutions."

"So, brother," remarked Hortense, addressing Mr. Melvil, "you were incorrect when you told me a moment ago Mademoiselle Arnold was less threatened by the ravages of the epidemic than was I."

Francis didn't respond to his sister's observation, and Henríquez resumed:

"If Mademoiselle Arnold is, as I suppose, the same young woman who looked after you so diligently, she doesn't, in fact, run as much risk—"

The doctor didn't finish his explanation. Valentine had just reentered her friend's room, and Hortense's brother had made a slight signal to the physician to alert him and impose silence upon him.

Mademoiselle Melvil saw this gesture, but wasn't surprised by it. She presumed Francis was afraid, now that she knew her friend was safe, that Valentine would be worried for her own sake in the current epidemic. And indeed, Mr. Melvil, as though he meant to corroborate his sister's opinion, suddenly changed the subject of the conversation, and, a few minutes later, Henríquez and he left, leaving the two young women together.

Doubly happy at feeling herself coming back to life and knowing that, in the person of her brother, she had such a sincerely affectionate and devoted protector nearby, Hortense then thought, for the first time, to inquire about Madame Deschamps's maid.

Although Mademoiselle Ridué's remarkably selfish character might not have keenly excited our readers' interest, we think, however, that they, too, want to learn what became of her after she left the Hôtel de l'Europe, for we've already said, when the slave woman called by the kitchen boy entered the dining room, the Parisian woman was no longer there.

It's because after awakening from her faint, which had lasted only a few seconds, the wretched girl, seized by a veritable panic, had fled from that house she perceived to be a hotbed of contagion.

For a good while, she'd wandered the streets, asking passersby what direction she should follow to reach one of the city gates. Yet among those whom she addressed, some, disturbed by her haggard look, mistook her for an escapee from a madhouse and continued on their way without answering her. Others, who knew English only, the most commonly spoken language in Louisiana nowadays, didn't understand her questions. Some people, finally, whether out of ignorance or out of malice—pranksters are to be found in every land—gave her false information, such that her strength was entirely depleted by the time she found herself out in the middle of the countryside at nightfall. Half-dead from fatigue and hunger, she sat beneath a tree in the middle of a cornfield and began to eat the pecans we saw her put in her bag. But this food wasn't enough to appease the demands of a stomach whose need for nourishment had already been keenly felt several hours earlier.

Nevertheless, Mademoiselle Ridué, whose worry concerning yellow fever increased all the more from the fear that solitude and darkness inspire in the weak-minded, drew the strength from the very excess of her terror to get up and drag herself to a cabin from whose window a light was shining.

This cabin was inhabited by a family of free blacks, decent folk who welcomed Mademoiselle Ridué quite warmly, and invited her to share their supper composed of a platter of potatoes baked under ashes and a bottle of tafia,[6] a liquor made from sugarcane, which blacks love with a passion and which they imagine to be a remedy for all manner of ills. They poured the Parisian maid a half-glass that she foolishly swallowed in a single gulp. One can guess what effect this intoxicating liquor had on the young woman's more or less empty stomach and already troubled mind.

"Oh!" she exclaimed, pressing one of her hands against her chest, as though, by means of this pressure, she might manage to smother the fire that was spreading from her throat into her guts.

But almost immediately her arms fell inert by her side; her head drooped upon her shoulder; then her suddenly stiff body fell heavily to the ground.

This time, it wasn't a passing faint. All her hosts' efforts to revive her were fruitless.

The next morning, an elderly woman who was a member of this black family, having gone to the New Orleans market to sell Turk's turban squash[7] and watermelons, the products of their gardens, told the cook at the Hôtel de l'Europe—which was one of their best customers, in fact—about the sudden death of the white woman who'd sought shelter with them. The cook, from the portrait of Mademoiselle Ridué that his supplier drew for him, recognized the Parisian maid and reported this occurrence to his mistress, who informed Mademoiselle Arnold in turn.

While the proprietress was delivering this sad news to the young woman in the middle of the stairs where the two women had crossed paths, Doctor Henríquez came by. Having overheard a few words that piqued his curiosity, the physician asked for further details, after which he declared the *subject* had succumbed to an attack of apoplexy or, in other words, a cerebral hemorrhage.

Thus, had that selfish girl—who'd not hesitated for a moment to abandon the two orphans temporarily entrusted to her care—rushed to the death she'd been fleeing. Had she not deserted her post, she most certainly wouldn't have been the victim of that entirely fortuitous accident; perhaps she wouldn't have fallen prey to the epidemic. And in the opposite case, she might have been among the number of those whom the knowledgeable Doctor Henríquez had almost miraculously saved. Such, at least, is our opinion, and such was the conclusion, too, with which Mademoiselle Arnold ended the account she gave to her companion of Mademoiselle Ridué's deplorable demise.

Once Valentine stopped talking, Hortense took her hands, which she pressed tenderly against her heart. Everything her friend had just recounted made it even more striking to Hortense the peril she'd been in and from which the Spanish physician's science would have had much difficulty to wrest her, had he not been seconded in his efforts by the tender care of her tireless nurse. The fear that Mademoiselle Arnold would end up contracting the scourge against which the latter had so valiantly defended her intensified Mademoiselle Melvil's impatience to leave the city. A very natural sentiment of gratitude, moreover, gave her the strength and—even more remarkably, considering the excessive indolence of her character—the highly determined willpower to depart for the Cyprière the following week.

Despite the scolding of Valentine, who characterized this determination as foolhardy recklessness, their departure took place on a July evening, two weeks after the two friends' arrival in New Orleans. Henríquez having declared that—come the moment when the young woman's convalescence was sufficiently advanced for her to tolerate movement—a change of air could only better her condition, Mr. Melvil had quickly consented to his sister's wishes, which conformed to his own, for that matter.

It's just that he'd have liked to return to the plantation by way of the steamboats that ceaselessly go up and down the great rivers of America, making light of the obstacles of tide and rapid currents that had hindered the progress of paddled boats in former times. But Hortense—whom the boredom of a thirty-five-day transatlantic crossing had rendered averse to any sort of boating—had so insisted on making the trek from New Orleans to the Cyprière in a carriage, he'd conceded once again on this matter.

It was agreed they'd travel at a gentle pace and by night, as the heat had gotten unbearable again during daylight hours. Consequently, Mesdemoiselles Melvil and Arnold, as well as Francis and a slave woman who was to serve as the two young ladies' maid, climbed into a carriage from which the top had been lifted and over which a gauze mosquito net had been improvised, both to let the air circulate inside the carriage and to bar entry to mosquitos, a veritable plague in tropical lands.[8]

The carriage was followed by a wagon containing the travelers' baggage, baskets filled with provisions, and various objects of an incontestable utility in a land where there are no villages, but only, and sometimes at a great distance from one another, plantations, isolated cabins, and a few inns that, being seldom frequented, are often lacking in essentials.

Because they'd decided to go only thirty miles each night for the length of their journey, both so as not to cause the convalescent too much fatigue and to spare the rented horses and their driver,

Figure 7. The restored, multicolored, raised big house of the Laura Plantation in Vacherie, Louisiana, a classic example of Louisiana Creole architecture, built on profits from sugarcane cultivation. Courtesy of Ruth R. Caillouet.

they might well be forced one day or another to camp out in the countryside. This was only a contingency, incidentally; per Mr. Melvil's calculations, they ought to find more or less comfortable shelter at each stop.

CHAPTER FIVE

· ·

A Plantation

The first morning after our travelers' departure saw them stop over at a lovely plantation,[1] one not for sugarcane but for oranges,[2] whose owner was a relative of the Melvils.

Forewarned the latter were passing through, he'd neglected nothing for their welcome to be a model of plantation hospitality. Although the sun was barely starting to peep over the horizon when the travelers arrived at the home of Mr. S***, he was already up and waiting for them, surrounded by his family, on the house's columned veranda. First, they were taken to the rooms prepared for them, each of which was adjoined by a washroom. Then, once they'd rested sufficiently, a slave waiting for them at the door of their rooms led them through a trellised gallery draped in bellflowers of all shades and other climbing plants into a gazebo shaded by one of those massive fig trees whose like would be vainly sought in our temperate regions.[3]

The structure of this octagonally shaped pavilion was perfectly suited for Louisiana's stifling climate. Immense, louvered shutters, supported at the eight corners of the building by light brickwork, stood in place of walls. Their green color contrasted gaily with a roof of flat cypress shingles painted a vivid red.

As for the gazebo's interior, it was comprised of but a single room and was continuously cooled by a jet of water, which sprang from the middle of a basin made of white marble, as were the vases filled with flowers adorning the corners and the slabs replacing the parquet floor. Marble, which is so common in Europe, is a luxury in Louisiana, an alluvial soil where no stone, not even a pebble, is to be found![4]

A splendid breakfast awaited the guests of Mr. S*** inside this cool sitting area whose entire furnishings consisted of a couch, a delicately worked marquetry table, and a few bamboo chairs. The planter's wife and daughters did the two friends the honors with that characteristic grace of Creoles.

What Valentine and Hortense liked the most about this meal, which was as varied as it was abundant, was a platter piled with a pyramid of bananas, guavas, coconuts, citrons, and pineapples.[5]

The guava, or pear of the Indies,[6] is a fruit of oval form, about the size of a pippin apple, with an excellent taste. People make highly appreciated jams and jellies from it. It grows on trees and is very common in the Antilles.

The pulp of the banana,[7] less delicate but more nutritious than that of the guava, is one of the favorite foods of blacks, for whom it often serves as bread. For their part, Creoles seldom ever eat it except grilled, fried, or even baked in the oven. Banana plants, otherwise called "Adam's fig tree,"[8] grow in both the East and West Indies; it's not a tree, but a plant or rather a sort of reed whose leaves, of a green that's very pleasing to the eye, sometimes grow to an extraordinary size.

As for coconuts, citrons, and pineapples,[9] it seems pointless to us to do a description. Who doesn't know that a coconut is a kind of palm tree, whose fruit or nut is comparable in size to a melon and contains a very refreshing milk and a delicious meat? And whom would we be telling that the pineapple is the most exquisite of fruits and the citron the most fragrant of lemons?

"Oh! Louisiana is such a lovely land!" exclaimed Mademoiselle Arnold. "What richness of vegetation! What a variety of products! I'm astounded emigration from Europe to America isn't more frequent and in greater numbers."

"Europeans are far from sharing your enthusiasm, which they'd call an infatuation, were they to witness it," said Mr. Melvil.

"Indeed," remarked Mr. S***, "they at least have the right to reproach us for yellow fever, which decimates them mercilessly."

"And for slavery!" added Francis.

"In that respect," countered the planter, "they're wrong. Slavery is one of the conditions for Louisiana's existence. Wishing to abolish it means desiring the ruination of this former colony of France. And whom would it profit, anyhow? Nobody, not even slaves, who aren't sufficiently inclined to civilization to benefit wisely from independence, the most precious of assets, the French affirm."[10]

There was a hint of irony in the tone with which the Creole accompanied those final words, and Mr. Melvil rejoined:

"Whatever the case, one cannot deny that here, as in other colonies where slavery hasn't been abolished, there are frightful abuses of property rights that whites wield upon blacks, and certainly—"

"Oh, my God!" exclaimed Mr. S***, who obviously didn't care to let his cousin go on. "Where will you find an institution that doesn't have its abuses, a society that doesn't have its prejudices? In France, for example, people claim mulattos are treated on equal footing, which seems absurd and revolting to us Americans—"

"The fact remains, my friend, unfortunately," Francis interrupted in turn, "that we could name more than one owner of a plantation and, consequently, of slaves, who engages with impunity in acts of atrocious barbarity towards the latter."[11]

"Oh! I know! You're thinking of that Creole woman who's an embarrassment to her sex, I'll admit, who—a dozen years or so ago—was accused of subjecting several of her slaves, who were guilty of more or less serious faults, to horrible torture. But you also know that—frightened by the general clamor that finally rose against her and the threat of raids on her plantation where, in fact, instruments of torture and the skeletons of slaves[12] were discovered in foul dungeons after her departure—she fled Louisiana and took refuge on a Spanish boat that bore her to Cuba."[13]

"And since nothing more vexing came of all this for her than being obliged to have a third party manage her plantation from

which she receives the revenue," resumed Mr. Melvil, "her example
has produced no impression upon masters who are often all too
willing to abuse their power. Near the Cyprière, there's a sugarcane
plantation much larger than my own, which belongs to a Creole
woman less barbarous—I like to think—than the one you just spoke
of, but whose tyranny is such that not a year goes by without several
of her blacks becoming maroons,[14] despite the harsh punishments
awaiting them once they're recaptured. It's truly deplorable the
magistrates of this land don't take charge of cracking down on such
reprehensible excesses, which, when they're committed by women,
become doubly odious."

"Are you personally acquainted with that Creole woman, brother?"
asked Hortense.

"No," answered Mr. Melvil. "Back when I bought the Cyprière,
I made no social calls in the area. Even if I'd done so, I wouldn't have
put in an appearance at the home of Madame A***. I never befriend
people whom it would be impossible for me to esteem."

Mr. and Mrs. S*** had listened in absolute silence to the young
lawyer's profession of faith. Perhaps, although disapproving of the
inhumanity with which a few planters treated their slaves, they didn't
share their relative's indignation, which was a mite exaggerated to
their way of thinking.

Often, one of the saddest consequences of despotism—that is to
say, authority exerted without control—is to lead the most generous
hearts and minds so far astray they gradually come to regard those
in submission to them as beings of too inferior an order in creation
for them to have to be concerned with their lot.

"According to what I hear," resumed the Creole with a slightly
sarcastic smile, the expression of which Francis alone noticed, "we
find in you, for all the slave-owner that you are, a staunch proponent
of the emancipation of blacks?"

"Without a doubt," answered Mr. Melvil, "if a wisely calculated,
progressively achieved emancipation were to supply peaceful citizens
and no further wrongdoers to our southern states, which are so vast

we welcome all fugitives without asking them for any show of papers or whether they're being pursued or have been condemned by sovereign vengeance or the justice of European tribunals."[15]

"But," objected the Creole man, "without slaves, what would become of our plantations?"

"The freedmen would cultivate them in exchange for wages."

"Experience has shown free blacks to be the laziest workers on earth."

"They'd cease to be so once they were familiar with civilization. Then they'd have new needs and pleasures. The desire to satisfy them would open their eyes to the necessity to work to which they'd apply themselves more half-heartedly, perhaps, in a state of liberty than in that of slavery, but always more efficiently than those indentured ones who come to us from Europe by the boatload, and of whom scarcely ten out of forty can be found who are capable of resisting the annoying and often deleterious influences of our climate."[16]

I hadn't suspected Mr. Melvil was a utopist, thought Mr. S***. In every land, people label those who dream of the perfectibility of man and society "utopists."

Whether Francis had fathomed his relative's thought or was no longer inclined to push the matter any further, he suddenly changed the topic of conversation, and turning towards Mademoiselle Arnold, he said with a cheerful air:

"Now that we've gone through all the serious reproaches Europeans lodge against us, let's pass to others comparatively much more frivolous, but whose accuracy can't go unrecognized."

"Indeed, cousin," exclaimed a laughing Mrs. S***, "one would think you mean to disgust our charming compatriot with her native land!"

At this accusation tossed out by the Creole woman in a jesting tone, a bright blush passed over Francis's brow. The half-light caused Hortense alone to notice it. At that moment, with a worried expression, the young woman had her eyes fixed upon those of her brother, which said more than words could have done:

Could it be true? Are you still trying to separate me from my friend?

The discomfort Francis had momentarily experienced—he, so loyal and so sincere that no question, however unforeseen or insidious it might be, had ever had the power to intimidate him, as both his enemies and friends would avow—this discomfort, shall we say, seemed to Mademoiselle Melvil to be an affirmative response to her silent query. Even so, her brother's gaze hadn't met her own. Neglecting, for good reason, to combat the assertion of Mrs. S***, he continued, still addressing Valentine: "So Europeans, especially French people who, while in every country around the world long for their own, complain about the perpetual variation of temperature that ruins the most robust constitutions—"

"As well as the most magnificent plantations," added Mr. S***.

"—About the countryside's monotony," carried on Mr. Melvil.

"It's true," added the Creole man, "traveling artists tramping over every hill and dale looking for picturesque sites to depict would be rather disappointed roaming about Louisiana. They'd find no crags, ridges, or valleys here."

"Your immeasurable prairies and ancient forests have their beauties," said Valentine.

"Unfortunately," Francis started up again, "our prairies or savannahs, whose grasses in some places reach the height of a man, don't keep their greenness very long, and our forests, which are swampy for the most part, are crawling with reptiles. As for mosquitos—"

"But, brother," interrupted Hortense, "it's bad of you to run down our homeland like this!"

"What does it matter?" said Mr. Melvil with a casualness that was too out of keeping with his personality not to conceal an ulterior motive. "Aren't we all natives of Louisiana? What's more, while I admit foreigners and even Creoles who were raised in Europe like mademoiselle and yourself have trouble getting used to our climate and—to our customs, I nonetheless appreciate the particular advantages offered to commerce by this lovely land's geographical location which, unbounded to the west, is bathed on the east by the gulf into which the magnificent rivers crossing this area flow.[17] Undoubtedly, too, the land here is fertile, and the vegetation is fast growing. We see before us several of its products, sugarcane in particular, grow and ripen in much less time than in the Antilles.[18] There, it's cut down only after a year and a half, but here in just six months! That enormous difference must be attributed mostly to this: in the islands where perpetual heat reigns, the earth is in a permanent state of ferment that depletes it, whereas in Louisiana, the soil obtains a new vigor in the few months of winter that follow the summer. Besides, our crops are of little variety. Plantation owners scarcely busy themselves with any other crops than that of sugarcane, cotton, and rice, which are, in truth, of great value."[19]

"Among the main objects that feed our external trade," he continued, "we still count the skins and furs that Indian tribes supply to us. The cultivation of our forests is also a fruitful source of riches. We don't have any factories, however. Our muslins[20] as well as our linens and silks come to us from Europe. Likewise, we bring in most of the fruits garnishing our tables from the island of Cuba where they abound, as well as sweet potatoes, whose roots, of an excellent taste and easily digestible, weigh between twelve and thirty pounds."[21]

"And this superb pyramid—" began Valentine.

"—Offers to your gaze a few samples of the delicious fruits our neighbors in Havana send to us in daily cargos," concluded Francis. "Neither banana, pineapple, guava, nor coconut trees have prospered in Louisiana, where people have likewise had to give up on cultivating coffee, a charming bush of which I possess a few plants at the Cyprière, which, perfectly positioned, haven't done so badly there."

"That we don't bring together in our gardens all of the fruits of which the Americas present such a great variety doesn't mean, however, that we don't also have a few lovely examples of local production to display to the eyes of foreigners," Mr. S*** said next.

While saying this, he signaled a slave, a butler of sorts whose duties, during the meal that was now coming to its end, had been limited to monitoring the service of the other slaves. The slave immediately left the gazebo but, a few minutes later, reappeared carrying a large basket containing a watermelon of extraordinary size and a profusion of oranges, pomegranates, figs, and pecans.

"Well, young ladies," asked the plantation owner, "are we as hard up as Melvil's words led you to believe, and wouldn't most people be content with a dessert like the one Ramma threw together in just a few seconds?"

"These fruits really do have an exquisite flavor," said Mademoiselle Melvil to Mr. S***, beside whom she was seated, and who'd just held out a branch upon which hung a dozen of those little violet figs called "celestes" in New Orleans and which Louisianans prefer, not without reason, to other more beautiful, but less fine, flavorful varieties.

Francis, meanwhile, was peeling two oranges of a reddish flesh like those that Malta alone produces in Europe. He then offered them to his female cousin and to Mademoiselle Arnold between whom he was sitting.

"So, were these oranges just picked on your property?" Valentine asked Mrs. S***.

"Certainly," answered the latter, "and if you need proof to be convinced, we'll give it to you," she added with a smile. "Ramma, raise the blind."

The slave immediately obeyed his mistress's order, revealing in its entirety a large, one-way mirror, till then masked by a taffeta blind covered in chinoiserie. Almost simultaneously, the louvered shutter placed behind that mirror opened by means of a spring activated by Ramma. As a result, a brightness replaced the aforementioned semi-darkness prevailing in the room, a glare softened, however, by the green foliage of a dense grove of orange trees of which this side of the gazebo had a view.

Astonished and delighted by this unexpected change of décor, Mademoiselle Arnold hurriedly arose and ran towards the mirrored panel, exclaiming: "Oh! What a magical effect!"

Whether it was due to the young woman's haste or of the distraction of Mrs. S***, who'd also gotten up and stared curiously at

Valentine's lovely face, the two women jostled one another slightly while passing by one another.

"Pardon me, madame!" said Mademoiselle Arnold, although she was by no means sure this brusque encounter could be attributed to her.

Rather than answer her as the rules of courtesy would seem to require, the Creole woman turned towards Hortense:

"Darling, aren't you tempted to take a short walk in this shade before nap time takes us back to our rooms?" Saying this, Mrs. S*** took from the hands of one of her slave-women two of those fans made of multicolored feathers with handles of ivory or ebony, which in Europe are used as screens.

"Here, cousin," continued the Creole woman, handing one of the fans to the young woman.

She kept the other, and the slave-woman gave the one remaining in her hands to Valentine.

"What must I do with this, madame?" asked Hortense.

"Whatever you'd like, my dear," answered Mrs. S***, heading towards the doors of the gazebo, which opened onto the grove.

"Valentine!" said Mademoiselle Melvil. "Come on!"

At her friend's call, Mademoiselle Arnold stepped away from that mirror through which she was admiring the grove of trees that have the privilege of bearing simultaneously and almost uninterruptedly both blossoms and fruits. Ever prompt in her movements, she reached the door Ramma had opened for his mistress, just as the latter was showing her relative through. She followed her immediately, thereby leaving behind Valentine, who didn't have time to notice this new discourtesy.

The plantation owner, after exchanging a few words in a low voice with Mr. Melvil, approached the young woman and took her by the hand to help her down the steps leading from the gazebo into the grove. Francis exited in turn and, passing them almost immediately, went to join his sister and Mrs. S***.

Since the path was too narrow for three people to walk there abreast, Hortense briefly surrendered her spot beside her relative and began to chat with the eldest of their hosts' daughters. The other children had remained in the gazebo.

They walked along in pairs, therefore, beneath the trees whose foliage formed a dome of greenery over their heads. All varieties of oranges were assembled there: the myrtle-leaved orange, as small as a walnut, and which is only eaten candied;[22] the bitter orange,[23] whose extremely sour juice is used to marinate game; the bergamot orange,[24] from which a delicious essence is derived; and many others besides, which would take too long to enumerate.

"I had, in fact, heard praise of the magnificence of the New World's forests," Mademoiselle Arnold was saying, "but I didn't suppose we'd find orange groves planted outside practically at the city gates."[25]

"This one may not be of as great an extent as you suppose," answered Mr. S***. "It contains only some two thousand trees."

"Two thousand!" repeated an amazed Valentine.

"We used to have the double of that here," continued the Creole man with a sigh, "and they were much more fruitful than these."

"To what cause do you attribute this decline?" asked Valentine.

"Mortality, rather," exclaimed the plantation owner, "for it was precisely that, twenty-five years ago, which ruined those like me who earn the bulk of their revenue from their orange groves. It was the result of one of those sudden changes in temperature Francis told you about earlier."

"In mid-February, for a whole week we experienced such a warm spell all the trees in our orangery—that's what we call our orange groves—were covered in blossoms and lots of still-green fruit ripened suddenly.[26] It was easy to foresee the unhappy consequences of this spring, or to put it better, of this premature summer, but there was no remedy for it. So, our consternation, but not surprise, was great when, one night, the wind blowing out of the southwest shifted to the northeast and suddenly brought us a chill of 15°F![27] The orange

Le Colibri léger gracieux, riche de parure, voltige de fleur en fleur.

Figure 8. Caption, translated, is "The violetear—light, gracious, richly adorned—flits from flower to flower." This illustration appeared in the 1845 edition of the novel.

trees, for the most part, froze. We had to cut them more or less down to the root. Some of them grew back, but many others perished."[28]

"Luckily," continued the planter, "we Louisianans are too accustomed to the vicissitudes of fortune and to temperature variations not to put up bravely with both the one and the other. Instead of being discouraged as Europeans almost always are in such cases, we actively occupy ourselves with defraying our losses and often succeed in doing so."

At that moment, Valentine dropped her fan while standing on her tiptoes to capture from a branch full of flowers a tiny little bird whose plumage gleamed with colors of topaz, sapphire, ruby, and emerald. Mr. S*** hurried to pick it up and kept it. Mademoiselle Arnold had stopped to follow with her eyes the flight of this charming bird that had fled, while sounding a very fine cry that we can translate into human language by this syllable: *zee, zee.*

"Isn't that a hummingbird?" asked Valentine.

"No, but it resembles it so much the error is quite excusable.[29] Like the hummingbird, the violetear—light, gracious, richly adorned—flits from flower to flower, existing off their nectar, and lives only in the lands where it multiplies. However, the hummingbird is even smaller than the violetear. Its faster, more continuous flight produces a sort of buzzing like that of a spinning wheel. Its call, *scrup, scrup,* demonstrates an impatient, even irascible liveliness of which it gives frequent proof, moreover, whether it's by tearing petals from flowers it unexpectedly finds to be withered or by pursuing with an incredible boldness birds ten times bigger than itself, which it attacks and riddles with blows from its needle-sharp beak, attaching itself to its enemy's body and allowing itself to be carried aloft by the latter.[30] Furthermore, hummingbirds and violetears are of a sensitivity that prevents them from living in aviaries no matter how vast they might be. These little beings, true jewels of nature, require immensity of space. They're not very mistrustful either, perhaps because they know the nimbleness of their movements makes them uncatchable."

"They're charming birds," said Mademoiselle Arnold.

"We have many others that, without deserving to be lumped together in relation to fragility and beauty, are still deserving of the naturalist's attention. See that gracious little bird with quills mixed with interchanging white and violet . . . it's the white-headed oriole of Louisiana.[31] That one with brown and orangey-yellow on its body and wings and whose head is covered by a small hood of downy black bears the name of one of the most business-minded cities of northern America—it's called a Baltimore oriole."

"It's really too bad," Valentine remarked again, "that, in lands where birds seem to borrow their most brilliant and harmonious nuances from flowers, nature has deprived them of a voice. Those that aren't entirely mute have a husky, sharp, monotone cry, which hurts your ear instead of charming it."[32]

"Your observation is just, with respect to a great number of winged inhabitants of tropical countries," rejoined Mr. S***, "but not for all of them, however. Among the exceptions to the general rule, we number the Carolina wren. It sings well, whirls in its flight, and doesn't abandon us during the winter as do many birds, including the hummingbird, which retires to the Floridas[33] or Mexico. We have the goldfinch, a little bird of the warbler kind, whose ample size and gentleness it possesses. Its plumage of a beautiful yellow on its neck, breast, and throat is shaded with different colors on the rest of its body. You can hear its rather pleasant song almost every month of the year.[34] I can also cite for you the olive oriole, particular to Louisiana; the waxwing, which has a very pretty warbling, to which it owes its French name of a *jaseur*.[35] Its coat is wine-red, its tail feathers quite lovely, and its head is adorned with a crest.[36] But unquestionably, the king of the singers is the mockingbird.[37] Many of them can be found in America's woods and grasslands. Besides its voice being extremely melodious, it's endowed to a truly prodigious degree with an ability to imitate all song, all cries that strike its ear. Although it loves its freedom, it isn't shy. Far from fleeing humankind, it willingly comes near homes, often builds its nest on neighboring trees, and, by treating it well, some do manage to tame it. It's regrettable that the natives of the land, whose

Cassique, de la Louisiane.

Figure 9. This hand-colored eighteenth-century plate from the French naturalist Buffon's volume on birds purports to depict a white-headed oriole of Louisiana. Lebrun derived her information on this bird from that source.

entire life is spent hunting, pitilessly destroy a great many of these charming virtuosos whose flesh, unfortunately for them and their admirers, is good to eat."

"I'd quite like to have the chance to judge the talent of those able musicians," said Valentine. "Indeed, monsieur," she added, making a movement to take back the feathered fan Mr. S*** had been waving around her, "I'm rather scatterbrained. The ornithological details you've had the kindness to give kept me from noticing till now—"

Figure 10. The alligator as depicted in Buffon.

"—That I'd taken it upon myself," concluded the laughing Creole, "to grab and use as a fan or fly-whisk, which you and your friend, as the true European women you've become, disdain to make use."

"Say that we 'neglect,' not that we 'disdain,'" responded Mademoiselle Arnold.

"Perhaps y'all's negligence wouldn't have lasted so long if both my daughter and I hadn't spared you two the discomforts of your lack of concern. Without the ceaseless fanning we were doing with these bouquets of feathers you'd been holding motionless in your hands as you might have done with flowers, sweat would be running down your faces, which myriads of mosquitos would've come to beleaguer.

Furthermore, in the parts of this path where the sunbeams pierce through the canopy of leaves, which isn't sufficient to intercept them everywhere, we've protected you from their reach by interposing these fans between the beams and your heads."

"Madame S*** was right, then," concluded Valentine, answering Hortense, who'd asked what she was to do with her screen during the stroll: "Whatever you'd like."

At that moment, Hortense turned back to share with her friend a pomegranate Miss S*** had just given to her. Pomegranates, while not greatly cultivated in Louisiana, succeed quite well there, however.

Miss Melvil's kind thought for Valentine interrupted the latter's conversation with the planter, and a short while later, they found themselves back in front of the gazebo.

Mrs. S*** didn't go back inside. Unaccustomed to walking, especially in such heat, she said she felt horribly fatigued by this short stroll.

Yet she was the very one who'd proposed it.

Whether her tiredness was feigned or real, the Creole woman, after embracing Hortense and addressing to Mademoiselle Arnold a slight inclination of her head, left along with her daughter. The two friends returned to their rooms, too, but by passing back through the gazebo and the trellised gallery in which Francis and his relative stayed to chat for a short while.

Valentine and Hortense's rooms connected with one another via a small sitting room where there were two sofas upon which the young women stretched out. Not yet having gotten into the habit of taking a nap, they'd lain down almost out of necessity to spend the blazing-hot hour of noon in inactivity, rather than to indulge in sleep.

Nevertheless, such was the need for rest they were unexpectedly experiencing that, after some ten minutes of chatting—a conversation of which the sole subject was Madame S***, with her fickle mood and disdainful, if not impertinent, manners—they fell asleep almost simultaneously.

CHAPTER SIX

A Storm

When Mesdemoiselles Arnold and Melvil awoke, they glanced at the clock and realized, not without surprise, that they'd slept for a good five hours. The recent illness of one of them, the successive vigils of the other, and the fatigue of a night spent in a carriage explained sufficiently, however, the length of their slumber.

A few moments later, the bell for dinner sounded, and the young women went down to the dining room. They were welcomed there by Mr. S*** surrounded by his four younger children. But his wife and eldest daughter didn't appear. The former, said the plantation owner in an apologetic tone, felt too indisposed to leave her rooms; the second had remained with her mother to keep her company.

As Mr. S*** was finishing these words, Francis also entered the room, and everyone sat down at the table.

"The heat's gotten unbearable," said Mr. Melvil. "I fear this will bring us rain . . . so I've already given orders to remove the carriage's mosquito net and to replace it with the leather cover."

"So you still mean to leave this very evening?" asked the master of the plantation.

"Right after dinner."

"You're not taking into account the weather, which upsets many a plan hereabouts."

"A storm would cool the air and make our travel more enjoyable," said Mademoiselle Melvil.

"The torrential rains that sometimes follow storms often, in very short order, make the roads unusable for several days," answered Mr. S***.

"You're trying to frighten us, cousin!" exclaimed Hortense.

"While our forecast might seem frightening to you," the Creole man replied gallantly, "they don't seem so for us, who'd find that a deluge's inconveniences wouldn't be too dear a cost for the pleasure of keeping you at our plantation for two or three weeks."

These gracious words seemed to be addressed equally to the two friends positioned beside one another. Smiling, they bowed. Francis, for his part, remained serious, however.

Mademoiselle Melvil began again, "I think my brother has important matters to conclude, which, despite your hospitable welcome, make him want our trip not to be delayed."

"Beyond the fact that the sudden indisposition of Mrs. S*** would make prolonging our stay here quite ill-mannered," added Francis, in a tone whose terseness seemed strange to Valentine.

Not having been a part of that conversation, she had perceived, moreover, in the features and tone of the plantation owner a hint of embarrassment and, in those of Mr. Melvil, an expression of discontent, which Hortense, obliged to partake in the conversation, hadn't noticed at all.

"The sky's gotten especially dark," remarked Mr. S***. "Have the shutters opened," he then ordered Ramma.

At that moment, a lightning bolt flashed across the immense, black cloud threatening to overrun the entire firmament and, almost simultaneously, a rapid, ear-splitting thunderclap rattled the plantation house's wooden walls. It was the only one. The cloud, torn asunder by the burst of lightning, dissolved into torrents of rain.

"It's impossible for you to leave today, my dear Francis," resumed Mr. S***.

"Who knows?" answered Hortense. "The sky's already starting to clear. In a few hours, perhaps, the rain won't be falling any longer."

"That's possible," said Mr. Melvil, "but in any case, the night will be too humid for a convalescent such as you. We must resign ourselves to waiting till tomorrow. With cooler temperatures, we'll be able to travel at least part of the morning and will make up for lost time that way."

Mr. S*** had gotten up from the table and, at that moment, was looking through the windowpanes at the weathervane set atop the roof of the gazebo in which he'd offered lunch to his guests. Hearing the end of Francis's response to his sister, he shook his head doubtfully.

Dinner over, they went into the sitting room. The evening was a dismal one, as is usually the case everywhere whenever the mistress of the house isn't in attendance. Everyone went to his or her rooms early, not without noticing that the rain was falling as fiercely as from the start.

Getting up the next morning, the young women first ran to their windows. The yard surrounding the house offered nothing more than the sad aspect of a pond.[1] Louisiana's flat, muddy terrain doesn't help the runoff of rainfall that, in some places, forms huge puddles whose fetid odors greatly contribute to the unhealthiness of the air that people breathe in that land.[2]

And still it continued to rain.

It lasted not only that whole day, but the following night and next day, too. Finally, the sun began to shine again, and Mr. Melvil had just given his orders for their departure when Ramma apprised him of the unhappy news of the overflow of the Red River and the Mississippi.[3] The road leading to the Cyprière was under water.

Who could say how long it would take those two rivers to return to their beds? While it was possible to reach Francis's plantation by means of another route, that way was passable only for travelers on horseback or afoot, and what's more, since it crossed through a forest, one couldn't venture it without a trustworthy guide.

This delay to which no precise end could be assigned was extremely irksome for Mr. Melvil. The affairs of several of his clients required his presence in New Orleans. Although the epidemic continued to run rampant there—once it manifests itself in an area, its ravages seldom cease before the beginning of the winter[4]—a great number of residents had stayed in the city. Those among them who, such as Mr. Melvil, had already had yellow fever were safe from its effects thereafter and attended to their ordinary occupations without fear.

But while the young lawyer was exempt of all personal concern in this respect, he rightly felt it with respect to his sister. Although she might have resisted the scourge's first attacks, she couldn't be considered invulnerable. Hortense also needed country air to recover entirely. A permanent lassitude, a lack of appetite, and an excess of indolence were indicative of a kind of general prostration, the natural consequence of the illness to which she'd nearly succumbed.

Francis could, it seems, have left the young ladies at the home of Mr. and Mrs. S*** for one or two months. Nonetheless, he positively refused the invitation extended to him by the Creole man on behalf of his wife, who persisted in keeping to her room.

Perhaps to Mr. Melvil this persistence—all the more singular since the patient's illness didn't present sufficient seriousness to warrant calling for a physician—seemed an inexcusable impoliteness. One would be tempted to presume such, based on the air of indifference with which he informed himself each morning of the health of that nonchalant or temperamental Creole woman.

To his daily inquiries, Mr. S*** invariably repeated the explanation he'd given the first day, namely: "That the nervous suffering to which his wife was prone, though making hustle and bustle unbearable to her, and sometimes lasting for quite a long time, wasn't of a nature to cause any worry."

An unexpected circumstance finally drew Mr. Melvil from this state of perplexity. Indians belonging to one of those tribes[5] from the west, who maintain business dealings with whites, passed by the plantation one day and stopped there to offer the cook some of the game they were carrying to New Orleans.

In fact, on market days in that city, one encounters whole families of these savages, ordinarily referred to by the generic name of "redskins."

Their sole garment consisted of a loincloth with which they envelop
their body from their lower back to their knees. As with the majority
of uncivilized peoples, women are the ones laden with the heaviest
burdens: the men busy themselves only with hunting and fishing.

Three of them stopped at the home of Mr. S***. Among them was
a young boy Mr. Melvil noticed while crossing the colonnade and
whose traits he thought he recognized. He approached the child,
spoke a few words to him in English, which the latter answered. He,
too, remembered having seen Francis at the Cyprière when he'd just
purchased it, that is to say, three years prior, and having sold Francis
a lynx or bobcat pelt.[6]

This animal with a spotted pelt, and whose gaze is simultaneously
gleaming and velvety, is about the size of a fox. It howls like a wolf,
walks and leaps like a cat, pursues squirrels to treetops, and boldly
attacks deer and horses even. Hunting this creature is not without
its perils. The one Mr. Melvil had bought from the young savage was
the first carnivorous animal he'd ever killed; what's more, Francis had
paid him handsomely for that skin, which was truly beautiful, and
since then, the Indian continued to go to the Cyprière from time to
time to sell game and live waterfowl to Maurice, the overseer.

Mr. Melvil was the first to get the idea of hiring him as a guide to the
Cyprière. Mitou—that was the Indian's name—had, in fact, just skirted
the forest they had to traverse to reach the sugarcane plantation; for
that matter, all savages know how to orient themselves so admirably
well that—even in woods entirely unknown to them—there's no risk
of going astray when being led by them.

If it had been a matter of only himself, Francis would've immediately set out with Mitou, but he was the travel companion and
protector of two young women, one of whom especially was delicate
and timorous, and there was no precaution he wouldn't take to spare
them not only of any sort of peril, but also fright.

Consequently, he wrote to Maurice to bring mules[7] without delay,
which are the gentlest and safest mount for women in every land where
paths present any danger. For—while there's no precipice to avoid, crag

to climb, or torrent to traverse in Louisiana—in these dark forests with horses, all of which are a bit skittish and prone to bolting, one must fear the hissing of snakes, the screams of lynxes—unknown noises or, at least, ones very seldom heard in lands inhabited by men—not to mention the obstacles presented to travelers' progress by gigantic tree trunks toppled by age or broken by lightning, enormous vines, and great pools of stagnant water.

Mitou consented all the more readily to serve as Mr. Melvil's messenger, because the latter promised him a double-barreled shotgun in payment and because Mr. S***'s cook had just relieved him of the deer he'd been carrying, laid across his shoulders, along with the leather belt attached around his lower back, from which were suspended a dozen of those little woodcocks or Louisiana quail, much prized in New Orleans and with which the Indians provision that city's market.[8]

Unlike him, Mitou's companions, having been unable to sell all their bits of game, continued on their way. The young Indian alone was heading back. Indeed, he didn't even need to go all the way to the Cyprière to fulfill his duty. Halfway there, he met Maurice. Based on the letter written by Francis to his overseer before departing from New Orleans, the latter had figured the rains and flooding would hamper the travelers' progress at a very short distance from the city.

And right away, he'd gone to get from the sugar plantation's stables five mules, upon two of which he'd put women's saddles. A third one had been loaded with food supplies, bulrush mats, and a piece of that fabric called sailcloth that is used for tents. For, although the way through the forest was much shorter than the one following the river's course, they couldn't go without camping out one night, either in the middle of the woods or on a prairie it was also necessary to cross. The other two mules would serve as mounts: one for Mr. Melvil, the other for Maurice and the slave-woman attached to the young ladies' service. As for the slave the overseer had brought along, he was a tireless walker and preferred to make the trip on foot.[9]

CHAPTER SEVEN

. . . .

Through the Forest

Mr. Melvil was rather pleasantly surprised to see his overseer[1] appear twenty-four hours sooner than he could have hoped.

They prepared to depart immediately. It was decided the carriage and wagon would remain at Mr. S***'s plantation along with the horses and two slaves who'd driven them there until Francis's return, for the young lawyer was planning to come back to New Orleans via his relative's plantation once he'd settled Hortense and Valentine at the Cyprière. As for the baggage the wagon contained, other mules would be sent immediately from the sugar plantation to transport it there.

Matters having been arranged thus, the travelers climbed onto their mules. Mademoiselle Arnold, more prompt in her movements than her friend, was already a few paces from the house when she heard a soft voice exclaim from a second-floor balcony:

"Have a good trip, cousin dear. 'Bye for now!"

It was Mrs. S***, who'd finally overcome the malaise she'd claimed to be experiencing for more than six days, in order to bid her young relative farewell.

Upon seeing her at her window, from which she was blowing kisses to Hortense with that childlike grace of Creole women, Valentine tightened her mule's bridle to stop. She was turning her head to make a polite inquiry to the supposedly ill woman as to the state of her health, when Francis—who'd just silently taken his leave of the planter with a handshake and of his wife with a ceremonious salute—approached the young woman:

"Mademoiselle," he said to her, "please continue going forward. My sister will follow your example. Otherwise, she's apt to waste precious time in an exchange of idle words. It's important we reach the forest's entrance before the sun shines its rays straight down on our heads."

While saying so, Mr. Melvil brought his mule alongside that of Mademoiselle Arnold who, while listening to the short speech of her friend's brother, had stopped restraining her mount. The result of this short scene, seemingly of very little importance, was to prevent Valentine from taking leave in any fashion of the mistress of the plantation from which the young woman was departing.

After two or three hours of travel, the party arrived at the entrance of the forest into which they plunged. Although Maurice knew well enough the direction to take to get to the Cyprière, he nonetheless let the slave, whom he'd chosen among all the others at the sugarcane plantation, lead the way along with the mule loaded with provisions. This was because he was more familiar than any of them with these woods, where he'd spent six weeks after escaping the plantation of Mrs. A***.

The "maroon" (that's what they call slaves who run away from the plantations to which they belong) had, during that time, lived off of roots, wild fruit, and birds he'd caught in their slumber. By day, he slept hidden in the leafy branches of tall trees; at night, he hunted squirrels. Those animals hardly move about until after the setting of the sun whose heat they fear greatly. The slave of whom we're speaking would hit them on the head with a stick he'd throw at them from a distance and would then profit from the stupor caused by this unexpected blow to grab them. He'd then sell them to the Indians who traded with whites and would get a few bottles of tafia from them in exchange.

But this delightful existence—because for a black slave, there's no happiness comparable to that of absolute idleness brightened by a few swigs of hard liquor—this existence, shall we say, didn't last long.

One day, when the overseer of Mrs. A***'s sugarcane plantation was crossing through the forest, he spotted the runaway cutting water vines² to slake his thirst.   *French*

This kind of vine differs from others in that its soft, spongy stalks, which resemble green cables, contain a fresh, clear water. For, in the majority of America's forests, particularly the one Mr. Melvil and his travel companions had just entered, the swampy soil dotted with ponds of stagnant water offers neither brook nor spring to quench the thirst of people passing through.

Pursued by the overseer, who was accompanied by two of those large dogs³ trained by whites for hunting maroons, the unfortunate black man had managed, however, to elude him. But, after a tiring race meant to confuse the dogs, the runaway's strength failed him. He fell exhausted amid the tall grasses on the edge of a prairie belonging to Mr. Melvil. There, slaves assigned to the latter's sugarcane plantation recognized him, got him on his feet, and, since he remained deprived of the use of his senses, brought him to the Cyprière.

Aware of his master's philanthropic sentiments and sure in advance of his approval, Maurice had gone without delay to Mrs. A***'s sugarhouse. The goal of this step wasn't to obtain mercy for the culprit from that inhumane woman—any attempt in that respect would have been fruitless. It was in order to bargain with her, through her overseer, concerning the purchase of two elderly slave-women of whom the Creole woman wanted to rid herself and then, afterwards, concerning that of the fugitive whom he well knew, he admitted, to have eluded the searches ordered by his mistress, but whom, probably, the runaway's own brother, a slave at the Cyprière, would manage to find and wrest from his errant, perilous life.⁴

After a bit of hesitation, Mrs. A*** agreed to the deal. In this instance, her cupidity silenced her maliciousness. A runaway slave is, in fact, subject to very harsh punishments whenever he falls back into the power of the masters from whose yoke he attempts to escape, and, judging by the tyrannical character of Mrs. A***, one must presume that, for her, it would be a true joy to see them inflicted on him. But it was becoming doubtful, based on the lack of success of previous pursuits at least, that they'd ever recapture him, whereas the sum at which he'd been valued was going to be paid to her immediately. Furthermore, Maurice, who was acting in the name of Francis and from whom he derived his authority, made the transfer of the Creole woman's rights over the runaway one of the conditions of the purchase of the two slave-women whom the overseer figured would be suitable for the personal service of Mademoiselle Melvil, whose pending departure from Europe, at that juncture, had been announced.

The deal had, therefore, been concluded, and, as Maurice expected, the runaway—happy both to find himself with a brother of whom he was quite fond and to pass under the dominion of a master as universally loved by his slaves as was Mr. Melvil—proved to be as submissive, hardworking, and zealous as he'd been lazy, careless, and intractable with his former mistress.

Mrs. A*** had learned of this transformation and the ruse employed by Maurice to shield the runaway from her vengeance. Thus was she impatiently awaiting Francis's arrival at the Cyprière to lodge a complaint in that regard.

Maurice had given all these details to Mr. Melvil when the young lawyer asked his overseer the name of the slave leading the little caravan's trek and who was entirely unknown to him.

Our young ladies had been traveling through the forest for about a half-hour, and the pair continued to maintain a silence that was the result of that religious contemplation into which, almost unconsciously, fall those who enter these imposing solitudes for the first time.

"Brother," Mademoiselle Melvil finally said, "why's our guide continually striking the vines and tall grasses on the left and right with the big stick he's holding in his hand?"

"It's to clear our way through," answered Francis.

"And also, I imagine," added Valentine, "to scare off reptiles and other harmful animals, which the hooves of our mules might startle in their sleep and whose abruptly aroused anger would be dangerous."

"That's true, too," said Mr. Melvil.

"Are there lots of snakes in these woods?" asked Hortense with a worried tone.

"Not only in these woods, but also on the prairies, in the sugarcane fields, and especially in the cypress marshes and stands and on the banks of the Mississippi, whose waters are extremely muddy after its confluence with the Missouri. During their annual floods, which levees built by the hand of man are insufficient to prevent everywhere, they deposit silt that's very favorable to the reproduction of all sorts of reptiles, from the alligator, the most fearsome of amphibious creatures, to the earthworm, the most inoffensive of all crawling animals."[5]

"If," he continued, "during your arrival at New Orleans, you'd gone up the river at daybreak, during that trajectory of some thirty leagues, you'd have seen thousands of caimans sunning themselves on tree trunks the Mississippi carries all the way to its delta, several of which will get entangled with one another and, perhaps, end up obstructing the river. Furthermore, over its course of some twelve hundred leagues in length, the Mississippi isn't the only one to sweep along the gigantic debris of the ancient forests it waters. In times of flood, the Red River uproots enormous trees that pile up in certain places, narrow the riverbed, and sometimes form solid bridges over which you can cross the river. Many centuries have no doubt passed since the first occurrences of this kind took place, for nowadays, these singular bridges are covered over with vegetation upon which there is growing a new forest, and that last word is no exaggeration in this case. These natural plantings growing on tree trunks are, in the direction of the river, more than twenty leagues in length. In truth, the river flowing below this embankment reappears every so often, but those intervals are growing smaller by the year and probably won't exist much longer."[6]

"What marvelous works are those performed by nature!" exclaimed Mademoiselle Arnold.

"There are others less grandiose, but more gracious, that would excite your admiration even more," continued Mr. Melvil. "In the western lands inhabited by tribes of redskins, there are large streams that people in

Europe would call rivers, above which Nature has cast elegant vaults of foliage. These vaults don't block the passage of the Indians' boats. Their rafts and pirogues, or dugouts made from a single tree trunk, glide and cross paths beneath verdant arcades filled with fragrance by the parasitical or climbing plants mixing their flowers among these branches."

"It must produce a charming sight!" said Valentine.

"Won't we make a stop soon?" asked Hortense. "It must be close to noon."

"Have you already gotten so into the habit of a nap that you know it's time for one without the help of a watch?" exclaimed Mademoiselle Arnold.

"I don't know that I've gotten used to it, but I do feel the need for one," answered the indolent young woman, whose eyelids were half-closed.

"Let's go a bit longer," said Mr. Melvil. "Maurice spoke to me of a clearing where we'll find more space than here to set up our tent."

"We're already there," announced the slave leading the string of mules.

And he stopped. The clearing was a square of ground recently stripped of ten or so trees.

"What's the point of setting up a tent and unrolling the mats?" murmured Hortense, getting off her mule and watching Maurice help the slave to sink stakes into the ground upon which they then stretched the piece of sailcloth; after which they covered the ground with green bulrush mats.

"These dense grasses rival the fluffiest bed, and the canopy formed overhead by the intertwined branches of those pecan trees and wild figs ought to be enough to shelter us."

"Yes," answered the overseer, "but a snake might fall on your head from that tree cover and—"

"Ah! That's true," said Mademoiselle Melvil languidly, interrupting the mulatto, as people of an apathetic, fainthearted character often do whenever someone tries to shield them from a physical or moral danger the sole supposition of which troubles their repose.

And the young woman lay down on the mat and fell asleep.

Instead of following her example, Mademoiselle Arnold remained at the tent's entrance watching the birds flitting about the foliage. She recognized the majority of those described to her by Mr. S*** during their stroll in the orange grove. However, she didn't spot the ones she desired most keenly to hear and admire—the mockingbird or hummingbird.

So as not to disturb Hortense's nap, she whispered her disappointment to Francis in this regard. "The hummingbird," Francis told her, "doesn't frequent the woods, where it would lack for sunlight, space, and flowers. But you'll surely find some on the great prairie, a part of which we'll pass by before arriving at the Cyprière. As for the mockingbird, we won't have too far to go to find some—and hey! Do you see that bird about the size of a robin, with a gray-brown plumage, rocking atop a pine tree on the black foliage against which the more cheerful green of that spray of ebony trees stands out?"[7]

Valentine nodded, and Mr. Melvil continued:

"It's the charming musician whose talent far exceeds that of the nightingale, which, were the latter to hear the former, would exhaust itself in vain efforts to equal it and soon die of fatigue and jealousy. Unfortunately, this one won't sing unless we keep silent. It's not accustomed to the human voice, which startles and troubles it. There it goes, flying away from its position up top to hide in the branches of that live oak. By not seeing us, it'll forget about us and, if we're quiet, maybe it'll sing."

So the two of them interrupted their conversation, and, a few moments later, the bird, thinking itself alone, sang as a prelude of sorts a few brilliant, perfectly sustained notes, which were followed by a series of roulades, arpeggios, and cadenzas of irreproachable flair and purity.

Mademoiselle Arnold was lending a charmed, attentive ear to these songs, when the virtuoso suddenly stopped in the middle of a delightful *fermata* to which it was putting a finish, an expressivity that would have done honor to our most capable opera singers, and abruptly abandoned the retreat it had chosen.

"Well now?" said Valentine.

In response to this exclamation, Mr. Melvil pointed out to her an animal rather similar to a fox, peacefully walking under the trees neighboring the one the mockingbird had just abandoned.

Scarcely had this animal heard Valentine's voice when, seized by a panic similar to the one it had itself caused the mockingbird, it instantaneously stood on its hind legs, accompanying this movement with a cry that caused all of its little ones, which, till then, had been wandering around the live oak, to come running. The latter immediately hurried into a sort of pouch positioned under the belly of their mother, who fled once she had them all safely stowed away.

Is there any need to spell out the name of this animal? Have our readers not recognized the female opossum?[8]

In the meantime, the slave-man and -woman had spread out on a big basket-shaped platter a portion of the provisions brought by Maurice and to which fresher ones had been added at the plantation of Mr. S***. Since Mademoiselle Melvil seemed plunged into a deep sleep, however, her brother and Valentine chose to delay lunch until she awoke. While they waited for her, Francis pointed out to Mademoiselle Arnold various kinds of trees, all of them magnificent and several of which were unknown to the young woman.

He showed her the sassafras tree, whose root and bark are very useful in medicine and also serve two particular uses for Louisianans. They make light infusions from the former, which many of them drink as a tea and, from the latter, make a powder they call *gumbo filé*,[9] with which they season various dishes. He also pointed out the *gossampin* or silk-cotton tree,[10] also called a *fromager* in the French West Indies: it was given the first of these names because of its resemblance to a pine tree. Its fruit contains a sort of very soft, fine, lustrous, pearl-gray cotton fiber. There were also some maples and cedars worthy of rivaling by their height and beauty those of Lebanon.[11]

Once Hortense finally opened her eyes, they had lunch; they then resumed their voyage. Before day's end, Maurice wanted to reach one of the forest's edges that verged on a vast prairie. As a result, they hurried the mules' pace and, shortly before nightfall, stopped at the opening to a spacious, gently rolling plain whose vegetation, mixed with an infinite variety of flowers, had preserved its greenness, thanks to the coolness sustained there by brooks of a remarkable clarity.

Upon arriving at this place, Valentine and Hortense could feel their lungs opening up and, comparing the sweet, pure air they were breathing there with the thick, humid air in the woods they were leaving behind, they told one another the overseer was right to want to get them out of there before dark.

Close to the spot where the tent was busily being set up again was an ajoupa,[12] a sort of cabin or shed, rather, made of bamboo stalks covered by bulrush mats. They are commonly encountered on the deserted plains where native hunters have built them. As the two friends approached to take a look, they saw Mitou emerge from it.

It was hereabouts that the young Indian had encountered the mulatto Maurice in search of whom Mr. Melvil had sent him. And presuming, not unreasonably, that Maurice would return with his masters by the same path, he'd been on the lookout for them in the meantime, with the probable intention of following them to the Cyprière where he was to receive the double-barreled shotgun Francis had promised. Nevertheless, since the young savage had only had to go halfway to the sugarcane plantation to acquit himself of his errand, the agreed-upon price really was a bit exorbitant. Mitou counted highly on Mr. Melvil's generosity, however, and his expectations were not disappointed.

"Come with us to the Cyprière," Francis said to the Indian.

Which meant:

"Come fetch your shotgun."

"What did you do while waiting for us?" he asked him next.

Mitou, who understood English passably well, although he spoke it with difficulty,[13] showed Francis, by way of a response, twenty or so skins of a reddish brown, about sixteen inches in length, some spotted, others with black stripes, spread out on the grass around the ajoupa to dry in the sun.

"How'd you kill those little animals?" asked Mr. Melvil.

"I caught 'em alive in their holes, not far from here," answered Mitou.

"I'd be curious to see 'em," rejoined Francis.

So, the Indian boy went into the tall grasses and, after a walk of five or six minutes, pointed out to Mr. Melvil and the young women who'd followed him a field located some distance away from the place where the four of them had just stopped.

"Do you see 'em?" asked Mitou.

"Yes," responded Francis, "and they're just what I'd surmised, prairie dogs."

And indeed, several prairie dogs sat peacefully atop a shaped mound formed of earth that these animals, which belong to the great family of rodents, cast out of the burrows they dig for themselves. Others were playing nearby.

Mesdemoiselles Arnold and Melvil thought they looked more like marmots or rats than dogs and shared their observation with Francis.

"It's true," responded the latter. "Thus, this animal, discovered only in 1807 in Louisiana, is classed in natural history under the name of *Spermophilus*.[14] The rather improper one of 'prairie dog' was given to it by hunters because of the resemblance they found between its cry of fright and a little dog's yapping. It's hardly ever to be seen except in flat, sandy areas. I once believed it only existed near the banks of the Missouri. It's a social animal. The ones you see getting fresh air around their burrow likely live in it together. These burrows, inside of which they spend the winter plunged in a lethargic slumber, are ordinarily one or two feet in depth and carpeted with a fine, dry grass. It requires boundless skill to capture them alive, as did this young Indian, for they're very fierce and bite viciously when provoked. I regret you can't see them a little closer up. Their big eyes and black whiskers give an air of strange savagery to their singularly large, flattened heads."

"Why don't we go closer to them?" exclaimed Valentine, taking a step in their direction.

Figure 11. Caption, translated, is "'How'd you kill these little animals?' asked Mr. Melvil." This illustration appeared as a frontispiece in the 1845 edition of the novel.

"They might lunge at us to bite us!" said Hortense, holding her friend back by her arm.

"Oh! Their short temper doesn't extend to prompting them to begin the attack first," continued a laughing Mr. Melvil. "But at the slightest alarm, they'll hurry into their burrows. As for you, mesdemoiselles, you'd do best to go back into your tent. Night is falling. The prairies are full of mosquitos, and we don't have any fly-whisks to shoo them away."

Saying so, Francis went back, and the two friends followed him.

Through Maurice's efforts, a meal composed of cold meats, fruits, and preserves was already served on the grass, which the slave had trimmed close to the ground, as well as in the tent, so that it now resembled nothing more than a green carpet. Once she returned to her mistresses after going to one of the nearby streams to refill the water in the gourds they'd gotten from the Creole's plantation, the slave-woman lit a grass fire beside the tent, the smoke of which is one of the best deterrents against mosquitos, which were starting to harass the travelers.

This fire had to be stoked until sunrise in order to keep away reptiles and wild animals. In any case, Mr. Melvil and Maurice planned to keep watch overnight outside, although Mitou would have given them his ajoupa. He asserted he was just as happy, if not more so, sleeping under the stars, a claim he proved by stretching out on the grass outside the tent occupied by the young women at the feet of whom slept the black maid.

The next day, at first light, they set out again, taking care to follow the edge of the forest, so that our travelers were sheltered by the trees against the ardent sunbeams and would, in the meantime, take advantage of the morning breeze cooled further by the water of the streams, whose surface it was rippling with its wind.

Nature was awakening gradually. Birds flitted from one branch to another, in their joyous movements shaking leaves from which dewdrops escaped. Broadleaf plantain, lemon balm, angelica, and all manner of ferns abound on these savannas, blending their pleasant aromas with the humid scents given off by the woods. Insects chittered in the grass, and the bees, abandoning their tree trunks in the hollow of which they deposit their honey, scattered, buzzing over the plain.

The large brown heron[15] of America and the reddish egret, whose species seems to be limited to Louisiana,[16] their feet in the water and their heads between their legs, were on the lookout for the passing fish they eat for nourishment. Their mournful aspect and immobility contrasted with the ebullient joyfulness of violetears and hummingbirds lifting themselves into the air. Some of those large grasshoppers, whose fire-colored wings contrast with the jet black of their bodies—which is called an eastern lubber grasshopper[17] in this country—would sometimes launch from the ground, covering in one jump a distance of three or four yards, and frightening by their sudden apparition the magnificent butterflies to whom flowers were opening their petals.

"Oh, what a beautiful land Louisiana is!" Valentine and Hortense repeated to one another over and over.

After two or three hours of travel, the small caravan stopped for lunch. That's when Mitou, whose visual and auditory organs had that keenness peculiar to the native inhabitant of the great solitudes, signaled the approach of a band of redskins several minutes before they were perceptible to Mr. Melvil and the two young ladies. The distance separating the white travelers from the Indians was so very far that the former were preparing to remount their mules by the time the latter joined them.

There were twelve of them, an equal number of men and women, not counting the infants carried by their mothers haphazardly along with unskinned skunks, stoats, and martens,[18] in hoods of a sort made from leather attached to their necks like sacks.

These savages' appearance was fiercer than that of the tribe to which belonged Mitou and the two other Indians from whom he'd parted company at the plantation of Mr. S***. Like the latter, they were clad in loincloths; a leather belt from which hung snipe and other wild game girded their lower backs. All of them bore their rifles on their shoulders, and one of them, spotting a grouse, a kind of pheasant native to these lands, slipping through the tall grass, shot and killed it without sighting it for even a second, so prompt and accurate is these savages' aim.

The rifle's bang, which the young ladies weren't expecting, caused them both to jump, and the slight cry of fright that Hortense blurted out seemed to flatter the hunter's pride greatly, for his till-then impassible face took on a sardonic cheerfulness that made his ugliness all the more repulsive.

Mitou took advantage of the encounter with these Indians to rid himself of the prairie dog skins he'd not forgotten while emerging from the ajoupa. In exchange for them, his brethren of the wilderness gave him a small gourd full of lead pellets.

While the youngster was trading with two of those savages, Francis approached the leader of the band and offered him a flask of brandy, which was among the various supplies Maurice had packed. After which, Francis began a conversation through signs with the Indian whom this largesse on the part of the "white chief" had suddenly humanized, and whose very expressive pantomime wasn't understood, however, by either Hortense or Valentine. All the same, despite the curiosity Mademoiselle Melvil felt to know the subject of this enigmatic conversation, the fright these armed savages had caused her prevented her from addressing to her brother any question on this subject before they parted company.

"So what was that Indian telling you in his pantomimed language?" she then asked Francis.

"He was explaining to me," answered the latter, "the path we must take to reach that stand of pines you see over yonder, without being forced to cross through a marsh. All the different kinds of snakes teeming there make passing through very dangerous. While there, he himself stepped upon and was bitten on his heel by a little black snake of the species called a 'moccasin.'[19] That's why he was shod—as you noticed for yourselves—with sandals of skin, shaped immediately by one his companions from those animal hides their women are carrying on their shoulders to New Orleans."

"But," said Valentine, "that shoe must be too slight to protect his feet against contact with stones."

"You're forgetting," answered a smiling Mr. Melvil, "there are no stones in the soil adjacent to our big rivers."

"That's true," answered Mademoiselle Arnold.

"Also," continued Francis, "that shoe only serves to hold below the sole of his foot the packet of herbs whose beneficial sap, when applied in time on the bite of even constrictors or rattlesnakes, neutralizes the terrible effects."[20]

"It's very fortunate that these savages, who are deprived of the succor of science in their nomadic and solitary life, can find, almost within hand's reach, the remedy alongside what's harmful," said Valentine.

"Without a doubt," responded Mr. Melvil, "and in this country as well as in Mexico, Brazil, and the West Indies, there are almost no plants, trees, or herbs, even, that don't contain within their flowers, fruits, or stem an agent against many ailments regarded as incurable. It is at least likely that if physicians—stirred by that love of science that should always derive from that of humanity—were to undertake the exploration of our savannas and forests and the study of an American flora so vast a man's entire life wouldn't suffice to become entirely familiar with it, they'd succeed, with the help of Indians and blacks, in discovering ways to cure hydrophobia, tuberculosis, and so many other maladies till now declared mortal by experts."

"I've heard it said in Europe," resumed Hortense, "that ammonia applied to venomous bites would close the wound and could even prevent the venom from getting into the blood."

"Yes," responded Francis, "but in certain cases, this precaution isn't enough. At the home of one of my friends, I saw a slave come back one evening from a cypress marsh with an arm that was all black and swollen. The poor fellow, having been bitten by a water moccasin, had sought in vain around the woods for the herbs that Indian easily found on the prairie. Since it was a long way from the place he was working back to the plantation, it was to be feared too much time had passed from the moment when he'd been bitten for him to

GATHERING THE CANE.

Figure 12. John William Orr, "Gathering the Cane," in T. B. Thorpe, "Sugar and the Sugar Region of Louisiana," *Harper's New Monthly Magazine*, June–November 1853, 760.

be saved. He himself figured he was doomed. But slaves aren't very attached to life and they're hard in the face of suffering. Thus, the fellow I'm talking about seemed entirely resigned to dying. So it was with a complete indifference that he let an alkali compress be applied to his arm, which soothed him only a little. I got the idea, though, of having him swallow a glass of water into which I'd poured a few drops of that corrosive. Without that dilution, it'd be a very active poison itself, and I had the good fortune to preserve that unfortunate slave's

SUGAR HOUSE IN FULL BLAST.

Figure 13. John William Orr, "Sugar House in Full Blast," in T. B. Thorpe, "Sugar and the Sugar Region of Louisiana," *Harper's New Monthly Magazine*, June–November 1853, 761. Along with depicting the reality of the industrial nature of sugar production, this drawing shows the slave cabins in the rear that housed the enslaved workers who made such industry possible.

life. Consequently, I've given that formula to Maurice who, happily enough, hasn't had occasion to use it yet. As for you, young ladies, since we're on this topic, I urgently recommend you two never go walking about the plantation's surroundings without having a little flask of alkali in your pocket."

While speaking thus, they'd arrived at the marsh mentioned by Francis as a haunt of reptiles and, to avoid it, they entered an already harvested field of corn, which Maurice affirmed to be part of the property of Mrs. A***. This field came to an end at a vast pine forest,

92   FRANK LESLIE'S ILLUSTRATED NEWSPAPER.   [OCTOBER 21, 1871.

Figure 14. An image of an animal-powered sugarcane mill published twenty-six years after Lebrun's novel in *Frank Leslie's Illustrated Newspaper,* October 21, 1871, 92.

Figure 15. An image of a steam-powered sugar mill, as depicted by John William Orr, "Sugar Mill," in T. B. Thorpe, "Sugar and the Sugar Region of Louisiana," *Harper's New Monthly Magazine,* June–November 1853, 764.

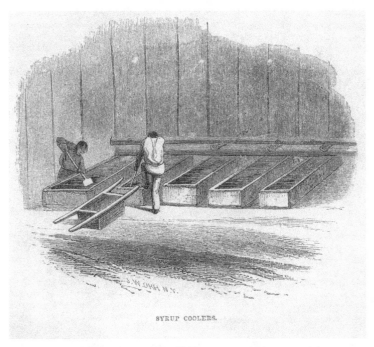

Figure 16. John William Orr, "Syrup Coolers," in T. B. Thorpe, "Sugar and the Sugar Region of Louisiana," *Harper's New Monthly Magazine*, June–November 1853, 762.

half of which belonged to the Creole woman and the other half to Mr. Melvil.

Around two in the afternoon, our travelers descended from their mules, a few steps from the Cyprière. Augustin, the little white boy, was the first to run to Francis, whom he considered to be his benefactor.

THE PURGERY.

Figure 17. John William Orr, "The Purgery," in T. B. Thorpe, "Sugar and the Sugar Region of Louisiana," *Harper's New Monthly Magazine*, June–November 1853, 763.

CHAPTER EIGHT

The Cyprière

Francis Melvil's plantation got its name from one of those vast swamps, some stretching to sixty or eighty miles, where the sort of green trees called cypresses grow.

These trees are very valuable because they have the priceless attribute of preserving their original hardness for centuries, especially once buried in the ground. People prefer to use cypress wood above all else for the construction of houses, very few of which are built of stone that's brought down from the northern states. Nevertheless, the majority of these houses must be elevated on pilings due to the soil's dampness. Because there is groundwater three feet down, the use of wood possessing a nondecaying nature is extremely important.[1]

The cypress forest that had once bordered Mr. Melvil's recently purchased plantation had been cut down some twenty years earlier. The boggiest part of the land it had occupied had been transformed into a rice farm. The other part, which had promptly dried due to the effect of the sunbeams to which it was then exposed, now formed a vast field of sugarcane, and a sugarhouse had risen there where once crawled reptiles, those vile creatures of the swamps.

A planter's house is usually located some distance away from the buildings that serve for sugar production. Such was the case with Francis's home.

Properly speaking, the yard—enclosed by a thick hedge of sour oranges to keep out animals—was simply a large field of grass crisscrossed by small streams and dotted with clusters of trees. Among the latter were to be seen magnolias and tulip trees, with foliage every bit as magnificent as flowers, maypops,[2] pink and white oleanders,[3] the shadows of which sheltered tufts of rhododendrons, yellow irises, and spiny cacti.[4] With their flexible branches, double jasmines coated the wooden house's brick-color painted walls and carried their fragrance to the large balcony or gallery enclosed by blinds, which stretched around the sole upper floor of this residence, on the ground floor of which were located the sitting room and dining room.[5]

It was into the first of these two rooms that Mr. Melvil first guided Hortense and Valentine. Augustin had told him Madame Launay was there at present.

Indeed, in the middle of the sitting room—whose gauze-curtained windows were opened in order to maintain in the room's interior perpetual drafts of air without which it would be impossible to breathe at certain hours of the day—sat half-buried in a vast, Morocco leather armchair a tiny, wrinkled old lady, whose extremely weakened vision was protected by green-tinted spectacles.[6]

On her knees frolicked a pet squirrel. It was so little that, at the softest noise, it would go hide in the pocket of its mistress's dress, to the belt of which it was attached, for that matter, by a long, silk ribbon that kept it from escaping. Right beside her, on a mahogany perch, slept a superb macaw from Brazil, with ruby-red feathers mixed with a deep blue and green.[7] Not far from it, they could see crouching on a bulrush mat a red-backed squirrel monkey, the gentlest, cutest, and most inoffensive of monkeys.[8]

At that moment, the one we're talking about was peeling an orange with a most entertaining seriousness.

Upon seeing Melvil and the two friends coming in, Madame Launay arose from her chair, saying in a cold, even curt, tone habitual to her:

"Good day, Francis. Of which of these young ladies are you the brother?" she added, looking at the young women through her glasses whose dark color kept one from seeing her little gray pupils, which, judging by the habitual acerbity of her mood, must have very rarely been animated by any kindly expression.

"Aunt," answered Hortense, taking by the hand Valentine, who'd remained a bit behind, "would you allow me to introduce my sister to you?"

"How's that?" said Madame Launay.

"It's a name of friendship that, in boarding schools, the boarders like to give to the dearest of their companions," explained Mr. Melvil.

"Ah!" said the old lady. "And mademoiselle is coming to spend the summer at the Cyprière?" she continued with a dour air after a short pause during which Francis and the two friends seated themselves on chairs placed around a pedestal table made of maple, just like the parquet floor, the paneling, and all of the room's furniture.

Upon that table were scattered a half-dozen boxes, some of tortoiseshell, others of bergamot bark, and three small baskets containing figs, pecans, oranges, and cakes.

"And how are you feeling today?" Francis asked his elderly relative with a concerned tone. "Maurice told me he'd left you in good health."

"That mulatto doesn't know what he's talking about," answered Madame Launay, emphasizing the word "mulatto" with a tone of scorn. "I've had no appetite or sleep these past three days."

"That's just awful, aunt," replied Mr. Melvil, "but I'll have you note that the Cyprière's overseer, having left the plantation four days ago, couldn't have known of your ailment."

"Possibly," murmured the old woman. "Anyhow, nephew," she continued in an acerbic tone, "since we're on the topic of observations, I'll also tell you your overseer's taking on the airs of a master around here, which don't befit for him, a man of color!"[9]

"For all that he's a man of color," Francis began again with a serious air, "Maurice has no less and, perhaps, has more intelligence, more integrity, I'll even add, than most whites entrusted with managing plantations in the owners' absence. My dear aunt, I don't know what your complaints about Maurice are. If, in some circumstance I can't imagine, he was disrespectful to you, please do tell me. I'll make the necessary rebukes in that respect. If, on the contrary, he's given you no cause to complain about him personally and if your dislike for that loyal, conscientious man has no other basis than the barbaric and truly ungodly prejudice of color, I'm forced to declare to you that, despite my desire to please you in all things, I won't be able to give you the satisfaction you're wishing for. So long as Maurice shows himself to be worthy of the position of trust he fills here, I'll keep it for him. I'll end this little explanation by asking you, aunt, to remember that, starting with you, all those who, for various reasons, become permanent or temporary inhabitants of the Cyprière must live here entirely independently of one another."[10]

This final sentence was pronounced by Francis with a tone simultaneously full of deference and firmness that astounded Madame Launay. Deep down, she loved her young relative, as much, at least, as the barrenness of her heart allowed her to love. Francis had always shown himself to be full of gentleness and thoughtfulness with her, and it was with a mixture of regret and worry that she said to him:

"My goodness, Francis, what solemn air has suddenly come over you? Have I offended you unintentionally?"

"In no respect, aunt. But I admit, your injustice, let me say, towards Maurice—"

"Come now, handsome nephew," interrupted Madame Launay with an almost gracious tone that bore witness to her sincere desire to make peace with Mr. Melvil, "be more indulgent with those who, unlike you, don't have the strength of mind or magnanimity to surmount their antipathies. Do think that, until you offered to let me retire to your plantation, my entire life had taken its course in South Carolina where prejudice—that's the expression you used—prejudice, I say, about color is perhaps more universally and more profoundly rooted than in any other colony.[11] Thus, people there can spot mulatto blood, even when it's flowing under skin of the whitest appearance. I myself was once quite skillful at discovering in the eyes and fingernails of individuals of mixed race barely perceptible signs of—reprobation."

This last word went unheard by Valentine and Hortense. The screeching of the lovely macaw just awakened by a light tap from Mr. Melvil's bamboo cane suddenly deafened them. At these cries, the little squirrel, probably curious to know the cause, peeked its pretty head out of the opening of its mistress's pocket where it had taken refuge at the appearance of three unknown figures. As for the squirrel monkey, which had long since finished peeling and eating its orange, it continued to make faces like someone speaking quietly and examined the group with a frightened air.

Meanwhile, Madame Launay hadn't noticed the mischief of her nephew who ordinarily was seldom inclined to pester the animals and who'd no doubt had recourse to this entirely uncharacteristic means in order to end a conversation he was starting to find tiresome. Madame Launay was too accustomed to the macaw's cries to be bothered or even to notice them, and she continued in a loud, shrill voice over that of her parrot:

"Now, my sight's gotten so bad that, even by taking off my pre-servers,[12] which make everything around me look green, from my dear niece and her young friend to my parrot Iago[13] and my monkey Janinet, it'd be impossible for me to tell a mulatto from a white man—"

"Aunt," interrupted Mr. Melvil, "is there no way to calm that macaw?"

The old lady's only response was to shake a silver bell placed on a chair within her reach. A slave-woman appeared immediately.

"Nina, bring this table closer," said Madame Launay, pointing the slave to the pedestal table, which was a little too far from her armchair for her to reach it without taking two or three steps.

"If I'd known what you wanted, madame," began Mademoiselle Arnold, "I—"

"Oh! My lovely, you're so French!" exclaimed Madame Launay with an ironic laugh and not allowing the young woman to finish her sentence.

"Say Parisian, aunt," continued Francis.

"I won't accept that compliment," rejoined a smiling Valentine. "I love my homeland too well for that."

"The homeland can be ungrateful at times," murmured Mr. Melvil, "and—"

He stopped. Perhaps he recognized the apparent untimeliness of this comment!

Meanwhile, the slave-woman Nina had rolled the table closer to her mistress who, having taken from one of the aforementioned baskets a bit of cake, brought it to her parrot herself. A tamed macaw likes all kinds of food: meat, bread, even passion fruit. But it especially likes pastries, so the bird's anger and anxiety calmed at once at Madame Launay's approach.

Had the latter been prompted to take this step out of a desire to please her relative by quieting the parrot immediately or solely out of a desire to bring an end to her dear Iago's apparent condition of nervous suffering?

We couldn't say. The fact remains that Nina, astounded to see the old lady moving around thus without any absolute need, remained beside the pedestal table as though petrified.

"Nina," Francis then said to her, "have some refreshments served for us. These young ladies will probably be quite delighted to retire to their rooms afterwards."

The slave-woman left to convey her master's orders to other slaves.

Once Madame Launay got back to her seat, she gave some pecans to the squirrel still nestled in her pocket and some figs to her squirrel monkey, who came running to get them once it heard itself being called by its name of Janinet. Afterwards, in obedience to a signal made by its mistress, it immediately returned to its bulrush mat, where it began to eat its fruits with all sorts of demonstrations of pleasure.

Scarcely a few minutes had passed since Nina's exit when Madame Launay shook her bell again. Nina wasn't back yet from the kitchen where she'd probably gone to order the refreshments requested by Mr. Melvil, so another slave-woman came into the sitting room. Madame Launay contented herself with pointing out to her the kerchief of fine cambric that had just escaped Hortense's hands. The slave-woman picked it up, returned it to the young woman, and withdrew.[14]

"Was that the only reason you rang for that woman?" asked an astonished Mademoiselle Melvil.

"That was sufficient cause, I imagine!" answered her aunt with a serious tone that seemed, in this circumstance, so amusing to Mademoiselle Arnold she couldn't stifle a burst of laughter.

This fit of gaiety offended Madame Launay, who, from that moment on, remained silent.

"The prostration into which a sometimes-scorching heat plunges not only Europeans but also Creoles, joined with the habit of being surrounded by slaves, makes idleness taken to its most absolute or, better put, most exaggerated regard singularly dear to the white people of this land," explained Mr. Melvil. "Here," he added smiling, "a woman who has a sense of her 'dignity' wouldn't do the slightest thing for herself, especially in the presence of witnesses. The ladies of Louisianan high society are almost always surrounded by five or six slave-women occupied with anticipating their merest desires. Those, such as our aunt, who prefer solitude or the company of their favorite animals to the constant company of their slaves, those women, I say, always have a bell at hand, at the slightest jingling of which their women immediately come running."

At that moment, Augustin and Nina appeared, carrying a small table upon which were served the refreshments, of which Madame Launay didn't partake. She spent the short duration this little meal lasted playing with her squirrel and repeatedly opening and closing her three candy boxes. One of them contained candied orange drops, the other, lemon drops, and the third, candied angelica. Creole women adore candies and preserves of all kinds.[15]

Once the young women arose from the table, Mr. Melvil ordered Nina to take them to their rooms. Before that, however, Valentine expressed the desire to wander around the plantation's outbuildings, which she'd only seen from the yard upon arriving, and Hortense agreed to go with her. Francis took them first to the sugarcane estate,

which, as we've noted previously, is always composed of several
buildings, namely: the actual sugarhouse, where the ovens and kettles
are found; two mills, one an animal-driven mill, the other steam-
driven; the purgery, where the sugar coming from the kettles is put
into troughs;[16] the cooler room, a hermetically sealed area in which
the sugar is dried by means of a low, constant heat; the rum distill-
ery, a workroom where the sugar spirits are made; the cooperage; a
vast shed under which is piled the pulp of crushed sugarcane from
which juice had been extracted;[17] the stable for mules employed in
the mill or for the transportation of the commodities produced; two
large barns; and a hospital for sick slaves. Not far from there were
the slave quarters, which, in Louisiana, is what they call the assem-
blage of cabins, otherwise called shacks, where the blacks used for
outdoor work live.[18]

After having visited this fine establishment in all its particulars,
Mesdemoiselles Arnold and Melvil looked around. On one side, they
saw the pine forest through which they'd arrived at the plantation,
and on the three others, fields of sugarcane, corn, and rice, bordered
by an immense curtain of cypress, the sole vestiges of the swampy
woods that had once occupied this fertile plain, and from which
Francis's plantation had derived its name.

Then, leaving Francis to chat with Mitou, who was wandering
among the sugarcane estate's buildings, waiting until the planter
was ready to give him the shotgun, the two friends returned to the
house, following a path of sycamores in the middle of which they
encountered Augustin.

This white boy was an orphan taken in by Mr. Melvil. Although
he wasn't exactly regarded as a servant at the Cyprière, nevertheless,
out of idleness and, also, out of gratefulness to the master of this
plantation, he endeavored to make himself useful and succeeded so
well in it that he was simultaneously the favorite of both Maurice
and Madame Launay. The overseer liked him because of his helpful
character and the swiftness with which he acquitted himself of the
errands with which he was charged. As for Francis's aunt, she couldn't

easily have done without the white boy . . . He alone could moisten to a suitable degree the *macouba*[19] with which she filled her snuffbox every morning and could prepare the sassafras tea, a cup of which she regularly drank every day after her supper.[20]

In addition, the child oversaw the farmyard whose prosperous situation did him immense honor. That's why he hurried to propose to the young women to take them there, which they accepted gladly.

This farmyard, located behind the house and at the extremity of the sycamore pathway, scarcely resembled those that we see in Europe. A high, wooden palisade masked by climbing plants surrounded it. A brook watered it and formed a pond there shaded by fig trees whose fruits were abandoned to the voracity of guinea fowl, grouse, and poultry of all kinds that frolicked within that vast, charming prison.

After spending a few minutes there and complimenting the white boy on the overall order and tidiness in the farmyard, the young women went back inside the house, at the door of which the four slave-women attached to their personal service were waiting to take each of them to their rooms. Among these women were the two slaves who, along with the runaway slave, had been sold to Maurice by the Creole woman whose sugarcane plantation neighbored Mr. Melvil's.

Valentine and Hortense came down to the sitting room only once it was time for dinner, for Madame Launay was accustomed to having three meals: one at nine in the morning, another at two in the afternoon, and the third at seven in the evening.

During supper, Mademoiselle Arnold again expressed her admiration of the land of Louisiana, the country of her birth, which, she added, she strongly hoped never to leave again.

"Europe may rightly boast of its scientific progress, its far-sighted legislation, its inventive spirit," exclaimed the young woman. "But I prefer America, with its lush vegetation, its radiant sky, and its variety of inhabitants."

Perhaps in her mind, she was also telling herself that this right of sovereignty that whites exercised in their plantations is an invaluable privilege. Who'd have blamed her for that? At the Cyprière, the slaves were happy—as much as the enslaved can be.

Mr. Melvil had heard the words uttered by his sister's friend without seeking, as on previous occasions, to temper her bursts of enthusiasm. Hortense concluded thereby that he'd abandoned his plan of diverting Valentine from the idea of moving to Louisiana for good. At any rate, she didn't have time to gain any certainty on this subject. That same evening, Francis, after bidding the three women good night, declared his intention of departing early the next morning with Mitou, who'd agreed to serve him as guide to the plantation of Mr. S***.

"Will you be back soon, brother?" asked Hortense.

"I hope so," responded Francis. "However, I can't be specific about the time of my return—but, in the meantime, both of you keep to yourselves here. I'm not acquainted with the neighboring families, and it's possible there might be some among their number whose society wouldn't be suitable for you."

In common accord, the two friends recognized the wisdom of this advice and promised to follow it.

CHAPTER NINE

A Summer Evening

A month had gone by since Mr. Melvil's departure. In keeping with his advice, Valentine and Hortense left the Cyprière only to go hear the Sunday Mass at Saint Paul's, the parish church for their plantation and many others for several miles around.[1]

This church being a bit far from Mr. Melvil's plantation, and the path leading there too narrow for a carriage to pass through, the young women made the trip there, as did Madame Launay, in palanquins borne by slaves. The favorite spot for Hortense's aunt was in the organ loft from which one could look out over the entire congregation without being seen. The two friends, who couldn't in all decency sit separately from the old lady, thus found themselves hidden from unwelcome looks, too, for the general curiosity was all the more deeply aroused with respect to the pretty denizens of the Cyprière by the fact that nobody from around there had met them.

As newcomers, it would have been up to them to pay the first calls on their neighbors, and, since they'd refrained entirely from doing so, no one had dared or attempted to appear at their home.

Mesdemoiselles Arnold and Melvil lived, therefore, in utter solitude, which the former coped with better than did the latter. Indeed, Hortense, whose recent illness had increased her innate laziness even more, spent her days sluggishly stretched out on a sofa; she barely felt the courage to read for fifteen straight minutes, whereas Valentine, endowed with great energy of body and mind, braved the blazing heat of the month of July and sought distractions in the pleasures of walking. In truth, though, she never went beyond the bounds of Mr. Melvil's property.

Once, however, towards the end of the day, while following a butterfly lovelier than any of those she'd admired so much on the savanna, she chanced to get lost in the middle of the pine forest that, it will no doubt be recalled, belonged in part to Mrs. A***.

Abandoning her pursuit of the butterfly then, the young woman tried to find the path back to the Cyprière. She wandered randomly for about a half-hour among those trees, the dark foliage of which contributed by its gloomy aspect to frighten her. Even though she didn't have a watch, she figured the time for sunset must be near and feared being caught by the dark in this solitude.

It's true, she thought, and this idea revived her courage temporarily, it's true that, once the stars start shining in the sky, by examining the position of some of them, especially the Big Dipper and the planet Venus, I'll be able to recognize the direction I need to go. But till then, Valentine next added with chagrin and in keeping with her habit of always being concerned for others, a bit more time will go by, and my good Hortense will be horribly worried!

It then occurred to her that the pines' height[2] and the small amount of open space between them would prevent her from seeing a suffi-ciently large stretch of the azure vault to orient herself successfully by means of the different constellations bestrewing it. Luckily, a few moments later, having followed another direction, Mademoiselle Arnold saw the forest was growing less dark. Was she approaching a field or just a glade?

Impatient to resolve this question of such great interest to her, Valentine quickened her pace. Suddenly, a cock's crow agreeably surprised her and reassured her mind by signaling a nearby dwelling. After the rooster, she thought she heard a hen clucking; next, a joyous voice began whispering to her ear a Creole song popular at the time, which Augustin would hum throughout the day.[3]

Was it the little white boy whom they'd sent from the plantation to look for her? Valentine opened her mouth to call out: "Augustin!" But that name faded on her lips. The suspicion had come to her that it might well be some stranger, white, mulatto, or black, whose physiognomy it would be prudent, at least, to judge before revealing herself to him. Right away, Mademoiselle Arnold slipped behind a big tree from where she kept an eye on the whistler's approach.

"So where's he hiding?" she asked herself, after a few minutes of useless waiting.

And then, her wandering eyes lighted on a gray bird of an average size, balancing itself not far from her on a pliant branch. It must be a mockingbird, for that's what was whistling and, probably, had imitated the rooster and hen so well earlier. Indeed, once it finished its Creole tune, it began the same songs over again and with as much success as before. It was an easy mistake to make!

But suddenly, the bird went quiet and became immobile, its eyes fixed on the ground—and among the grasses surrounding the foot of the tree there was a light movement accompanied by an even lighter noise still and rather similar to the one produced by brushing a silk dress. This movement and noise were caused by a snake raising its head above the branch upon which the mockingbird, no doubt fascinated by the reptile's gaze, was hanging tightly instead of fleeing from its enemy by flying away.

Trembling with fear, Valentine started running through the pines, with no other goal than escaping the serpent, of which the poor bird was surely going to become the prey. When she stopped next, feeling like she was almost out of breath, she noticed happily she was at the edge of the woods, at the entrance to a vast field of sugarcane. In the distance, she could see a house neighbored by several other buildings. It was, no doubt, Mrs. A***'s sugar plantation.

Based on what she'd heard Mr. Melvil say concerning that woman's cruelty towards slaves, Mademoiselle Arnold felt a feeling of revulsion towards her, which would have made it difficult to ask for hospitality at her plantation. While the young woman was wondering, now that she was out of the woods, whether it wouldn't be possible for her to return to the Cyprière without a guide, she thought she saw the cane waving a few steps from her. It was still unripe, but already high and dense, and it seemed more difficult to make one's way through it than through a bushy thicket.

Still troubled by the scare that her encounter with the snake had caused her, Valentine imagined that perhaps a bobcat being pursued by hunters had sought refuge in the sugarcane—but the waving lasted only a few seconds. Mademoiselle Arnold felt her courage returning to her when she saw, truly quite far from the place where she'd stopped, an individual running towards her at tremendous speed.

This individual was a black man, and Valentine hoped to get information from him concerning the path that would lead her back to the Cyprière. At first, her hopes were disappointed. The black man passed by her without seeming to notice her and plunged so hurriedly into the cane plantings that Mademoiselle Arnold didn't have time to ask him a question. Scarcely had he disappeared when muffled moans reached the young woman's ears. Without asking herself whether or not there was any peril in going forward, she entered the field, which she managed to do by fiercely parting the canes with her arms.

There she beheld a sad sight. The black man was kneeling beside a child stretched out on the ground, whose spasmodically agitated features betrayed awful suffering.

They were both runaways. Slaves still the previous night, they'd escaped the nearby sugarcane plantation the morning of that very day, before the hour for work had sounded.[4] The father, exasperated by a cruel punishment inflicted upon his son for an oversight of which he'd been "guilty," had carried the bruised and bloodied boy away in his arms. Deeming that some place close to the plantation would be exactly where no one would think to look for them, they'd both huddled among the sugarcane, waiting for the darkness of night to come and further their escape. It was there, just recently, that a snake—perhaps the very one Mademoiselle Arnold had seen making the mockingbird so uneasy—had bitten the young slave's leg.

In vain, the father, forgetting the risk he ran of being recaptured and returned to the sugarcane plantation, had gone in search of the plants whose sap is an antidote for the reptiles' venom. All his efforts had gone unrewarded, and he was returning in all haste, before it was too late to attempt another means of treatment rarely employed because of the mortal consequences it might have for the one who puts it to use.

At the moment when Valentine appeared, the slave was getting ready to suck out the wound despite the child's resistance. Mademoiselle Arnold, whom the black man informed by a few words broken by sobs of the motive for this touching struggle between him and his son, stopped this burst of paternal devotion.

"Before using such a perilous remedy," she said, "let's try another one that's at least as effective."

While saying so, she pulled from her pocket the flask of ammonia she'd taken precaution to bring, per Francis's advice. She then poured a few drops of this corrosive on the wound of the young slave, who felt an instantaneous relief. Nonetheless, his leg was still swollen, and his mind was groggy. Seeing this, Valentine cried out:

"If we just had some water!"

"Me get you some right away," said the old black man.[5]

"I don't want it for myself, but for your child," replied the young woman.

The runaway slave didn't hear her answer. He'd run back into the woods from which he soon returned, dragging behind him an enormous vine from which he made water flow into Valentine's cupped, white hand. And the slave's surprise was great when he saw the young woman mix a bit of her flask's contents in that limpid water that she then offered to the child to drink.

Scarcely had he swallowed that concoction when his leg's swelling began to decrease, and his despondent face came back to life.

Avant d'employer un si périlleux reméde, dit-elle, essayons
d'un autre au moins aussi efficace.

Figure 18. Caption, translated, is "'Before using such a perilous remedy,' she said, 'let's try another one that's at least as effective.'" This is the final illustration in Lebrun's original edition.

These visible signs of a cure overjoyed the old black man. His gratitude towards the woman who'd saved his son manifested itself by excessive demonstrations. After crawling to Mademoiselle Arnold's feet to kiss the hem of her dress, he remained for a few minutes in contemplation of her, laughing and weeping by turns.

Once Valentine was certain her treatment had succeeded completely, she thought of getting back to the Cyprière as promptly as possible. Indeed, the slave was familiar with that plantation to which he'd belonged in his youth, long before Mr. Melvil was its owner. So he gave to Valentine directions by means of which she had no fear of going astray again.

"Now," the black man next said, upon seeing the young woman preparing to leave, "now his life and mine belong to you. Old Benjamin and young Dominique can't forget an offense or a good deed."

Night had already fallen when Mademoiselle Arnold encountered the young white boy some ways from the Cyprière. He, along with Maurice and several other black men sent in different directions by Mademoiselle Melvil, had been searching for her for more than an hour.

While they walked, Augustin pointed out to Valentine many glowing insects, otherwise known as fireflies, which, rising into the air, were shining there like sparks. These singular *hymenopterans*[6] are usually called *lucioles* in France, from the name given to them in Italy where they're rather common and infinitely smaller than in America. In Louisiana and Cuba, some as big as maybugs can be found. By enclosing them under a glass, they can serve as night lamps. If Mademoiselle Arnold hadn't been in such a hurry to bring an end to the worry Hortense was feeling about her, she'd certainly have tried to capture one of these flies; but she postponed that pleasure till some other evening.

As for Madame Launay—whom Mademoiselle Arnold's prolonged absence hadn't prevented from having her third meal at its accustomed hour—she remained in the middle of the sitting room on her big Morocco leather armchair beside her marquetry pedestal table, surrounded by her three pets, slowly savoring the cup of sassafras tea the white boy had hurried to take to her, though he'd only just arrived. For the old lady, very systematic in her habits, had obstinately refused that Nina should, out of the ordinary, prepare her favorite tea that night. Thus her bad mood with respect to Valentine—who'd been the involuntary cause of the delay regarding one of her surefire enjoyments—vented itself in stinging, sarcastic words about young people brought up in Europe.

In part to avoid the repetition of these complaints and reproaches in her friend's presence, Mademoiselle Melvil had hurried to take Valentine into the dining room. Once they were seated at the table, they signaled the female slaves who served them to leave, for they wanted to be alone in order to converse freely.

Hortense, too, had interesting news to communicate to her companion and, once the latter had finished the tale of her walk, she placed two opened letters before her. One was from Francis, the other from Madame Deschamps. Mademoiselle Melvil had received them a few moments after Valentine had left the plantation house.

CHAPTER TEN

A Party

Francis's letter contained a marriage proposal he'd taken upon himself to convey to his sister.

The hopes of this excellent brother were coming to fruition . . . Doctor Henríquez had determined that Mademoiselle Melvil, of all the young people whom he'd hitherto encountered, was the one best suited to him as a wife.

Hortense, for her part, had given very little thought to the Spanish doctor, so she needed to refresh her memory and to corroborate it with that of Valentine in order to form for herself a positive opinion concerning him.

The result of the two friends' consultation on this grave matter was that Doctor or *Señor* Henríquez, as Mr. Melvil sometimes called him, was a very kind, refined young man and that his proposals presented under the auspices of her brother, in whose judgment one could have complete confidence, certainly deserved to be accepted.

As for the letter from Madame Deschamps, it was simply an invitation addressed to the two young women for a housewarming she was giving the following week at one of the properties she'd inherited. The one in question was a cotton plantation nicely situated a short distance from the Mississippi at a place where a levee protected the locals from flooding.[1]

Already sharing Creoles' excessive taste for luxury and pleasures, Monsieur and Madame Deschamps, scarcely having moved into their new home, wanted to bring together there not only their neighbors, but also a great number of prominent inhabitants of New Orleans. Consequently, one of the steamboats regularly traveling up and down the river had been booked exclusively by the Cotonnerie's owners for the day appointed for the ball in order to ferry to a landing very close to their plantation a complete orchestra and the many people invited to the party, whether from the city or from the plantations scattered, so to speak, along the length of the river.

Madame Deschamps had taken care to indicate in her note to the two young friends the times at which the boat would stop to board travelers at different places. Furthermore, she let them know, to remove any pretext for a refusal, that Mr. Hervey, the New Orleans notary—who'd be accompanying his sister both to and fro—would also be at their disposal, in case Mr. Melvil wasn't at the Cyprière at present. In a nutshell, the terms in which the invitation from the Cotonnerie's owners was conceived expressed a keen impatience finally to see their former travel companions once again. The sincerity of this impatience was, moreover, sufficiently proven by the efforts they'd been required to make to learn of the two friends' current whereabouts.

Nevertheless, Valentine was, at first, of a mind not to go to this get-together; she reminded Hortense of her brother's express recommendation not to leave the Cyprière during his absence. But Mademoiselle Melvil, eager for entertainment and amusements, asserted that this recommendation was a precaution by Francis to keep the two of them from forming any relationships with neighbors whose company might be inappropriate for young people and could not, consequently, concern a respectable family to whom they'd been entrusted by their schoolmistress to make the crossing from Europe to America. This reasoning not being entirely devoid of accuracy, Mademoiselle Arnold sided with her friend's point of view.

This big question having been resolved, the young women occupied themselves with choosing their outfits. They each selected dresses made of Indian muslin with the only differences being that the knotted shoulder ribbons[2] and belt would be of a blue color for Hortense and poppy red for Valentine, the former proposing to wear a set of pearls, the latter, coral jewelry.

Everything having thus been settled during their supper, the two friends got up from the table and went back to the sitting room to inform Madame Launay of their plan, of which she neither approved nor disapproved.

The following week, therefore, on the day indicated in the invitation, the two friends climbed into a carriage around four in the afternoon and arrived at the junction of the Red River and the Mississippi at six in the evening.[3]

They didn't wait long for the passage of the steamboat upon which, just as Madame Deschamps had told them, they found Mr. Hervey. But the latter's sister wasn't accompanying him, having preferred to go overland to the Cotonnerie, which wasn't very far from her home.

Upon seeing Mademoiselle Arnold boarding the boat with Mademoiselle Melvil, the notary made an involuntary gesture of surprise. Hortense supposed he hadn't recognized her companion and was going to tell him her name when Mr. Hervey, taking them both by the hand, led them down into the boat's sitting room where, however, there was absolutely no one. All the travelers or, better put, all of the Deschamps's invitees—since no one else had taken passage on this ship—were gathered under the tent shading the ship's deck.

"In every respect, you'll be infinitely better off here than up there," said Mr. Hervey to the young women, who together cast an inquiring look at him. "I'll send you some refreshments," he added immediately, as though to avoid explaining himself further.

And then he left them with a haste that Mesdemoiselles Melvil and Arnold attributed to an excess of thoughtfulness. Indeed, some slave-women soon brought them lemon and pineapple jellies and iced orangeade. As for the notary, he didn't reappear. Far from taking offense at this conduct, Hortense and Valentine were grateful to him for it as proof of his discretion. Likewise, they presumed he'd led them into the solitary sitting room because he deemed it inappropriate for such young people to mix with a large assortment among whom there were no women of their acquaintance. Anyhow, their seclusion didn't last very long. From the place of their embarkation, the trip by water to the Cotonnerie was quite short, and it was only seven o'clock when the steamboat stopped for the final time.

The Deschamps family welcomed both Mesdemoiselles Melvil and Arnold with equal enthusiasm. The party was as cheerful as it was splendid. There was a dazzling profusion of lights and flowers. The women there were, for the most part, remarkable in their elegance and beauty. Hortense and Valentine ranked among the prettiest.

Right from entering the ball, they'd been separated from one another. Mr. Hervey, having offered his arm to Mademoiselle Melvil, led her into the dance rooms where his sister was, whom he wished to introduce to her and beside whom the young woman took a seat. Then, after a crowd of dancers surrounded the charming Creole woman, the latter had been unable to rejoin Valentine, who'd remained in the first sitting room alongside Madame Deschamps, who was soon forced to leave her to attend to other guests.

Next, desiring to enjoy the sights this glittering gathering offered, Mademoiselle Arnold positioned herself in the frame of a window where she long went unnoticed. She then grew bored with her isolation, and the temptation overcame her to take part in this party herself. So she went to sit on a bench among other young women, intending to mingle in the conversations and various dances in which she saw people of all ages participating.

But Mademoiselle Arnold soon regretted bringing attention to herself. Her neighbors, after looking her up and down, turned away from her with an unequivocal air of disdain and spoke to one another in low voices. Reacting very naturally, Valentine looked into a large mirror supposing there was something wrong with her outfit that made her look ridiculous. There was nothing of the sort, however.

While she was looking at herself curiously, seeking in vain to unravel the mystery of such ill will, an elderly lady, beside whom she was sitting, left her place and headed towards the mistress of the house who, at the moment, was standing at the second sitting room's entrance and who seemed simultaneously both astonished and very discomfited by the message she'd just heard. This little scene went unobserved by Mademoiselle Arnold, whose attention was just then focused on her impertinent neighbors who continued whispering among themselves. At the moment when the young woman was wondering silently if she should try to rejoin her friend or leave the ball immediately, Madame Deschamps's elder son—a twelve-year-old boy—was sent to her by his mother to invite her to dance. Afraid she might wound the self-esteem of a schoolchild, Mademoiselle Arnold got up, and they both took their places in a quadrille then taking shape. Nevertheless, as the first dance figure began, they still had no opposites. The Deschamps boy had to call upon his little sister, whose partner was a child like her.

Once the contra dance was over, Valentine returned to sit in the window frame, fearing that, by leaving too soon, she'd let people guess the humiliation she felt from these repeated tokens of a disdain that, to her mind, was inexplicable. With the exception of Monsieur Deschamps, who came several times to chat with her about pointless things, no one approached the forlorn girl, either to ask her to dance or to address to her one of those banal phrases used by people who don't know one another, but whom a similar purpose, serious or frivolous, has brought together in the same sitting room.

As for Mademoiselle Melvil—dizzied by the whirl and animation of the dance in which she was indulging herself, along with the mad compulsion the most lackadaisical of Creole women feel for pleasures—she didn't think to go rejoin her friend.

Once it was suppertime, a multitude of small tables set for four guests was brought into the sitting rooms. The younger Deschamps led Valentine to one of those tables where they sat by her side. Nevertheless, the fourth seat remained unoccupied.

There was in this series of bad manners on the part of Monsieur and Madame Deschamps's guests a demonstration of scorn so systematic that the young woman, even though it was impossible for her to guess its cause, had great difficulty holding back her tears. She told herself that the incomprehensible conduct people were showing towards her in the very presence of those who'd invited her would, in Europe, have constituted a true lack of consideration towards the masters of the house, and she was dumbfounded to see the latter seemed more distressed than offended by it.

Immediately after supper, Valentine retired to the apartment reserved for her, but she didn't sleep a wink the whole night. Day was barely starting to break when she furtively left the house. With the exception of a few people who, along with herself and Hortense, had been invited to stay on a few days at the Cotonnerie, everyone was getting ready to have breakfast before returning to the steamboat parked in the waters of the Mississippi, awaiting the return of the large party it had brought and with whom, as one might well suppose, Mademoiselle Arnold didn't care to find herself again.

She therefore waited for the passage of another steamboat coming down the river and which, at her repeated signals, stopped at the Cotonnerie's landing. Naturally, she was forced to make a long walk on foot to the Cyprière from the place where she later disembarked.

CHAPTER ELEVEN

A Fire

"Well, my dear young lady, did you have a good time?" Madame Launay first asked Valentine, when the latter came to have lunch in the dining room where the old lady, who'd arisen later than usual that day, was finishing her morning meal. "Hey!" she continued, without giving the young woman time to answer her, "where did you leave Hortense?"

"At the Cotonnerie, madame, where we were both invited to spend a few days, as you know."

"How did my niece agree to stay there without you, her inseparable companion, her bosom friend, her chosen sister?—for such are the titles she's pleased to give you."

Mademoiselle Arnold was struck by the sardonic tone with which Madame Launay spoke these words, and it was with a curt tone that she said: "Since it no longer suited me at all to extend my stay at Madame Deschamps's, and since I didn't wish to upset Hortense's plans in the meantime, I left this morning without having told anybody except with a note she'll be given once she awakens."

"It didn't suit you to extend your stay at Madame Deschamps's!" replied Madame Launay, emphasizing each syllable, as though she sought some mysterious meaning in Valentine's response. "Weren't you satisfied with that lady's welcome?" Madame Launay then added, in a low voice, as though she were talking to herself, "But she's a French woman!"

"But, madame, never have I claimed that courtesy was the exclusive share of women of the country where I was raised—"

"And which you ought never to have left, my poor child," concluded the old lady with a tone of compassion.

"Meaning, madame?" demanded Mademoiselle Arnold.

"Truly," Madame Launay murmured again, "hearing her, you'd suppose she didn't even suspect."

"I asked you a question just now, madame, and you don't answer!" Valentine exclaimed sharply. "Who authorizes you to treat me with this disdain?"

"My goodness, my dear, I'd no intention of offending you—But come, since you wish it so, let's explain ourselves frankly—Anyhow, I really do need a basis for all this—Unfortunately, I can't judge anything on my own, and Maurice claims, as do the slaves, to have noticed nothing—apparently they're acting on my nephew's orders—because Mrs. A*** couldn't be wrong—"

Like most elderly people who usually live alone or surrounded by animals, Madame Launay had gotten so into the habit of talking to herself, she'd lapse into it right in the middle of the most animated conversation.

"What connection is there between Mrs. A*** and myself?" interrupted again Mademoiselle Arnold, who was tired of these ramblings seemingly calculated to prolong the state of painful uncertainty into which she was plunged.

"A little patience, mademoiselle, and you'll understand me, I hope. Mrs. A***, the owner of the sugarcane plantation located on the other side of the pine forest that this plantation backs up to, so to speak, came over yesterday, a short while after you two left, to ask me for information concerning two slaves, a father and son, the former named Benjamin, the latter, Dominique, who ran away from her plantation about eight days ago."

"She hasn't found them?" asked Valentine, whose interest for those two blacks, one of whose life she'd saved, made her temporarily forget her personal preoccupations.

"Good Lord, no!" responded Madame Launay. "Otherwise, she'd have suspected Maurice—whom she accuses, not without cause, of encouraging marronage by protecting runaways—of providing shelter to the two I just named."[1]

"That's true! And then?"

"Then, after I said no, she had the courtesy to invite us to dinner in three days at her home. I thought I should accept."

"Not for me, I imagine!"

"She gave me no occasion to do so."

"I understand. You've left her unaware of the presence at the Cyprière of Mademoiselle Melvil's close friend, and I'm very happy with that omission."

"Quite the contrary, I named you first."

"Ah!"

"But at that name of Arnold—"

"Well?" said Valentine, troubled strangely by Madame Launay's affected hesitation.

"She cried out," continued the old lady, "and asked me if you were kin to the Arnolds, merchants in Mobile who both died in Natchez ten or twelve years ago from yellow fever."

"I'm their daughter," said Mademoiselle Arnold with a feeling of noble pride. She knew her parents had left behind in the world of commerce an unassailable reputation of good faith.

"You're their daughter!" repeated Madame Launay. "In that case, my dear child," she continued after a short pause and assuming a tone of protective familiarity, "you were wrong to expose yourself, as you did by going to Madame Deschamps's ball, to a very disgraceful reception, especially for you who are practically a foreigner in this land and whom American customs—"

At that moment, Madame Launay's voice was drowned out by the piercing cries made by the parrot in the sitting room where its mistress had left it.

"Oh, good Lord!" said the latter, hurriedly getting up, "Janinet and Iago might be fighting!" And she hurried out of the dining room.

Mademoiselle Arnold ran and shut herself in her bedroom. Hardly had she gone in there when she let herself fall onto a seat, crying out: "Oh, my God! Have I been humiliated enough?"

While lending an ear to the half-explicatory words of Madame Launay a short while before, the young lady had made a quick review of the past. She remembered the mulatto woman's ambiguous responses at the Saint Louis Cathedral, the conversation of the two free women of color while leaving the church service, and several incidents that had occurred during her stay at the plantation of Mr. Melvil's cousin. She then believed she understood why her parents had sent her as an infant to France, which, for the first time, she regretted ever leaving.

But in this thorny circumstance, the habitual pluck and courage of her character didn't fail her. Wishing to clarify her remaining doubts—feeble ones, it's true—concerning the social position she'd be occupying in Louisiana, she took up a quill and wrote to a lawyer in Mobile whom she'd heard Francis mention several times and whom she presumed to have been connected to Mr. and Mrs. Arnold in the past. Valentine asked him for written confirmation to her letter, requesting he address it to her, care of Mr. Hervey, notary in New Orleans, for she was planning to leave the Cyprière before Hortense even got back. A final farewell would have been too painful for her to utter, but she did mean to sever forever her relationship with the one-time friend whose equal she no longer found herself to be.

Once Mademoiselle Arnold had finished her letter, she rang for the black maid and ordered her to find Augustin to whom she wished to speak immediately.

The child didn't keep her waiting long. Valentine gave him her letter, enjoining him to take it discreetly to the closest town where there was a post office. It was important to the success of her plan that Madame Launay have no knowledge of it. Then, she told the little white boy to have a horse saddled for her at seven in the evening.

"You'll accompany me to the river's edge and bring the horse back here," she added.

"If mademoiselle would consent to delay her departure until I've served Madame Launay her sassafras tea—" ventured Augustin.

"Agreed," answered Valentine who, in spite of the sad thoughts weighing on her mind, couldn't keep herself from smiling at the white boy's extreme punctuality in fulfilling his duty. It was, for that matter, of little difference to her whether she departed an hour earlier or later, so long as it was that evening, for it was possible Mademoiselle Melvil might come back to the Cyprière the following day.

Valentine, after resting a bit, busied herself with preparations for her trip, then she sat on her balcony where she remained, contemplating the landscape spreading before her eyes, waiting for the hour of her escape to sound. For it truly was as a fugitive that she was fleeing this plantation where she surely foresaw Hortense would try to keep her, if she arrived in time to do so. And since she had no doubt the motive for her unforeseen departure would be promptly divulged by Madame Launay to her niece, she traced out for the latter only these few words that were disheartening for each of the two friends: "Farewell forever!"

Night was falling. Silence and calm prevailed around the plantation. Suddenly, however, Mademoiselle Arnold thought she saw two figures outside of the yard, slipping along the hedge of sour oranges. No doubt, they were slaves from the sugarhouse who, before returning to the slave quarters, were coming to the overseer's shack to get orders concerning the next day's work. She was absently following them with her eyes when a strange spectacle drew her gaze to the other side.

Across from the plantation, a reddish brightness was illuminating the sky— One might have said it was a magnificent aurora borealis.

At that instant, a child's voice could be heard below the young woman's window.

"Here! Here!" it was saying. "Mitou never wrong about directions."[2]

"Who's there?" Mademoiselle Arnold asked sharply.

"Old Benjamin and young Dominique never forget a good deed," responded a slave climbing up the balcony.

"What does that mean?" exclaimed Valentine.

"You not understand?" said Benjamin, extending his arm towards the blazing horizon. "The sky be the mirror of the ground," he added.

"I really don't understand," responded Mademoiselle Arnold, surprised by the black man's use of poetic language, even though that's what primitive people ordinarily use the most in solemn circumstances.

"Blacks have their days of anger, too," explained Benjamin. "Cruel white woman be ruined tomorrow."

"Are you speaking of your mistress?"

"Cruel white woman no longer mistress of old Benjamin or young Dominique. They run away to land of Mitou's brothers and come back to land of whites only to save you!"

"Thank you for your devotion, but I've nothing to fear. You're the one threatened by a dire fate. If you were recaptured!—"

The black man shook his head no.

"Cruel white woman have no more slaves now. All slaves revolted at once—at a signal, set fire at twenty places at the Sucrerie[3]— Mitou found out about plot and warned us. All the buildings burn at same time— Run away, no time to waste."[4]

"But I repeat to you, I've nothing to fear here. The distance separating this plantation from that of Mrs. A***—"

Benjamin interrupted Valentine:

"Fire eat both sugarcane field and pine woods. Wind drive flames towards the Cyprière."

While saying this, the slave had leapt onto the balcony's balustrade to take a look over the roof of the house towards the pine forest whose conflagration was reflected in the sky. Already, one could hear in the distance the noise caused by the falling of trees devoured by the flames. From one moment to the next, if the wind that had risen continued to blow, the inhabitants of the Cyprière might find themselves encircled by fire. The runaway slave was telling the truth: they had to flee!

Mademoiselle Arnold hurriedly went back into her room and rang for her women, but none appeared. All of them, upon seeing the danger threatening the Cyprière, had gone in search of the overseer. Unfortunately, he'd left on horseback two hours earlier for Natchez on business for his master, which would take several days. The foreman alone, who, as well as the other slaves, resided in the slave quarters, was informed of Maurice's absence. Valentine then called for Benjamin, but he'd run to the quarters to sound the alarm.

The only one left in the house was Madame Launay, who still suspected nothing and was peacefully enjoying her cup of tea in the company of Janinet, Iago, and the squirrel. However, her advanced age and near total blindness made her situation extremely perilous. Valentine, therefore, saw to her safety first.

"If you truly are devoted to me, follow me," said the young woman to Benjamin.

And she led him into the sitting room. There, she explained to Madame Launay in a few words the necessity for a prompt escape. Upon hearing her, the old woman screamed in terror and let herself be carried by the old black man, who lifted her in his arms as he might have done with a child. While leaving the house, Valentine saw the horse Augustin had prepared for her, attached by a bridle to a tree. She was preparing to climb onto it when the old black man stopped her.

"No use! Dangerous!" he said. "Animal not been trained for fire."

Without entirely sharing the slave's fears, Mademoiselle Arnold yielded to his opinion and followed him on foot with Dominique. Burdened as he was, Benjamin was forced to stop several times to catch his breath.

Meanwhile, the fire continued to progress. Even at a very great distance from the heart of the blaze, the heat of the air became so intense that, in various places, the tall, already dry grasses spontaneously burst into flame and, to avoid them, the escapees had to walk in a stream for a long while. As they got out of it, they entered a cypress forest and reached the Mississippi around the middle of the night. There, they found shelter in a shack inhabited by half-civilized Indians living peacefully there off the product of their fishing.

The next morning, two steamboats crossed paths at the same hour in front of this shack. Madame Launay took passage on the one going up the river, and Mademoiselle Arnold on the other.

The old lady asked that they stop at the landing of Madame Deschamps's Cotonnerie, at the home of whom she'd find Hortense.

The young woman, for her part, went to New Orleans.

As for the runaway slaves, they likely returned to Mitou's lands, for they were never to be seen again.

CHAPTER TWELVE

The Departure

Now we'll ask our young readers to transport themselves in their imagination into one of the most beautiful houses on Royal Street in New Orleans. Beside the window of an elegant sitting room located on the ground floor of this house, Hortense Melvil and Doctor Henríquez are seated facing one another. The young woman is serious and pensive; the physician looks extremely unhappy.

"So," he said, "you persist in wishing to delay our wedding until you've found Mademoiselle Arnold?"

"Yes, doctor. The painful uncertainty I'm in concerning her fate is making me feel so sad and ill-tempered!"

"So what are you saying?"

"Honestly, I should be forgiven for this sadness and sullenness coming from a grief that's all the deeper because it's mixed with remorse."

"Remorse! Now, let me just tell you, that's a very exaggerated expression—"

"Not at all. If I'm using that word instead of 'regret,' it's because I'm conscious of my guilt! Indeed, if, on that fateful evening, the last one I spent with my dear Valentine, I hadn't let myself get distracted and caught up in the pleasures of the ball to the point of forgetting that excellent friend entirely, I wouldn't have to lament over her loss now, for she's lost to me, Señor Henríquez. 'Farewell forever,' she wrote to me. What harsh reproach in those simple words traced by a trembling hand!"

"Come now, it's not your fault if—"

"Oh! I'm not blinding myself to my failings, doctor! I'm quite sure my presence in the same sitting room as Valentine would have prevailed over that envious society attempting to take vengeance upon the great superiority of such a beautiful person by crushing her through their insolence."

"You're mistaken," murmured the physician.

"And the next day," Hortense carried on, "once I learned of her hasty departure from the Cotonnerie, ought I not to have guessed how much her noble heart had been wounded! How did I not chase after her to keep her with me by my pleas, my caresses, and my tears? But no, the indolence of my character didn't keep me from resisting Madame Deschamps's insistence that I stay two whole days at her home. How I despaired once Madame Launay arrived and I learned from that pitiless woman of my cherished companion's flight and the motive for that desperate resolution!"

"You must admit," replied Henríquez with a tone of indifference that produced a disagreeable impression upon his young fiancée, "you must admit Melvil acted very inconsiderately in all this—If he'd informed Mademoiselle Arnold and yourself—"

"Good heavens!" Hortense interrupted sharply. "If my brother erred in this awkward circumstance, it was only out of an excess of prudence and sensitivity.[1] He'd hoped to convince Valentine to return to Europe before she discovered this secret, which he hesitated to confide in me, out of fear, I can see, that the weakness of my mind might cause me to consider the position of my adoptive sister in a different light than he did. This mistrust of the stability of my sentiments has opened my eyes to the duties that friendship and gratefulness impose upon me. For you will remember, doctor, I'm indebted to that devoted friend's cares and vigils for saving my life. You've told me so yourself often enough."

"No doubt," responded the Spaniard, with a hurriedness indicating his desire to put an end to this conversation. "And," he added, with the evident goal of diverting attention from the ideas preoccupying Mademoiselle Melvil's mind, "tell me, please, is it really true Mrs. A*** is more or less ruined?"

"Good Lord, yes! Last week, Maurice, who came to fetch Madame Launay—who likes staying at the Cyprière much better than in New Orleans, where she's ceaselessly haunted by the fear of yellow fever— Maurice assured us that inhumane woman's entire plantation, her forests, and this year's harvest of sugarcane were consumed by the fire. She herself nearly perished amid the flames."

"Really! And yet your brother's property wasn't harmed by that devastation?"

"Very luckily, no! At the moment when the fire started to reach the portion of pine forest belonging to Francis, the wind suddenly changed direction, and my brother suffered no other loss than twenty or so trees."

"Very little, indeed."

Then there was a silence during which the two fiancés, both of whom seemed deep in serious thought, kept their gaze immutably fixed on the windowpanes.

"Francis still isn't back," Henríquez finally continued. "I sure would have liked to talk with him a bit."

"He won't be long," answered Mademoiselle Melvil. "Oh, my God!" cried out the young woman, "what's that I see? Doctor, look, will you?"

"Who . . . or what?" asked the physician.

"That sister of Misericordia,[2] whom we'd call a 'sister of charity' in France . . ."

"Well?"

"I saw her in profile when she passed by on the other side of the street and found a striking resemblance in her to Valentine."

"That's an illusion—"

"Oh! I do hope not—and if I'm not mistaken, it won't be long before we're reunited, never again to be separated!"

At this declaration, a cloud of discontent darkened Henríquez's face.

"You're not serious?" he said.

"How can you doubt that?" asked an astonished Mademoiselle Melvil.

"Well, you're fully aware now what distance American society's customs set between white women and mulatto women. The cruel experience Mademoiselle Arnold had of it at Madame Deschamps's should have opened the eyes of both of you as to the necessity of conforming to established customs."

"You mean prejudices, doctor!"

"It doesn't matter, if those prejudices have acquired either as much or more force than laws."

"If people highly placed on the social ladder dared to combat them, they'd vanquish them."

"I doubt it. As a matter of fact, you wouldn't find a soul here willing to undertake that struggle."

"Not even you, Señor Henríquez?"

"As a foreigner—I was born in Spain, as you know—I must, more than another perhaps, respect that which you call prejudice."

"Well! I'll brave it," exclaimed Mademoiselle Melvil, with a heated indignation.

"Take care, for it's strong enough to crush you. Judge for yourself: Mademoiselle Arnold's father, an American from New York, living in Mobile, fell in love with a woman of color full of grace and virtues. Despite the advice of his relatives and friends, he was foolhardy enough to marry her. From that point on, of all his relations with whites he kept only the purely commercial ones. Never was Madame Arnold admitted to any parlors, and whenever her husband accompanied her to church or the theater, he was forced to separate himself from her or to place himself at her side among mulattos. You see that. General reprobation would weigh upon you and no less upon your friend, were you to persist in living with her on a footing of equality that's so horribly shocking in the eyes of whites."

"That's enough, doctor. I'm sufficiently enlightened."

"So," began Henríquez, "you understand—"

"—That there are points upon which we shall never be in agreement," concluded Hortense.

The Spaniard looked at her with a dumbfounded air.

At that moment, the parlor door opened. Mr. Melvil appeared, holding the hand of Mademoiselle Arnold, into whose arms Hortense went running.

"So I wasn't wrong after all!" she cried out.

Indeed, Valentine was wearing the habit of the Sisters of Misericordia, among whom she'd taken refuge, meaning henceforth to devote her life and fortune to the comfort of the wretched. As is known, these sisters don't pronounce any vows.[3]

"You were luckier than I in your search," said Hortense to her brother.

"Happenstance—what am I saying? Providence meant for me to run into mademoiselle a few steps from our door," answered Francis.

"Cruel friend!" said Mademoiselle Melvil. "What amends don't you owe us for having judged us so badly!"

Valentine, profoundly moved, responded to these marks of friendship with naught but her tears.

"My dear sister!" she stammered finally.

"Persuade her to turn that title into a true one," said Mr. Melvil to Hortense.

"Oh! That's impossible," said Valentine.

"Here, perhaps. Not in France!" the brother and sister responded simultaneously.

As for the Spanish doctor, he'd furtively exited the parlor when he saw Hortense's friend entering it.

Two weeks after this touching scene, Francis Melvil and Valentine Arnold were joined in wedlock at the Saint Louis Cathedral by the bishop[4] of New Orleans. That same day, they embarked for Europe, taking with them Hortense, who got married in Paris a few months after arriving there.

Thus were Louisianans deprived of one of their most learned legal minds, and Doctor Henríquez lost a charming wife, whom he remembered wistfully more than once. But every day, the paupers of New Orleans bless the name of Arnold, for Mr. Melvil refused that there be any change to the charitable projects of Valentine, whose personal fortune was employed in the foundation of an almshouse where ailing paupers are welcomed with no distinction among races.

NOTES

· ·

Introduction

1. For the information synopsized here, see the entry on "LEBRUN (Pauline Guyot, connue sous le pseudonyme de Camille)" [Pauline Guyot, known under the pseudonym of Camille] in volume 10 of Larousse, *Grand dictionnaire universel du XIXè siècle*, 294. As pianos go in Lebrun's life, the Viennese-born Henri Herz (1803–1888), the concert pianist, composer, piano builder, and Conservatoire de Paris professor and her contemporary, dedicated one of his pieces in her honor: his Opus 33, the "Rondo caractéristique pour le piano forte sur la barcarolle de Marie, dédié à Mademoiselle Pauline Guyot" [Characteristic Rondo for the Pianoforte on the barcarolle of Marie, dedicated to Mademoiselle Pauline Guyot] (Leipzig: Frédéric Hoffmeister, n.d. [circa 1826 or 1827]). Coincidentally, around the same time as the publication of Lebrun's novel, Herz undertook a voyage to America in 1845–1847 and later published a book concerning his travels titled *Mes voyages en Amérique* [published in English as *My Travels in America*, trans. Henry Bertram Hill, 1963]. The volume's sixteenth chapter depicts Herz's visit to New Orleans, where he is gladdened to find a bit of France in the New World and pleased to be able to speak French. True to travelogue form, he describes the city and includes comments on its law courts, a notable inhabitant, yellow fever, marriage customs in the United States, the perilous propensity towards dueling, and a humorous anecdote about a sixteen-person piano concert. He also discusses the area's pervasive racial prejudice and reports a disturbing scene in which he witnesses a female slave threatened with a dunking in the well by her mistress, a hotel-owning *quarteronne* [quadroon] (293–95).

2. The entry on our author in Part 2 of Vapereau's *Dictionnaire universel des contemporains* notes that the *Miroir* is a collection of "tableaux historiques" [historical portrayals] (1052).

3. Monicat, in *Devoirs d'écriture: modèles d'histoires pour filles et littérature féminine au XIXe siècle*, does touch upon the novel, while providing a synopsis of it (61n21). Concerning the paucity of information about many women writers in the nineteenth century, Monicat notes: "Peu d'éléments biographiques sont disponibles au sujet de la plupart de ces auteurs, malgré les travaux de plus en plus

nombreux qui enrichissent notre connaissance de l'histoire des femmes, et plus particulièrement celle de leur histoire littéraire" (8n5) [There are few biographical elements available concerning the majority of these women authors, despite the increasing number of works enriching our awareness of the history of women and, more particularly, that of their literary history].

4. Editions of the novel appeared in 1845, 1848, 1850, 1852, 1857, 1859, and 1861.

5. Later in the century, as with an undated edition of Lebrun's *Histoire d'un caniche blanc*, secular groups vetted such books, and their approval was noted in the volume: "Cet Ouvrage a été approuvé par la Commission des Bibliothèques scolaires et des Livres de Prix" [This work was approved by the Commission of School Libraries and Prize Books].

6. Although neither author is close to being a model for belief in racial equality, both men were abolitionists at heart. For Biart, see his 1876 travelogue titled *A travers l'Amérique* [published in English as *My Rambles in the New World*, trans. Mary de Hauteville, 1877], especially in two chapters that recount events from the late 1850s. In "Le jour de Noël à la Havane" [Christmas Day in Havana] (151–72), Biart proclaims himself an "ennemi juré de l'esclavage" [a sworn enemy of slavery] (160), but mistakes a traditional day of (relative) freedom for enslaved persons for the consequences of a bloody rebellion. In "De la Havane à la Nouvelle Orléans" [From Havana to New Orleans] (173–208), which includes a subheading of "La question de l'esclavage" [The matter of slavery] (175), he has a long conversation with a slaveholding Louisianan general named Dumont, who is shocked that Biart continues to express his support for emancipation. Dumont encourages the Frenchman not to disembark in New Orleans, for "l'air y est malsain pour ceux qui ont vos idées, surtout en ce moment où, rampant le pacte de l'Union, les Etats du Nord menacent de nous asservir" (177) [the air is unhealthy for people with your ideas, especially at this moment when, breaking the pact of the Union, the northern states are threatening to subjugate us]. Biart asserts that he will not foment rebellion among the slaves, but shall limit his preaching, as he puts it, to the masters (177). This, of course, includes the general himself, who considers himself to be as humane as possible to his enslaved individuals; after all, he claims, "mes nègres sont mes enfants et ne portent pas de chaine" [my slaves are my children and aren't enchained], to which Biart replies that "one swallow does not a summer make" (177). For Verne, see specifically his novels *Un capitaine de quinze ans* (1878) [*Dick Sand, A Captain at Fifteen*] and *Nord contre Sud* (1887) [*Texar's Revenge, or, North Against South*], but also various characters in such works as *L'Ile mystérieuse* (1874–1875) [*The Mysterious Island*].

7. Miller, *The French Atlantic Triangle: Literature and Culture of the Slave Trade*.

8. Lebrun would revisit the matter of slavery in an entry titled "Colonies françaises, 2ᵐᵉ étude: La Martinique" in her magazine *Le Miroir de la France* (Paris: Bureau de la Direction du Miroir de la France, 1850), 291–307. This entry includes remarks about Creole women and maroons, thoughts about the recent emancipation of enslaved persons in France's overseas possessions, and even a brief history

of slavery that one could certainly say minimizes the French role in the development of slavery in the New World (303). For a history of royal policies and cultural attitudes with regard to slavery in metropolitan France and its colonies, see Peabody's *"There Are No Slaves in France"*: *The Political Culture of Race and Slavery in the Ancien Régime* and Palmer's *Intimate Bonds: Family and Slavery in the French Atlantic*. Slavery is also a marked feature of Lebrun's story "Le vieux Noir et le jeune Blanc" in *Contes Moraux*. This story is set in Martinique in 1841, before the liberation of enslaved individuals there, and presents a young white man saved from death on multiple occasions by people of color.

9. To counterpoise our assertion, we do note that Lebrun and her volume figure as entry 785 in a compendium of published accounts by French travelers to the United States amassed by Frank Monaghan in his bibliography *French Travellers in the United States, 1765–1932*, 48.

10. *Le Dauphiné. Histoire, descriptions pittoresques, antiquités, scènes de mœurs, personnages célèbres, curiosités naturelles, châteaux et ruines, anecdotes, monuments et édifices publics, coutumes locales.*

11. For a taste of such in Woillez, see her two otherwise excellent and oft-republished novels *L'Orpheline de Moscou, ou la jeune institutrice* (1841) [*The Orphan-girl from Moscow, or the Young Schoolteacher*] and *Le jeune tambour, ou les deux amis* (1846) [*The Young Drummer-boy, or the Two Friends*]. Monicat summarizes it well when she notes, "*Amitié et dévouement* est représentatif des récits sur lesquels pèse un fort poids moralisateur" (58) [*Friendship and Devotion* is representative of stories upon which weighs a strong moralizing burden].

12. Lebrun's acquaintance Herz details a rueful account of an invitation to perform for free people of color in New Orleans, which he feels obliged to decline for fear of losing any future white audiences. According to Herz's secretary Ulmann, "Si vous commettiez [. . .] la faute inexcusable de jouer pour des nègres, soyez assuré que vous n'auriez jamais un auditeur blanc à la Nouvelle-Orléans" (292) [If you committed [. . .] the inexcusable error of playing for blacks, be assured that you'd never perform for a white audience in New Orleans].

13. For a fuller discussion of this misogynistic tradition, see Johnson's "Can Women and Men Be Friends? Writings on Friendship in France's *Ancien Régime* and C. B. Fagan's Comedy *L'Amitié rivale de l'amour*."

14. As with *Amitié et dévouement*, this novel was never translated into English. "C'est affreux, [. . .] c'est affreux n'est-ce pas, de se reconnaître victime d'aussi basses machinations? Voila donc [. . .] où m'a conduit cette amitié de femme!" (309) [It's awful, [. . .] it's awful, isn't it, seeing oneself the victim of such despicable machinations. That's where this friendship of women has led me]. Lucile's reaction is not exaggerated: her erstwhile "friend" had disposed of her money-grubbing, former lover by arranging his marriage to Lucile. This novel is available both in reprints and for free download from the Gallica site of the Bibliothèque Nationale de France: https://gallica.bnf.fr/ark:/12148/bpt6k5681632o?rk=64378;o.

15. For a fuller treatment of friendship tropes in French literature, see Johnson's *Once There Were Two Friends: Idealized Male Friendships in French Narrative from the Middle Ages through the Enlightenment.*

Preface

1. Lebrun consistently capitalizes "*États*" when referring to the states in the USA.

2. Concluded in 1803, the treaty for the Louisiana Purchase transferred claims to a vast swath of North America from France to the United States. The modern-day state of Louisiana is but a small portion of the purchase, which became fifteen states in all and extended into modern-day Canada. For Americans now and probably in 1845, too, Lebrun should certainly mention Mississippi and Tennessee to the east, whereas Texas entered statehood in 1845.

3. Reflective, no doubt, of the historical sources she is using, Lebrun's knowledge of Native American peoples' homelands is not entirely precise, especially concerning the Creeks and Cherokees. As Colin C. Galloway notes: "Cherokee traditions tell that their ancestors originated in the southern Appalachians, in what is today the western Carolinas and eastern Georgia and Tennessee" (50). On the other hand, the Cherokee language is one of the Iroquoian languages, which is perhaps how Lebrun's unknown source came to make a connection with Canada and the northern United States where the Iroquois confederacy and other peoples speaking Iroquoian languages were located.

4. Lebrun here uses the equally dated, offensive equivalent *Peaux-Rouges* [redskins].

5. Lebrun here means the area encompassed in the Louisiana Purchase, not the American state.

6. Giovanni da Verrazzano (1485–1528). The Verrazzano-Narrows Bridge in New York City is named in his honor. Jacques Cartier, a Breton, is usually attributed with the "discovery" of today's Canadian maritime province Nova Scotia in 1534.

7. The original edition of Lebrun's novel incorrectly indicates this expedition by the French Jesuit missionary Jacques Marquette (1637–1675) and the explorer Louis Jolliet (1645–1700) occurred in 1773, rather than a century earlier. Along with other infelicities, the later Mame editions of the novel correct this error, which was repeated in the second Pornin edition.

8. René Robert Cavelier, Sieur de La Salle, or Robert de La Salle (1643–1687). Although a prominent figure in the colony after his arrival and granted a fiefdom on the island of Montreal, this famous explorer was never a "governor" of Canada. He is credited with establishing the village of Lachine (now a borough of Montreal). Lebrun seems to be confusing La Salle with the governor who encouraged his explorations: Louis de Buade, Comte de Frontenac et de Palluau, who

is commonly known as Frontenac (1622–1698), the two-time governor of New France.

9. In honor of the Sun King, Louis XIV (1638–1715).

10. Pierre Le Moyne d'Iberville (1661–1706), a French Canadian nobleman, also known as the Sieur d'Iberville. "Yberville" was an alternate spelling of his name in the seventeenth century. Iberville Parish in Louisiana and the city of D'Iberville in Mississippi are named in his honor.

11. Philippe II, duc d'Orléans (1674–1723), served as the regent of France from 1715 to 1723, after the death of the Sun King, until the majority of the king's great-grandson, Louis XV.

12. This secret agreement between France and Spain, signed on October 1, 1800, purported to exchange the Louisiana territories for some in Italy.

13. The sale of French claims to that swath of North America in the Louisiana Purchase was for fifteen million dollars.

14. The original edition of the novel says *Maures* or "Moors" here, a word that makes little sense in context. The Mame editions of the novel correct this word to *mœurs* [morals or customs].

15. Given the cultural and racial distinctions she is drawing concerning Creoles, Lebrun here means white (and free) people born in the former colonies of French and Spanish ancestry versus those who came to the colonies directly from France or Spain. See chapter 1, endnote 5 for a more in-depth discussion of the designation *Creole*. See chapter 2, endnotes 7 and 14 for more discussion relating to Creole people and language; Lebrun does not use any specifically Louisiana Creole language.

Chapter One: The Arrival

1. *La Nantaise* means "The Girl from Nantes." Nantes, like New Orleans, is a city on a river with maritime access. Nantes, along with La Rochelle, Bordeaux, and St. Malo, was home to slave ships and wealthy slave traders who regularly plied the French Atlantic and Indian Ocean Triangles, thereby greatly enriching the French city and its merchants in the eighteenth and nineteenth centuries. Lebrun is perhaps making an oblique allusion here to France's legacy of slave trading and enslavement with this ship's name. While US involvement in the international slave trade officially ended after 1807, New Orleans continued to be one of the most important markets for domestic slave trading in the United States for another half-century, when Union forces ended the sale of enslaved persons in the city.

2. This derives from an Algonquin word, according to vol. 1 of Scharf's *History of Saint Louis City and Country, from the Earliest Periods to the Present Day*, 13–14n2. For Lebrun's purposes, *Namesi-si-pou* is possibly gleaned from Barbé-Marbois, *Histoire de la Louisiane et de la cession de cette colonie par la France*

aux Etats-Unis de l'Amérique Septentrionale [*A History of Louisiana and the Cession of This Colony by France to the United States of North America*], 111.

3. The distance represented by leagues varied in many countries but is roughly three miles or four kilometers. Even now, interestingly, there are competing claims as to the length of the Mississippi River, as the US National Park Service (NPS) notes on its webpage on facts concerning the river: https://www.nps.gov/miss/riverfacts.htm. The NPS credits the river with being 2,350 miles in length.

4. As we can see in her 1848 travelogue *Le Dauphiné*, Lebrun enjoyed writing poetic descriptions of such water scenes. Here she describes her trip on the Rhône River, while traveling from Lyon to Vienne, a small city thirty-five kilometers down the river from Lyon: "Nous descendions rapidement le Rhône, dont les flots verdâtres miroitaient aux rayons ardens [*sic*] du soleil. Dans l'éther bleu et transparent nageaient des nuages dorés, et une fraîche brise nous apportait les senteurs délicieuses qui émanaient des massifs de lilas et d'autres arbustes odoriférans (*sic*), au milieu desquels semblaient se blottir les habitations éparses sur les rives du fleuve" (2–3) [We were rapidly going down the Rhône River whose greenish waters reflected the sun's ardent rays. In the blue, transparent ether swam golden clouds, and a fresh breeze bore to us the delicious scents emanating from beds of lilacs and other fragrant shrubbery, among which the scattered dwellings on the river's banks seemed to nestle].

5. "Creole" in the nineteenth-century French sense means having been born in or raised in the then French or Spanish colonies. For instance, Balzac's *La Fille aux yeux d'or* (1835) [*The Girl with the Golden Eyes*] contains a reference to a "Créole" from the Antilles. Baudelaire's "A une dame créole" [To a Creole Lady] was written in Reunion in the 1840s and published in *Les Fleurs du Mal* (1857). In contemporary Louisiana, the term "Creole" can refer to people (or things) that came into being in Louisiana as opposed to the Old World; thus, this contemporary definition is very similar to the nineteenth-century French one. However, another definition of a Louisiana Creole does not emphasize the importance of having colonial French or Spanish ancestors. This broader definition allows for people with virtually any combination of European, Native, and African heritages in Louisiana to be Creole, if, linguistically, they come from French, Spanish, and/or Creole-speaking families. Hortense embodies one current Louisianan definition of Creole: she has an English father and a Martiniquais (French) mother, but was not born in colonial French or Spanish Louisiana, if the character is contemporaneous with the book's publication. In chapter 2, we will discuss more of the meaning of Creole in Louisiana, which connotes race. In eighteenth- and nineteenth-century literature, when explaining the phenomenon alternately as the result of sultry climes, tropical illnesses, the mixture of races, and the effects of slavery, it was a common trope to describe the colonial descendants of European settlers as lazy. As Miller notes, too, "the Creole as someone who has been morally compromised, in some unstated way, by the institution of slavery [is] a commonplace in the nineteenth century" (156).

6. The European settlement of Mobile began in 1702, when the French built *Fort Louis de la Louisiane* as the first capital of *Louisiane*. French Canadian brothers Pierre Le Moyne d'Iberville and Jean-Baptiste Le Moyne, Sieur de Bienville founded Mobile. Bienville became royal governor of French Louisiana in 1701. Bienville founded New Orleans in 1718, and this city has remained in the French and American collective imagination as a former capital of North American French colonial holdings to a greater degree than Mobile has. The latter, albeit having been the first capital of Louisiana, became a part of the British West Florida colony in 1763, and its French history is less commonly known. In 1763, the Treaty of Paris ending the Seven Years' War ceded French territories east of the Mississippi River to a victorious Britain. Mobile was also Spanish from 1780 to 1812 and then became American once Alabama entered the United States as the twenty-second state in 1822.

7. For more information on yellow fever in the New World, see https://scope blog.stanford.edu/2019/01/28/how-yellow-fever-shaped-19th-century-new-orleans -a-qa/.

8. Louisiana Creoles of means often sent at least one of their children to France for education and work experience. This practice also allowed free Creoles of color liberties of which they were otherwise deprived in the United States. The plays of Louisiana-born, free man of color writer Victor Séjour (1817–1874) met with success at the Comédie Française. He is also credited with penning an indictment of slavery in his 1837 tale "Le Mulâtre" [The Mulatto], one of the earliest known pieces of published fiction by an American writer of African descent.

9. In the second story of her *Contes moraux* (purportedly cowritten by F. de Saint-Léger, another pen name for Pauline Guyot), Lebrun sets up the plot of her story "Le vieux Noir et le jeune Blanc" in a similar fashion, but here for a young man. Octave Blainvilliers, the eighteen-year-old, orphaned son of Creole parents, grows up and is educated in Paris, but returns to his parents' homeland of Martinique, where he is to begin to learn how to conduct himself as a plantation owner (34–35). In a short book published in 1875 titled *Les enfants bienfaisants* (after the first of the volume's three tales), Lebrun revisits the themes of bonds of friendship, Creoles, epidemics, and the cultural hybridity of the nineteenth-century Atlantic world in a subplot of the third story, "Le poney du Cardigan." As the story opens, the English Lord Mowbray is visiting his sister, now the "baronne de Ligny" [baroness of Ligny]. Promising the gift of a pony to be sent from his Welsh estate to his nephew Casimir, Mowbray must return to London to meet his ward, Alice Merton, the seventeen-year-old daughter of an "amie intime" (59) [intimate friend] of Lady Mary, the sister of the lord and baroness. Alice, born on Barbados, has been orphaned by an unnamed epidemic that ravaged the Antilles. Leaving behind her magnificent plantation and traveling with "une famille créole" (71) [a Creole family], she is returning to Europe to live with her much older brother, who has a German wife. Alice survives first a shipwreck and then a near stranding at sea before arriving in Le Havre rather than her intended destination. Her brother is able to

borrow the obliging Casimir's pony to hurry to that port, where Alice has neither family nor friends to greet her.

10. The narrator here means those careers requiring specialized training, such as lawyers, pharmacists, and doctors, which American English speakers generally simply characterize as professions. As a counterpoint to Lebrun's assertions about the prestige of professional positions in American society as contrasted with Louisiana's Creole society, consider the recollections of the wealthy heiress Laura Locoul Gore (1861–1963) in her *Memories of the Old Plantation Home*. Her father, Emile Locoul (1822–1879), was sent to Bordeaux for education in a military school as a thirteen-year-old. After his graduation, a celebratory tour of Europe, and return to Louisiana:

> Father wished to study law, of which he was very fond. I have no doubt he would have made his mark extensively. Often Father would discuss the law with his plantation neighbor, Judge (later, Governor) Roman, and he could have passed the Bar examinations, if he so desired.
>
> But the family opposed his going into law bitterly, for a "southern gentleman had to be a planter." Professional men were not regarded with favor, nor had the same prestige. When a sugar planter walked the streets of New Orleans with his cottonade britches, alpaca coat, panama hat and gold-headed cane, he was looked upon as the king of creation and everybody bowed down to him. (20)

In this respect, therefore, Francis Melvil has attained higher social status by purchasing a sugar plantation.

11. *Cyprière* refers to a stand of cypress trees. See chapter 8, endnote 1 for more on cypresses.

12. Because of human-made changes beginning in 1831, the Red River was cut off from the Mississippi: "Historically, the Red River joined the Mississippi here [50 miles south of Natchez] while the Atchafalaya flowed out of the system as a distributary to the Gulf of Mexico." Campanella, *Bienville's Dilemma: A Historical Geography of New Orleans*, 87.

13. The language of race has been extensively and intensively studied. Arguably, among the most commonly used words in general usage to refer to persons of supposedly mixed race is mulatto. Lebrun surely is using the term in its commonly used sense. The difference between American and French usage will emerge as one of the book's themes.

14. Lebrun's use of "piaster" is accurate. It was simply the former Spanish silver dollar, the *peso de ocho*, or "piece of eight," which was widely used legal tender in the United States until the passage of the Coinage Act in 1857. Like Francophone people in Quebec, Louisianan French-speakers still refer to the dollar as a *piastre*. Of historical note, the French version of the 1803 treaty for the Louisiana Purchase prices the transaction in piasters.

15. France's central bank, first chartered in 1800 during the period of the Consulate.

16. The oldest school of medicine still in existence, the prestigious École de *Médecine* dates back to 1137.

17. This is in contrast with a pre-Haussmann Paris or any number of "unplanned" French cities. New Orleans and Mobile were laid out by Adrien de Pauger, an eighteenth-century French engineer. New Orleans's *Vieux Carré* or "Old Square" is noted as an example of early urbanism, for this area is laid out in an orderly, almost perfectly symmetrical grid. Figure 1 at the beginning of this volume shows the layout of New Orleans in a cutout. Paris, prior to George Eugène Haussmann's renovations from 1853 to 1879, was a medieval and labyrinthine agglomeration of villages; the orderly New Orleans grid probably appeared very neat and organized to French visitors.

Chapter Two: The Saint Louis Cathedral

1. Built in 1727, the Saint Louis Cathedral church is one of the oldest continuous congregations in the United States. Destroyed in the great New Orleans fire of 1788, the second building was constructed in the 1790s. With the separation of Louisiana from the Diocese of Cuba in 1793, the church was dedicated as a cathedral on Christmas Eve of 1794. When Lebrun was writing *Amitié et dévouement*, plans were under way to overhaul the site for a third building, in 1850, that gave the cathedral its current look and size.

2. Rented pews were the norm throughout American Christendom in this period. There may well have been separate sections for free and enslaved people of color in antebellum Catholic churches in Louisiana. Established in 1841, Saint Augustine Church in New Orleans bears a 2004 commemorative plaque at the shrine of St. Augustine called "The Tomb of the Unknown Slave." The plaque proclaims the St. Augustine Church was "the only parish in the United States whose free people of color bought two outer rows of pews exclusively for slaves to use for worship." Segregated seating in churches was a manifestation of white supremacy not limited to the South, as historian Jelani M. Favors notes: "In spite of the egalitarian rhetoric often associated with the Quakers, [Sarah Mapp] Douglass had her own run-in with the segregationist policies observed by the religious group [. . .]. Writing to William Bassett, an English Quaker in an 1837 letter, she noted, 'There is a bench set apart for our people, whether officially appointed or not I cannot say, but my mother and myself were told to sit there and a Friend sat at each end of the bench to prevent a white person from sitting there'" (27). The AME Church famously came into being in 1816 in Philadelphia after Black preachers at St. George's Methodist Episcopal Church rejected discrimination in the church, which included segregated seating. Contrasting the practices of Protestant and Roman Catholic congregations, Slawson notes, "A final difference between southern Protestantism and Catholicism was the virtual absence of separate Catholic churches for the races. People of both races attended the same churches, though

blacks usually had to sit in special pews or galleries" (143). Elsewhere in the South, this phenomenon is reflected in separate catechisms for white people and Black people, as notes Tate in *Catholics' Lost Cause: South Carolina Catholics and the American South, 1820–1861*, 18. For his part, Stern asserts, "While the church segregated organizations and activities such as parish societies, catechetical instruction, and processions, black and white Catholics worshiped together in the same churches and until the 1890s—the same pews" (77). While it is conjecture, perhaps news of more expansive 1840s segregationist policies favoring whites in Louisiana made its way to France. Living conditions for free people of color in Louisiana began to degrade after the 1830s, however. See https://lib.lsu.edu/sites/all/files/sc/fpoc/history.html#historydecline. Given that the first edition of *Friendship and Devotion* was approved by the archbishop of Quimper, it seems plausible that Lebrun depicts an unfortunate reality of pew segregation within the New Orleans cathedral. Perhaps the Louisiana Catholic leadership had fallen prey to justifications for slavery and white supremacy, as Tate identifies elsewhere in the Antebellum South. While the Irish-born John England (1786–1842), the first bishop of the newly created Catholic diocese in Charleston, sought to strike a *via media* that condemned sudden abolition of slavery while hoping for its eventual end, his successors "failed to maintain an independent course, eventually capitulating to the position of the dominant culture in which they lived" (Tate 201).

3. In the original French, Lebrun uses the term *de couleur* [of color] to delineate these women as being different from the "négresses" in the other enclosure (30).

4. According to Allison Plyer and Laman Gardere in *The New Orleans Prosperity Index*, 58 percent of the city's population in the 1840s were whites, 23 percent were enslaved Blacks, and 19 percent were free Blacks (table titled "Share of Historical Population by Race, New Orleans"). By the 1850s, the percentage of free Blacks had decreased by over half.

5. Lebrun's novel, like many of her other works, appears in a series called the "Gymnase moral d'éducation," the "Moral school of education." Given the series' nature, it is understandable why such a book might criticize racial segregation in a Catholic church in the former French colony, disapprove of Valentine's vulnerability to pride, the foremost of the seven deadly sins, or take up other concerns of a moral nature.

6. Prior to Vatican II in the Roman Catholic Church, a missal was a book containing the prayers and rites used during the Mass. A shortened form called a "missalette" has now largely replaced missals in common congregational usage.

7. "Two degrees" refers to supposed whiteness. In *Africans in Colonial Louisiana: The Development of Afro-Creole Culture in the Eighteenth Century*, Gwendolyn Midlo Hall reports there were at least ten racial descriptors once commonly in use in Louisiana.

8. Although English speakers commonly think of the pope as "the" pontiff, a pontiff is any bishop, and the pontiff's vestments are called "pontificals."

9. A church official who serves as an usher and caretaker and who leads processions with a "verge" or rod of office in hand.

10. We note that, by making this young man not a verger or usher of the church, Lebrun gives the cathedral an out: it is not the church that is sanctioning pew segregation, but a racial policing performed by the congregants themselves.

11. While it is currently difficult to imagine such a dramatic change in temperature in June in New Orleans, we should recall that the climate in North America in the first half of the nineteenth century was still under the declining effects of the Little Ice Age and that early summer weather conditions may have been more variable then than they are now.

12. A portico or enclosed area in front of a church.

13. In the original French, it is not entirely clear whether "she" is referring to Mademoiselle Arnold or Mademoiselle Ridué. Either Mademoiselle Ridué had found seating in a side chapel of the nave or that which was earlier described as something akin to a box pew is now a separate chapel.

14. In a modest attempt to add local color to her story, the author indicates this young man is making this statement in a non-standard French patois that changes the gender of *voiture* and does not accurately replicate the Louisiana Creole variety: "*Moi* en amener un à *vous* tout-à-l'heure" (38–39), which would be on the order of "Moi, je vais vous en amener une tout à l'heure" in standard French. Emphasis by Lebrun.

15. The French word *suivante* is ambiguous. That person is not a servant, but a subordinate companion, a personal assistant of sorts. As we see here, it is not a relationship of parity.

16. *Les Dames de la Providence* was founded in New Orleans in 1839 as an organization of "women to care for the poor and sick," according to Baudier in *The Catholic Church in Louisiana*, 367. It was an association of laypeople who raised money for charitable causes. During the 1840s, the city's main newspapers reported on their activities. The gift of five hundred piasters indicates Lebrun's awareness of the wealth and piety on the part of New Orleans's free people of color. This would have been a generous charitable offering, equaling thousands of dollars in present-day US currency.

17. In the portion of her posthumous tetralogy *Violetta la Quarteronne*, Sidonie de La Houssaye gives a rather different interpretation of the appearance and generosity of women of color at the Saint Louis Cathedral, here as affected by the anger of the adulterous and ironically named Pierre Saulvé, with respect to his mixed-race paramour, Violetta, and her despised Aunt Aspasie. The author notes, too, that Violetta "avec un grand fracas—pour attirer l'attention du public—entrait dans un des bancs de derrière, réservés à la couleur" [with a great racket—to attract the public's attention—would enter one of the rear benches reserved for people of color]. She goes on to note that the quadroon women there made so much noise that they eventually lost the corner "reserved" for them. See *Les Quarteronnes de la Nouvelle-Orléans*, 240–41.

18. Like "mulatto," the meaning of the term "Creole" has been variously used and interpreted. As she did in the novel's preface, Lebrun seems to be using it in the nineteenth-century Louisianan sense of virtually everyone who was born in Louisiana. Thus, the main characters, Valentine and Hortense, are Creoles because they were born in Louisiana, speak French, and are Catholic. Most contemporary scholars take it as axiomatic that early nineteenth-century Louisiana was an overwhelmingly Creole society.

Chapter Three: Yellow Fever

1. Yellow fever tormented New Orleans throughout the nineteenth century. It is a mosquito-vectored disease endemic in sub-Saharan Africa, which spread to other parts of the world, including Europe, along with the slave trade. In the toxic phase of the disease, the afflicted became jaundiced, hence the name. "In the 100-year period between 1800 and 1900, yellow fever assaulted New Orleans for sixty-seven summers. Many victims were immigrants and newcomers to the city, and for this reason it was also referred to as the 'stranger's disease.' The worst epidemic years coincided with some of the highest levels of Irish and German immigration into the city: 1847, 1853, 1854, 1855, and 1858," notes Kelley in "Yellow Fever." In the New World, during the novel's era, the disease was borne by the "yellow fever mosquito" (Aedes aegypti), but nowadays the invasive tiger mosquito (Aedes albopictus) is a carrier, too. Readers of this novel should keep in mind that the novel's characters reveal flawed information about the disease, its contagiousness, its victims, and those who might have a relative immunity.

2. Due to its involvement in the slave trade, Europe was not immune to outbreaks of the disease, but they were rare, given that yellow fever mosquitos prefer warmer climates. The mosquitos also breed in standing water, which is almost omnipresent in New Orleans due to its high amounts of precipitation annually and lack of adequate drainage. New Orleans is behind only its Gulf Coast peers Mobile and Pensacola for annual amounts of rainfall in US cities.

3. The yellow fever season coincided with what was and is the hurricane season (June to November), when mosquitos would have been especially rampant.

4. By contemporary French standards, this salary was a fantastic sum. In France in 1853, a female domestic would have earned between 163 and 190 francs annually, depending on her role, according to Emile Chevallier in Les salaires au XIXè siècle, 72.

5. Cassava, also known as yucca and manioc, is a New World plant cultivated and eaten in many tropical places, including the Caribbean, but it is not a traditional Louisiana food and likely would have been imported.

6. Pecan pralines are a traditional Louisianan sweet. They are round in shape and made out of sugar, cream, and usually pecans; they are different from French pralines, which are caramelized, sugarcoated almonds.

7. Collecting pecans was typically children's work.

8. One should keep in mind that, in the vocabulary of that era, dinner was a large meal in the afternoon, with supper in the evening. In modern American English in the rural South, at least, this vocabulary usage still prevails only in the idea of Sunday dinner or Thanksgiving dinner not being evening meals. In Louisiana French, *le déjeuner* is breakfast, *le dîner* is lunch, and *le souper* is supper.

9. A *salmis* is a classic French dish in which slices of game bird meat are reheated and served in a rich sauce. "Topinambour" is the edible tuber of a sunflower-like plant native to North America also called a "Jerusalem artichoke" or "sunchoke." It is commonly eaten in France nowadays.

10. This assertion is only somewhat accurate. With mosquitos as the vector, the disease would have spread anywhere the mosquitos lived. Since New Orleans was more densely populated than rural areas, outbreaks of the disease would have been more spectacular and reported in news sources. Tens of thousands died of yellow fever throughout the United States in the eighteenth and nineteenth centuries.

11. Many diseases struck nineteenth-century Louisiana besides yellow fever. The heat, humidity, and frequent summer outbreaks of cholera, smallpox, and malaria in New Orleans caused people to flee the city for rural and coastal areas, which were viewed as more salubrious. Other coastal cities of the era experienced similar phenomena: the city of Summerville, South Carolina, owes its existence to a similar flight of wealthy whites from Charleston.

12. In this instance, "Creole" refers to people of European descent living in the former French colony.

Chapter Four: Sundry Events

1. The *Sœurs grises* [Grey Nuns], also known as Sisters and Daughters of Charity, are a charitable order founded in the early eighteenth century in Montreal where their headquarters remain. New Orleans's *L'Hôpital des Pauvres de la Charité*, which eventually became Charity Hospital, was founded on May 10, 1736. This hospital for the indigent was the second oldest public hospital in the United States; it closed due to political concerns regarding its charitable mission after Hurricane Katrina (2005) and despite the building not having suffered extensive damage. The Daughters of Charity began their ministry in health care in New Orleans at Charity Hospital in 1834 and established Hôtel Dieu Hospital in 1859. The Daughters of Charity still offer low-cost and free medical services in various clinics across New Orleans, and their former website stated: "Our mission, similar to that of other [Catholic] ministries, is to improve the health and well-being of our community and to be a presence of the Love of Jesus in the lives of all we serve and with whom we partner" (http://dchcno.org/main/about_us?loc=general). It should be kept in mind that hospitals in the novel's era were more akin to

almshouses and hospices than our current idea of hospitals being solely a place for surgery and medical care.

2. Francis here echoes Dr. Henríquez's later implication that, due to her African heritage, Valentine has a greater resistance to the disease than do European new-comers to New Orleans. While it is true that people in areas of sub-Saharan Africa, where the disease is endemic, might acquire immunity through exposure as chil-dren, the disease is a deadly one there, too.

3. In nineteenth-century France, the formal second-person pronoun *vous* was far more widespread than it is today. In that era, *vous* was sometimes used even among family members, with children addressing their parents formally while parents used the informal pronoun (*tu*) with their children. In English at that time, the informal "thou" had yielded to the second-person plural pronoun "you." The word "you" became the sole second-person subject pronoun in most parts of the English-speaking world by the eighteenth century. Today "thou" is used only in some Yorkshire and Lancashire (Northern England) dialects and Scots, but remains recognizable in American English given its frequency in commonly avail-able texts such as the King James Bible or works by Shakespeare. Lebrun observes that Hortense's brother uses *vous* when speaking to his sister in French, but mis-takenly suggests that it was, in some manner or other, the English formal register. The paragraph does lead one to wonder whether Lebrun thought English speakers were still commonly using "thou" and "thee" when speaking to their loved ones.

4. Inexplicably, Lebrun has Francis saying "Don" Henríquez, even though that title is only appropriate with a first name in Spanish. Francis is the only white male in the novel whose first name is frequently used, and even he is often referred to as "Mr. Melvil."

5. The distance of forty leagues is roughly one hundred and twenty miles, with people on horseback traveling twenty to thirty miles a day, depending on the road conditions and the horse's conditioning. Such a trip might take as long as a week.

6. A kind of cheap rum, tafia (or taffia) is not as processed as the better-known product and is thus cheaper to produce and purchase. Antoine Simon Le Page du Pratz, an eighteenth-century Dutchmen raised in France, who lived in Louisiana from 1718 to 1734, refers to tafia in his three-volume, 1758 publication *Histoire de la Louisiane*. In a chapter devoted to the "Maniere de gouverner les Négres (sic)" [The Manner for Governing Slaves], he mentions serving up tafia as a reward for the day's labors. He also explains the word in a footnote: "Le Tafia est une liqueur forte faite avec le marc de sucre, que les Négres aiment beaucoup" (1:347) [Tafia is a strong liquor made from the dregs of sugar, which slaves love greatly]. Tafia is mentioned in C. C. Robin's *Voyages* (2:214) and also figures in Lebrun's story "Le vieux Noir et le jeune Blanc," when, as we paraphrase here, the narrator tells us that tafia is a part of the enslaved persons' entertainment on Saturday nights, when they leave their slave quarters to run to some ajoupa to spend the night there smoking, drinking tafia, and dancing the bamboula (85).

7. A heritage variety of squash originally from France.

8. In the original, Lebrun adds a bit of local color in French; instead of calling mosquitos *moustiques*, she calls them *maringouins*, a term used in Francophone North America (Canada, Martinique, Guadeloupe, Haiti, Louisiana) and even in parts of France. There is a small town in Iberville Parish in Louisiana that goes by this less than enticing name! The word originates from the indigenous South American language Guaraní. An American equivalent for this word is "gallinipper."

Chapter Five: A Plantation

1. The chapter title in French is "Une Habitation." *Habitation* in Caribbean and Louisiana French means the master's house (also known as the "big house" in English) on a plantation, the outbuildings, and the fields. In English, "plantation" does not necessarily connote a house or home. There were thousands of *habitations*, mainly owned by cotton and sugarcane planters who were at the head of great fortunes and society in Louisiana. Typically, a *habitation* consisted of many buildings and homes: smaller houses included the overseer's home and the enslaved persons' houses. A *habitation* is comparable to a small village. Large *habitations* had gardens, a well, barns, fields, and even a smithy and cotton gins; enslaved people tended to all of these facilities. *Habitations* had houses for those enslaved, usually arranged in rows typically located behind the big house. The wealthiest plantations had their own "sugarhouse," called a *sucrière* in this text (see Figure 12). Having this means of production was an integral part of many sugarcane families' wealth, due to the savings of being able to make sugar on site rather than having to haul one's crop to someone else's sugarhouse. Thorpe claims that, in 1853, there were "nearly fifteen hundred sugar plantations in Louisiana" (758).

2. Louisiana's best-known citrus fruit is the satsuma, a small tangerine-like fruit introduced to the Gulf Coast in the eighteenth century.

3. Versus those climes in France, the narrator means.

4. In the nineteenth century, Louisianans imported marble, granite, and slate. As such, stone and stonework were rare; however, Louisianans decorated their homes with faux finishes, and wooden architectural and structural features like mantels were painted to look like marble.

5. The chapter later explains many of these products were imported to the area from Caribbean islands.

6. "Guava" comes to English via Spanish *guayaba,* derived from the Arawak word for the fruit: *guayavu.*

7. Although Lebrun's text specifically refers to *banane*, she means the starchier "cooking" banana or plantain, not today's common banana. In *Banana: The Fate of the Fruit That Changed the World* and its section on the expansion of the world's most consumed fruit to the United States, Koeppel notes, "Bananas were available in the United States immediately following the Civil War. But they were a luxury item, like caviar, consumed more for status than taste[. . . .] plantains, for cooking,

however, had been a staple in the southern parts of the hemisphere since Spanish times" (52). The *Louisiana Advertiser* of June 1, 1820, gives notice of the schooner the *Grey Hound*, which bore a cargo of "coffee and plantains." The same issue of the *Advertiser* also notes the "Brig *Mary Ann*, Selby, Havana" bore "sugar, coffee sweetmeats, segars, pineapples, cocoanuts, tamarinds, limes, oranges." Our thanks to Dr. David Shields of the University of South Carolina for unearthing this reference. Later, the *Louisiana Advertiser* of January 12, 1826, reported in the "Marine Journal" that a hundred loads of plantains and a hundred bunches of bananas arrived from Havana. In Louisiana French, bananas were called *figues*, as they are in various Creole dialects around the world. Bananas were not widely eaten in the United States until the late nineteenth century.

8. While Lebrun's assertion about *figuier d'Adam* is true for French, "Adam's Figs" in English are a common fig in South Africa.

9. Perhaps stemming from native people's traditions in the Caribbean, the pineapple—a fruit native to the New World and first taken to Europe by Columbus—was a symbol of hospitality. It is not a Louisiana crop.

10. In her reflections in *Miroir de la France* on slavery and emancipation in Martinique, published five years after *Amitié et dévouement*, Lebrun admits mixed feelings about emancipation and betrays concerns not unlike those of Mr. S***, noting: "Aujourd'hui que le fait accompli de l'émancipation des noirs a tranché, peut-être un peu tardivement et sans aucun doute trop brusquement, une question qu'il eût été prudent de résoudre plus tôt et avec circonspection, on ne peut que déplorer les secousses qu'il aurait été possible d'éviter, en déterminant à l'avance l'époque où cette émancipation devait avoir lieu en y préparant graduellement une race trop longtemps avilie par l'esclavage pour ne pas être d'abord étourdie par son état de liberté, en ménageant enfin aux colons des ressources positives pour assurer l'exploitation de leurs propriétes" (305–306) [Now that the fait accompli of the emancipation of blacks has been settled, perhaps a little late and, without a doubt, too abruptly, a question that it would have been prudent to resolve sooner and with circumspection, one can only deplore the jolts it would have been possible to avoid, by determining in advance the time when this emancipation was to occur, by gradually preparing a race too long debased by slavery not to be stunned at first by its state of freedom, by arranging, lastly, substantive resources for farmers to insure the cultivation of their properties].

11. Mr. Melvil's assertion concerning abuses of enslaved persons echoes the contention of Palmer in *Intimate Bonds: Family and Slavery in the French Atlantic*. Building on the work of Malick Ghachem concerning slavery in French Saint-Domingue prior to the Haitian Revolution, Palmer notes: "In the Caribbean, the Code Noir placed judicial limitations on the physical abuse of slaves [. . .] and also making killing a slave a criminal offence. However, these limitations on owners' authority were virtually never enforced [. . .]. For all intents and purposes, owners in Saint-Domingue could torture, beat, rape, starve, and otherwise abuse those

they called chattel [. . .]. Harsh treatment went unnoted for the most part, and even killing a slave seldom occasioned more than a fine. For practical purposes, owners had almost unlimited control over their human property" (48).

12. Unlike Mr. Melvil, who refers to these unfortunate souls as *noirs*, Mr. S*** starts by saying *noirs,* but then switches to the more pejorative *nègre*, which almost always referred to enslaved persons.

13. Francis is relating the tale of Marie Delphine (née Macarty) LaLaurie or "Madame LaLaurie" (c. 1780–1849), a contemporaneous New Orleans socialite accused of torturing and murdering her enslaved individuals. She fled to France under threat of mob justice, yet ultimately suffered no other consequence than the inconvenience of moving away from her French Quarter mansion on Royal Street to live and, eventually, die in Paris. Slavery remained legal in Cuba until its abolishment by royal decree in 1886.

14. Maroons were enslaved persons who had run away from their owners. In Louisiana, maroons sometimes took refuge with indigenous peoples who were able to survive in undesirable swampland and with whom they formed communities. The English word "maroon" derives from the French Antilles derivation of the Spanish word *cimarrón* that referred to an escaped domestic animal that returned to the wild. Maroons also established communities in colonial French Indian Ocean islands. From the eighteenth-century writings of Bernardin de St. Pierre to the contemporary writings of Edouard Glissant, maroons and marronage play a significant part in Francophone fiction and criticism dealing with slavery.

15. Francis apparently is referring to the historical immigration of criminals and prostitutes to the Americas. Louisiana was a home to *forçats* [convicts]. One of the famous novels of eighteenth-century France, *Manon Lescaut* (1731; 1753), depicts the deportation of its eponymous character to Louisiana.

16. Louisiana, like all of its Caribbean neighbors, depended enormously on the labor of the enslaved and indentured laborers. Many indentured servants, particularly those of German descent (Alsatian, Lorraine, Swiss, and Baltic), came to Louisiana throughout the eighteenth century and into the nineteenth, beginning with their recruitment by the financier John Law. Because the French had heard conditions were so harsh in the Louisiana colony, they proved to be unwilling recruits; thus, Law resorted to finding Germans to people the colony. These indentured servants' health and survival rates were frequently noted as being poor—the ships they arrived in were even called "pest ships," with "pest" being a derivation of the French word for plague, *la peste*. Once across the Atlantic, like Hortense, many of the indentured servants fell gravely ill upon arrival. See the following: Le Conte, "Les Allemands à la Louisiane au XVIIIe siècle"; Alice D. Forsyth and Earlene L. Zeringue, *German "Pest Ships," 1720–1721* (New Orleans: Genealogical Research Society of New Orleans, 1969); and https://www.hnoc.org/research/german-settlers-louisiana-and-new-orleans. See also Carrigan's "Privilege, Prejudice, and the Strangers' Disease in Nineteenth-Century New Orleans."

17. Only a small portion of the modern state of Louisiana juts into the Gulf of Mexico where alluvial deposits from the Mississippi River created land, but that area does include New Orleans itself.

18. Sugarcane is cultivated in much of the world, and its harvest varies widely.

19. Then, as now, farmers grew cotton mostly in the northern, drier part of the state, whereas the greater humidity of southern Louisiana was optimal for rice and sugarcane cultivation. It is likely that the hasty six months explained by Francis, versus the usual eight to nine months for production, was the result of guesswork by farmers of the era trying to decide when the first freezes would arrive and potentially ruin crops. It is possible that the different varieties of sugarcane grown in that era, like the once-common ribbon cane, may have affected production time. In recent years, inspired in part by the growth of interest in heritage crops, the purple ribbon variety has been reintroduced for cultivation in coastal Georgia, particularly on Sapelo Island. According to T. B. Thorpe in his 1853 essay "Sugar and the Sugar Region in Louisiana," the four most common varieties of cane in that era in Louisiana were the bourbon, the ribbon, the otaheite, and the creole (749); he also notes, "Nine months from the time that it is planted are required in Louisiana to ripen the cane" (756).

20. Some modern interpretations of the Deep South's cotton and sugarcane cultivation suggest the production was industrial. The fields and contingent industries (sugar mills and cotton gins) were factories in the fields, an idea that becomes clearer in Figures 11–15 in this volume. Thorpe notes the implication of both northern and southern states, if not globalization, in this slavery-based industry when he elaborates: "The mill, the steam-engines, the complicated vacuum-pans, the bone-black, the wrought iron moulds, the iron of the railway, the mules, the wagons, the carts, the food, the clothing for an army of negroes, and the ten thousand not recollected but expensive items, are all produced at the North and West; and hundreds of families in those distant portions of the country are just as dependent for their living as the planter himself upon the successful cultivation of the sugar-cane crop" (759). Lebrun fails to connect that the cotton for "our muslins" would have come from cotton plantations that were not in Europe and most likely would have come from the American South. In the first half of the nineteenth century, American cotton production outweighed that of other regions.

21. Lebrun may be referring to the African or Caribbean yam when she says *igname* (*dioscorea*) in the original, which is not a sweet potato or *patate douce* (*Ipomoea batatas*). Louisiana has historically been a large producer of sweet potatoes. One popular variety developed in the 1930s was, in fact, marketed as a "yam." See https://www.lsuagcenter.com/portals/communications/publications/agmag/archive/2012/spring/sweet-potato-louisianas-most-popular-vegetable.

22. This fruit, also known by its Italian name of *chinotto*, is an important ingredient in the liqueur Campari, which came into being only in 1860, well after this novel's first publication. Its presence in Louisiana is noted in the "Flore louisianaise" [Louisianan Flora] section of the third volume of C. C. Robin's *Voyages;*

see 3:474–75, a section that also alludes to the creations of hedges of sour varieties of oranges.

23. Also called the Seville orange, the bitter orange, or sour orange and commonly used for making marmalade and marinades, such as Badia Sour Orange (*Naranja Agria*). Describing the environs of New Orleans in his account of his travels in Louisiana, C. C. Robin notes: "on y voit des avenues de magnifiques orangers de ceux surtout au fruit acide, se parant d'une année à l'autre de leurs pommes rajeunissantes" (2:63) [you can see avenues of magnificent orange trees there, of the kind with an acidic fruit especially, bearing their rejuvenating fruit from one year to the next].

24. The source of bergamot oil used in teas and perfumes.

25. In most of France and certainly in Paris, as in much of Louisiana, oranges cannot be grown in the open without running the risk of tree-killing, fruit-ruining winter and spring freezes.

26. Ordinarily in English, as in continental French, an orangery or *orangerie* would be akin to a greenhouse meant to protect the trees from low temperatures.

27. In the original text, and in a nice touch of adding local color, Lebrun has Mr. S*** express this temperature in Fahrenheit rather than the expected Celsius.

28. Mme Laure Andry, in her 1882 *Histoire de la Louisiane, racontée aux enfants louisianais* [History of Louisiana Told to Louisianan Children], refers to a similarly memorable climactic event occurring in the same decade that Mr. S*** evokes (if we think the novel is set in the 1840s): "Le 16 Février 1823, un froid violent se fit sentir, les bords du fleuve furent glacés, l'on patina sur les marais. Tous les orangers furent détruits, ce qui fut une grande perte pour les petits propriétaires dont ils constituaient le revenu principal. On trouva morts de froid des bateliers dans leurs embarcations, des nègres dans leurs cabanes, des bestiaux dans les forêts" (119) [On February 16, 1823, it grew fiercely cold; the banks of the river were icy; people skated in the marshes. All the orange trees were destroyed, which was a great loss for the small landholders for whom they constituted the main income. Boatmen in their skiffs, slaves in their cabins, and beasts in the forests were found dead from the cold].

29. In colloquial French, there is no distinction between *oiseau-mouche*, which translates literally as "bird-fly," and the widely used expression *colibri* (violetear), which scientifically should be limited to four species in the family of *Trochilidae* but which is commonly used to describe the more than three hundred species. Clearly, Lebrun means to draw a distinction between two birds in the larger family.

30. Lebrun drew the language to describe this bird and subsequent ones from the writings of Georges-Louis Leclerc, Comte de Buffon (1707–1788) who, with the help of others, produced a hugely popular, encyclopedic, thirty-six-volume *Histoire naturelle, générale et particulière*, nine volumes of which were devoted to birds and appeared from 1770 to 1783. (These nine volumes are available for free download from Gallica.) In the sixth volume of those devoted to birds, Buffon notes concerning hummingbirds: "Rien n'égale en effet la vivacité de ces petits oiseaux,

si ce n'est leur courage, ou plutôt leur audace: on les voit poursuivre avec furie des oiseaux vingt fois plus gros qu'eux, s'attacher à leur corps, & se laissant emporter par leur vol, les béqueter à coups redoublés, jusqu'à ce qu'ils aient assouvi leur petite colère (n). Quelquefois même ils se livrent entr'eux de très-vifs combats ; l'impatience paroît être leur ame ; s'ils s'approchent d'une fleur & qu'ils la trouvent fanée, ils lui arrachent les pétales avec une précipitation qui marque leur dépit ; ils n'ont point d'autre voix qu'un petit cri, *screp, screp,* fréquent & répété" (6:6) [Nothing equals, in fact, the vivacity of these little birds, if not their courage, or rather their audacity: they've been seen to pursue furiously birds twenty times larger than themselves, attach themselves to their bodies, & letting themselves be carried along by their flight, pecking at them with redoubled blows until they've sated their bit of anger. They sometimes even wage very intense battles among themselves; impatience seems to be their soul; if they approach a flower and find it wilted, they tear off its petals with a precipitation that marks their spite; they have no other voice than a small, frequent, repeated cry: *scrup scrup*]. Lebrun's description is not unlike the one that appears late in the 1812 classic by Johann David Wyss, *The Swiss Family Robinson,* which was soon translated into French in 1813 by Swiss writer Isabelle de Montolieu (1751–1832). Notes the narrator in the novel's fifty-fourth chapter: "Our beautiful flowers also attracted numerous guests: there were the hummingbirds: and it was one of our greatest amusements to watch these little birds flying around us, sparkling like precious stones, and hardly perceptible by the quickness of their motions; it was an amusing spectacle to see these passionate, choleric little fellows attack others twice their size, and drive them away from their nests, and at other times they would tear in pieces the unlucky flower that had deceived their expectations of a rich feast" (291).

31. The *cassique de la Louisiane* also appears in the third volume of Buffon's *Histoire naturelle des oiseaux* (3:242). Unfortunately, the bird is thought to be extinct, if indeed it truly was an oriole. According to Hume in *Extinct Birds*, it is "Known only from the plate of Daubenton and the descriptions of Buffon and Pennant. McAtee (1963) considered it a partial albino, and unidentifiable. Clearly not an Old World oriole and if anywhere perhaps placed with the icterids" (428). In line with that last comment, it is quite likely the bird is simply a piebald grackle. Our thanks both to Gwen and Tom Barnett and to Ruth Caillouet and Barbara Holland for their help in tracking down information on this bird.

32. Lebrun draws this idea about birdsong in the New World from Buffon's frequent contributor, the naturalist Philippe Guéneau de Montbeillard. Concerning the mockingbird, Buffon observes: "Nous trouvons dans cet oiseau singulier, une exception frappante à une observation générale faite sur les oiseaux du nouveau monde. Presque tous les Voyageurs s'accordent à dire qu'autant les couleurs de leur plumage sont vives, riches, éclatantes, autant le son de leur voix est aigre, rauque, monotone, en un mot désagréable" (3:325) [We find in this singular bird a striking exception to a general observation made about the birds of the New World. Almost all Voyagers agree in saying that however much the colors of their feathers are

vivid, rich, striking, the sound of their voice is equally acerbic, croaky, monotonous, in short, disagreeable]. Notes Montbeillard: "La Nature, qui peignit des plus riches couleurs la plupart des oiseaux du nouveau monde, leur refusa presque à tous l'agrément du chant, & ne leur donna, sur ces terres désertes, que des cris sauvages" (Buffon and Montbeillard 5:166) [Nature, which painted the majority of the birds in the New World in the richest colors, refused to almost all of them the agreeableness of song & gave them, in these deserted lands, but savage cries].

33. In the original, this character refers to the antiquated plural of "Les Florides." Following the 1763 Treaty of Paris, the British took possession of a large swath of formerly French and Spanish lands from the Mississippi River to the Atlantic. They divided the new possessions at the Apalachicola River into West Florida, with its capital in Pensacola, and East Florida, with its capital in St. Augustine. They kept these lands until the American Revolution and the 1783 Treaty of Paris returned both Floridas to Spanish control, albeit with a new territorial line at the Suwannee River to the east. In the new American republic, West Florida would become the "Florida parishes" in Louisiana and the Gulf access for the states of Mississippi and Alabama. To excuse Lebrun's characterization, however, Florida only became a state in 1845, the year of this novel's publication.

34. Lebrun also seems to derive information about the goldfinch from Buffon and Montbeillard (5:165).

35. Meaning that it is a bit of a chatterbox, too. Some etymologies of the word "jazz" claim the French verb *jaser* as its antecedent. Jazz was originally spelled "jass." See Merriam and Garner, "Jazz: The Word."

36. Lebrun seems to be describing the coloration of a Bohemian waxwing. The state of Louisiana does not list that particular bird; see http://www.wlf.louisiana. gov/wildlife/birds-louisiana. The website lists only the cedar waxwing, which has touches of red only on its wingtips. Images of the latter bird are available at the following website: https://www.allaboutbirds.org/guide/Cedar_Waxwing/id. Latham's volume 1, part 2 of *A General Synopsis of Birds* simply translates this bird as an "olive oriole" (444).

37. In the original text, Lebrun also refers to this bird by the name of "merle cendré de Saint-Domingue," which Montbeillard thinks is simply a mislabeled mockingbird (Buffon and Montbeillard 3:320). Of the seventeen species of mockingbirds, the one most commonly found in North America is the northern mockingbird, which is the only variety listed on the website on Louisiana birds cited in note 36.

Chapter Six: The Storm

1. Because flooding was so common in nineteenth-century Louisiana and ground floors became inundated so frequently, most plantation houses near waterways were built atop pilings. Typically, the ground floor was built not to house

people, but to store goods, food, and wine, which could be brought to higher levels in the event of a flood. See Figure 6 of the Laura Plantation for an example.

2. In the nineteenth century, there were various theories about why epidemics happened in New Orleans during the summer. One widespread theory was that the abundant humidity in the air and on the ground could be miasmic. People believed that a miasma in the air caused disease and that a miasma was identifiable by a fetid smell. The word "malaria" originates from *malus* (bad) and *aer* (air) in Latin.

3. Disastrous spring flooding from "crevasses" in the levees was common in Louisiana. A particularly bad one inundated New Orleans in June 1849; it was dubbed "Pierre Sauvé's Crevasse" because the fissure occurred on Sauvé's plantation. Landowners were responsible for the upkeep of the levee on their property. See Campanella, "Long Before Hurricane Katrina." T. B. Thorpe discusses the matter in his essay on the sugar-growing areas of Louisiana: "Throw one too many waves over the levee, or force one drop of water too much through its feeble walls, the barrier dissolves away, and the fountains of the great deep seem to be broken up, as they roll undisputed over the country, carrying terror and ruin, with the cry, '*The crevasse! the crevasse!*'" (755).

4. Winter weather brought a decline in the numbers of mosquitos, the vector for malaria and yellow fever. Consequently, city dwellers went to rural and seaside areas in the summer and fall months because they figured the air there was better, there were fewer people and, thus, there was less likelihood of contracting diseases. "The most deadly diseases to strike Louisiana during the antebellum period were cholera, smallpox, malaria, and yellow fever. In an epidemic year, the mortality rate could reach as high as sixty percent of those who contracted a disease. The death rate in New Orleans ranged from a low of 36 per 1,000 in the late 1820s to a high of 1 in 15 during the summer of 1853. Over 12,000 people died of yellow fever in New Orleans that year, with still more deaths in rural areas in south Louisiana, marking the single highest annual death rate of any state during the entire nineteenth century. Because people died faster than graves could be dug, the popular saying was that, pretty soon, people would have to dig their own graves," notes the Louisiana State Museum's Online Exhibits; see https://www.crt.state.la.us/louisiana-state-museum/online-exhibits/the-cabildo/ antebellum-louisiana-disease-death-and-mourning/index.

5. Perhaps Lebrun refers to the Tunica people, who were frequently guides for the French.

6. While McDermott, in *A Glossary of Mississippi Valley French, 1673–1850*, defines Lebrun's term as "chat-tigre, n.m. Louisiana French for cougar" (49), since that animal has a spotted coat we prefer the primary translation in Valdman and Rottet's *Dictionary of Louisiana French*, which defines *chat sauvage* as a bobcat (125) and *chat-tigre* as an "ocelot, bobcat" (125), while also acknowledging McDermott's earlier term.

7. Thought to be calmer, more surefooted, and better suited than horses to withstand extreme heat, mules remain the preferred work equine in Louisiana.

8. The city's market most likely refers to an area today known as the New Orleans French Market, which was originally a Native American portage from the Mississippi River to Lake Pontchartrain.

9. In this situation, it is telling which member of the group gets or "wants" to walk and who is not obliged to do so. There is a similar scene in Lebrun's tale "Le vieux Noir et le jeune Blanc." As the story opens, before we even know the characters' names, "on vit avancer, monté sur un cheval de petite taille, un jeune homme de dix-sept à dix-huit ans [. . . à] côté de lui marchait un nègre d'une cinquantaine d'années. D'une main, il tirait par la bride un mulet chargé de bagages; de l'autre, il soutenait un vaste parasol au-dessus la tête de l'étranger qu'il accompagnait et que nous présenterons sous le nom d'Octave Blainvilliers" (34) [we could see advancing, mounted on a small horse, a young man of seventeen to eighteen years of age [. . .] beside whom was walking a fifty-something-year-old slave. With one hand, he was pulling by the bridle a mule loaded with baggage; with the other, he was holding up a vast parasol over the head of the foreigner he was accompanying and whom we'll introduce to our readers by the name of Octave Blainvilliers]. This spectacle of a healthy young adolescent being shaded by an elderly enslaved man certainly contributes to the notion of the lazy Creole and also speaks to Lebrun's notion that Europeans arriving in the slaveholding colonies are quickly seduced by the local customs and lifestyle.

Chapter Seven: Through the Forest

1. Lebrun opts for the more neutral term *géreur*, which is more a manager than an overseer, and uses neither *économe* nor *contremaître*, the two designations that usually refer to a plantation overseer in French.

2. While there are plenty of vines in the American South that a person could, in a pinch, cut open for water, the particular one called a "water vine" (*Vitis tiliifolia*) does not seem to be common in Louisiana, although it is widespread in Mexico. There is one reference to its being in Louisiana, however, by Tulane University Professor of Botany R. S. Cocks, under the heading of *vitaceae*, in "A List of the Shrubs of Louisiana," 178. Interestingly, Cocks notes that it would grow in "sandy soil," which is not the soil one would expect in the forest near La Cyprière. See http://botanicus.org/item/31753003541742.

3. The use of ferocious dogs to track runaways was commonplace in the Americas and other slaveholding areas. The dog is an important figure in literature relating to enslaved people, for they were quite familiar with the dogs on a plantation, yet these same animals were used to track and ensnare runaways. Martiniquais and Prix Goncourt-winning author Patrick Chamoiseau's *Le vieil esclave et le molosse* (1998) (translated as *Slave Old Man* in American English and *The Old Man and the Mastiff* in British English editions) depicts a runaway (a maroon) and his complicated relationship with a mastiff-like dog. Bernardin de Saint-Pierre's

hugely popular 1788 novel *Paul et Virginie* also alludes to the hunting of escapees
with dogs on the island of Mauritius.

4. Louisiana regulated the sale and treatment of enslaved people through a set
of laws called the *Code Noir* from 1724 to 1803, with some modifications during
Spanish rule of the colony. While this set of laws authorized the harsh punishment
of enslaved individuals and of recaptured runaways, the *Code Noir* did not allow
the separation of enslaved parents from children who were minors or spousal
separation, but otherwise families, even elderly enslaved family members, could be
separated from one another. Louisiana adopted US laws in 1803, which did allow
for family separation, so Lebrun points out that, among enslaved people, their
friends and family members were subject to painful losses for all. See Code XLIII
at http://french.centenary.edu/codenoir.htm: "Voulons néanmoins que le mari, sa
femme et leurs enfans impubères ne puissent être saisis et vendus séparément, s'ils
sont sous la puissance du même maître : déclarons nulles les saisies et ventes sépa-
rées qui pourroient être faites, ce que nous voulons aussi avoir lieu dans les ventes
volontaires, à peine contre ceux qui seront lesdites ventes, d'être privés de celui ou
de ceux qu'ils auront gardés, qui sont adjugés aux acquéreurs, sans qu'ils soient
tenus de faire aucun supplément de prix." The English translation of this article is
credited as Article XLVII: "Husband, wife and prepubescent children, if they are
all under the same master, may not be taken and sold separately. We declare the
seizing and sales that shall be done as such to be void. For slaves who have been
separated, we desire that the seller shall risk their loss, and that the slaves he kept
shall be awarded to the buyer, without him having to pay any supplement" (http://
chnm.gmu.edu/revolution/d/335/). Whether slaveholders observed the provisions
of this set of laws is quite another matter, as Spear relates concerning the abusive
behavior of one Joseph Chaperon in the 1720s (*Race, Sex, and Social Order in
Early New Orleans*, 52–53). The narrator (or author) in Lebrun's "Le vieux Noir et le
jeune Blanc" seems rather naïve in asserting that, in Martinique, "il était très-rare,
disons-nous, que les tribunaux eussent à sévir contre un abus de pouvoir" (39) [it
was very rare, we say, that the courts had to take action against an abuse of power].

5. In the original French, Lebrun first refers to the alligator as a "crocodile"
(156). The latter word is commonly used in modern American English, however,
to distinguish the North American members of the subfamily of *Alligatorinae*
from the crocodilians (order of reptiles) of the subfamily of *Crocodylinae*, a coastal
species of which appears in the southern tip of Florida. Later, Lebrun uses the
word *caimans*, which in English refers to the alligator-like crocodilians native to
Central and South America. In French, the word *reptile* is not as limited as it is
in common modern American English and means any creature that crawls on its
belly. Note the definition from Bescherelle's *Dictionnaire classique et élémentaire
de la langue française*, which was contemporary with the publication of Lebrun's
novel: "Reptile. adj. et s. m. animal rampant qui se traîne sur le ventre" (270). In
Louisiana, French speakers use *alligateur/alligator, caiman,* and *cocodrie* to refer to
alligators. See Valdman and Rottet, *Dictionary of Louisiana French*, 22, 100, 140–41.
C. C. Robin also remarked upon the presence of alligators and other reptiles in

this area, noting: "Ces eaux dormantes et livides fourmillent de reptiles, surtout de crocodiles" (2:62) [these still, pallid waters are teeming with reptiles, especially alligators].

6. Francis underscores the shifting nature of the area's alluvial land, known as the Mississippi alluvial plain. Were it not for the ubiquitous levees along the waterways nowadays, the seasonal flooding of the Mississippi River and its tributaries would constantly rearrange and renew the sinking land.

7. It is not clear to us which tree exactly Lebrun means when she refers to *ébéniers* (161). The only ebony tree in the United States is the persimmon tree (*diospyros virginiana*). The Texas ebony is not native to that area.

8. Opossums are native to the Americas and do not typically emerge before nightfall. In Caribbean French, the opossum is known as a *manicou*, whereas, in Louisiana French, the name is *rat de bois* (woods rat). Le Page du Pratz mentions this creature (2:94–97) and includes an image of this animal and others, which can been seen at the website https://jcb.lunaimaging.com/luna/servlet/detail/ JCB~1~1~947~115902676:Chat-Suavage--Rat-de-Bois--B%C3%AAte-pua. Pratz mentions that the flesh of this creature is "d'un très-bon gout" (96) [of a very good taste]. See also Valdman and Rottet, *Dictionary of Louisiana French*, 524.

9. Gumbo filé or simply filé is a powder made from sassafras leaves (*Sassafras albidum*), but, as Lebrun notes, the sassafras roots and bark also have medicinal and culinary uses, including flavoring and thickening of soups, especially gumbo, the signature soup of Louisiana cooking. The term "Gumbo file" has several conflicting etymologies—one is that gumbo may have derived its name from the Choctaw word for filé powder: kombo. Another explanation is that the soup's name (gumbo) derives from *gombo* meaning okra in various Bantu (Central African) languages. Okra is a major ingredient and thickening agent in some kinds of gumbo (the soup); typically, however, okra gumbo is neither cooked nor eaten with filé powder. Finally, *fil* in French means string or thread, and filé powder makes the gumbo (the dish) thicker, hence able to hold together in thick or glutinous threads (as explained to RW by Houma Indian Jamie Luster, personal interview, April 2019).

10. We can currently find no source saying that this tree (*Ceiba pentandra*), although common to the tropics of the Americas and the Caribbean, grows in Louisiana. It is also known as the kapok. Lebrun proposes that one of its names in French, *gossampin*, derives from the fact that the tree resembles a pine tree, which is not true.

11. While Lebrun is not very specific here, we believe she is referring to swamp red maples and eastern red cedars.

12. According to the online dictionary maintained by the Oxford University Press, "ajoupa" is a word adopted into English from French and used in the Caribbean for structures much like Lebrun describes. See https://en.oxforddictionaries .com/definition/ajoupa.

13. In addition to the experience of the ill-fated French lady's maid after her flight from the Hôtel de l'Europe, this is one of the few instances in the novel where the characters are explicitly said to be speaking English to one another.

14. The five species of prairie dogs were once classed in the genus of *Spermophilus*, which includes forty species of ground squirrels, but are now classed under the genus *Cynomys*, both genera being in the tribe of *Marmotini*.

15. The Louisiana heron (*Ardea ludoviciana*) is partially brown, but its plumage is mostly blue.

16. The reddish egret (*Egretta rufescens*) is found along the Gulf Coast, the Caribbean, and Central America.

17. Lebrun accurately calls it a *cheval du diable*, a term that should not be confused with the similar French Canadian expression for a variety of mantis. See the definition for "grasshopper" in Valdman and Rottet, 130.

18. While skunks and stoats do live in large swaths of North America, martens are not considered to range as far south as Louisiana, unless they once did formerly and were hunted to extinction in the southern reaches of the continent. Although Lebrun uses the word *putois* in her text, the usual word for skunk in Louisiana French is *bête puante* (stinking beast); see Valdman and Rottet, 71.

19. According to McDermott's *Glossary*, Lebrun's choice of the word *Congo* in the original text (176) is accurate insofar as it is the Louisiana French "name for the water or cotton-mouth moccasin" (55). See also the third entry for the same word in Valdman and Rottet, 151.

20. While Native Americans would clearly have needed to devise treatments for bites from widely common venomous snakes like coral snakes, moccasins, copperheads, and rattlesnakes, North American constrictors (Lebrun specifically refers to "boas," 177) are not venomous, although a bite from one could certainly become infected. As in modern-day Florida's Everglades, there have been invasive species like boa constrictors in Louisiana; see https://www.nola.com/environment/index.ssf/2016/10/9-foot_boa_constrictor_killed.html. The Frenchman Albert Calmette, who was also instrumental in the development of a tuberculosis vaccine, did not invent modern antivenins until 1896. The entry on rattlesnakes titled "BOICINGA, ou SERPENT A SONNETTE" in volume one of La Chesnaye-Desbois's *Dictionnaire raisonné et universel des animaux* (1:312) describes different remedies for serpents in the *Amériques*, including the use of the animal itself as cure. Snakebite is also a plot point in Lebrun's tale "Le vieux Noir et le jeune Blanc." Octave is bitten on the heel by a fer-de-lance, Martinique's endemic venomous snake, which Lebrun compares to Louisiana's moccasin (82). Octave is saved by the herbal knowledge of Maga, the aged mother of Timothée, the *vieux noir* of the story's title.

Chapter Eight: The Cyprière

1. The bald cypress (*Taxodium distichum*)—Louisiana's state tree—is remarkable for its nondecaying nature, an attribute noted early on by Europeans. Pratz, for instance, describes "cœurs de Cyprès" [cypress heartwood] as "incorruptibles"

(3:16). On the bottom of the Gulf of Mexico, near the coast of Alabama, two hundred miles from New Orleans, the remains of a sixty-thousand-year-old cypress forest were discovered in 2004. The ancient forest's submerged wood has not decayed. Ben Raines's *The Underworld Forest* (2018) documents the millennia-old cypress wood's extraordinary durability; see https://www.nola.com/environment/2018/02/underwater_forest_in_the_gulf.html.

2. This plant is also known as the wild passion vine or purple passionflower, names rendered in French as *grenadille*. C. C. Robin describes it as "une jolie espèce de *grenadille*, fleur de la passion, plante vivace qui couvre et pare les buissons" (3:518) [a pretty example of *Passifloraceae*, or passionflower, a perennial plant that covers and adorns bushes].

3. While very common around the world, oleander is a poisonous plant. There is one legend from the Myrtles Plantation in St. Francisville, Louisiana, in which Chloe, an enslaved girl, in an ill-considered attempt to win back the affections of her abusive owner, Judge Clark Woodruff, baked a dessert laced with oleander, which resulted in the deaths of the judge's wife and two daughters. Chloe's fellow enslaved persons, fearing retribution, purportedly hanged Chloe and threw her body into the Mississippi. "Other sources, however, indicate Sarah and her children died of yellow fever," reports Maria Carter in an article dated October 11, 2017, appearing in the online version of the popular magazine *Country Living*. On a tour of the Myrtles Plantation that EJJ took on August 31, 2019, the guide recounted that, for the offense of repeated eavesdropping, the judge sliced off Chloe's ear before banishing her from the big house for the misery of work in the kitchens.

4. Cacti are not common in modern-day Louisiana, outside of saline prairies in the northwestern tip of the state and in Webb Parish, although Cyprière-like plantations could certainly have had this and other imported plants for ornamental purposes.

5. In this era in the South, it was common for kitchens of the well-to-do to be in a separate structure adjacent to the main living area, so as to avoid needlessly heating the home or risking fires.

6. While it is tempting to think of Madame Launay's glasses as an early kind of sunglasses, the intent of such eyewear was not to protect eyes from sunlight. It was thought, rather, that the tints would protect eyes from fatigue or would help to conserve failing sight.

7. Lebrun seems to be describing the red and green macaw. Also known as the green-winged macaw, it is native to northern and central South America.

8. Excepting tropical areas of Mexico, monkeys are not native to North America, but people in the Americas and Europe did keep them and other exotic animals as pets, especially as global maritime travel increased in the seventeenth and eighteenth centuries and sailors brought home various animals as curiosities. Madame Launay's possession of them speaks to her wealth, however, for she possesses pets that serve no practical purpose on a farm, as a dog or cat might. As David Diop explains, there is a history of European travel writers linking the

domestication of monkeys with the same processes used to transform entrapped Africans into slaves. Creating an equivalence of the words *"singe"* [monkey] and *"nègre,"* a racialized term also meant to convey "slave," this process relied upon anthropomorphizing the animal, while dehumanizing the human. As we see, Madame Launay does use food and bonds to control her pets. Her possession of them echoes in her use of slaves for especially frivolous tasks, which Mr. Melvil will explain as being due to an exaggerated sense of pride on the part of white women of the land. For further discussion on the trope of the "lazy Creole," see chapter 1, endnote 5.

9. It is of note that Madame Launay voices a manifestation of white supremacy based on the biracial hierarchy dominant in contemporary South Carolina, which clashes with the triracial culture of Louisiana. From her perspective, people are either purely white or of color, whereas Louisiana culture of the era, according to Lebrun, posits white, mulatto, and Black, all the while policing those distinctions and maintaining white supremacy.

10. The trustworthy manager also figures in Lebrun's story "Le vieux Noir et le jeune Blanc." Young Octave Blainvilliers can afford to do a sort of plantation-owner internship with his guardian M. Fabre in the town of Carbet because there is a trustworthy *gérant* at Octave's plantation near the town of Macouba (35–36).

11. It is interesting and perhaps telling that Madame Launay chooses to use the archaic word "colony" for one of the original thirteen states.

12. Madame Launay uses the then-dated word *conserves* to describe her glasses, which were meant to protect her vision, not to shade her eyes. Thus, "preservers" is indicated as the third translation for the word *conserve* in Thunot and Clifton's *Nouveau dictionnaire anglais-français et français-anglais*, 90. In a definition dating back to the 1694 edition of their dictionary, the sixth edition (1832–1835) of the Académie Française's dictionary defines the word thus: "CONSERVES au pluriel, se dit d'une sorte de lunettes qui grossissent peu les objets, et qui conservent la vue. *Il se sert de conserves. Il met des conserves. Il prit ses conserves*" (374; emphasis in original) [Preservers, plural, said of a kind of glasses that magnify objects very little and which preserve sight. *He makes use of preservers. He put on his preservers. He took his preservers*].

13. Iago is the villainous character jealous of the Moor Othello in Shakespeare's play, so it appears to be an overdetermined name referencing the color prejudice and bitter mindset of the bird Iago's owner, Madame Launay. We would like to thank Eduardo Febles for this insight in his presentation, "The Construction of Racial Identities in Camille Lebrun's *Amitié et dévouement ou Trois mois à la Louisiane,"* on November 2, 2018, at the biennial conference of the American Society of Quebec Studies in New Orleans.

14. Lebrun would reuse this idea about the indolence of Creole women. In her previously mentioned article in *Le Miroir de la France,* she notes: "La vie, aux îles, puise son plus grand charme dans une nonchalance qui n'est peut-être pas tant une conséquence du climat que le résultat de l'introduction de l'esclavage dans les mœurs européennes. La créole, habituée dès son enfance à être entourée de

négresses, elles-mêmes si peu actives qu'il en faut au moins six pour faire le travail d'une femme de chambre française, la créole ne comprend pas comment une femme libre, une blanche, peut se donner volontairement la fatigue de ramasser le mouchoir tombé de ses mains à terre" (294) [Life, in the islands, draws its greatest charm in an indolence that is, perhaps, not so much the consequence of the climate as the result of the introduction of slavery into European mores. The Creole woman—accustomed from her childhood to being surrounded by slave-women, themselves so little active that at least six of them are necessary to do the work of one French maid—doesn't understand how a free woman, a white woman, can voluntarily go to the trouble of picking up a kerchief fallen from her hands to the ground]. Similarly, in her tale "Le vieux Noir et le jeune Blanc," we see a description of the ailing Mme Fabre reclining on a chaise longue, surrounded by a half-dozen enslaved women fanning her and slowly doing needlework.

15. Candies, preserves, and other sugar-based foods figure prominently in Caribbean and Louisiana cuisine and are reflective of the sugarcane cultivation the novel describes. A recipe for *fleur d'oranger praline* [orange blossom praline] is available in the nineteenth-century *Cookery for English Households. By a French Lady* (London: Macmillan and Co., 1864), 252.

16. In the purgery, the cooled, crystalized sugar was put in hogsheads and drained of molasses (Thorpe 763).

17. The word Lebrun employs for pulp, *bagasse* or *bégasse*, is the kind of dry pulpy residue left after the extraction of juice from sugarcane. Louisianans in sugar-producing regions continue to refer to the pulp as *bagasse*.

18. For the names of the various sugar-production buildings and the rooms in the "sugarhouse," we used the expressions as listed in T. B. Thorpe's account concerning the production of sugar in Louisiana (759–63).

19. In the original French, Lebrun uses this word of local color that is also possible in British English. *Macouba* is a snuff scented with attar of roses. The word is derived from the name of a tobacco-growing town in northern Martinique, a connection that reminds the reader of both the origins of the mother of Francis and Hortense and the long-existing trade networks in the Caribbean and the Gulf of Mexico, which would bring such goods to wealthy Louisianans.

20. Perhaps Lebrun is recalling to readers the inherent contradiction regarding Madame Launay's Creole nature as she indulges in native products—tobacco and sassafras—both of which were introduced to Europeans through colonization of the Americas. Macouba is the variety of tobacco cultivated at the Martiniquais plantation belonging to Octave Blainvilliers in Lebrun's tale "Le vieux Noir et le jeune Blanc."

Chapter Nine: A Summer Evening

1. There are several Saint Paul Catholic churches in contemporary Louisiana, but none predate the twentieth century except Saint Paul the Apostle on 1879

L'Eglise Street in the town of Mansura, which was established in 1796, about thirty miles from the younger city of Alexandria, on the Red River in Rapides Parish. Mansura is in Avoyelles Parish, named for the Avoyel Native Americans, and is well known for its French and Native American heritages. Today the Tunica–Biloxi people are one of four federally recognized tribes in Louisiana (the three others are the Chitimacha, the Jena Band of Choctaw, and the Coushatta). The Tunica–Biloxi Tribe has a reservation in Avoyelles Parish. Although probably an imaginary plantation, the Cyprière could have been located in or around Avoyelles Parish.

2. "Piney Woods" is the forest descriptor for most of northern and central Louisiana, where the Red River and Avoyelles Parish are located. See https://www.nfwf.org/whoweare/mediacenter/feature/Pages/Conserving-Forests.aspx.

3. The mockingbird's call has been compared to a traditional trumpet riff in Louisiana. While Abrams and Reckdahl's article "Which Came First: The Mockingbird or the Musician?" claims the trumpet imitation of the mockingbird dates from the late 1800s, "It probably started amongst the older musicians when brass band music was in its beginnings in the late 1800s," muses [trumpeter Leroy] Jones. "It's something that's been passed down for generations among the brass bands."

4. As early as 1700, the Jesuit writer Paul de Ru notes, during his voyage with Bienville, the existence of a community of runaways,: "On a appris dans tous les villages qu'un grand nombre de nègres et de mulâtres avaient déserté et s'étaient établis dans un canton séparé où ils persistent dans leur révolte" [We learned in all the villages that a great number of blacks and mulattos had run away and had established themselves in a separate community where they persist in their revolt]; quoted in Villiers, "Extrait d'un journal," 134. Marronage was common all over the Americas and wherever else there was chattel slavery. *The Freedom on the Move* database of fugitives from North American slavery lists 202,525 advertisements for runaways. See https://freedomonthemove.org/#about.

5. Like many other contemporary French writers attempting to portray local patois of French, Lebrun depicts the runaway as using a nonstandard French that evokes Creole versions of the language, here using *moi* as the subject of the sentence rather than *je*. This translation attempts to convey the same effect in English.

6. Lebrun mistakenly calls the "luciole," or firefly, a *hymenopteran*, which is not the correct order, for insects in that order are typically stinging insects (ants, wasps, and bees, for instance). Fireflies belong to the *coleopteran* order, that of beetles.

Chapter Ten: A Party

1. Lebrun opts to describe this plantation as "a" cotton farm, with the conceit that the plantation's name would be the same thing in French, i.e., "the" or *la Cotonnerie*. Henceforth, we will use the term as the place's name.

2. According to Félice's *Encyclopédie, ou Dictionnaire raisonné des connoissances humaines*, "Nœud d'épaule, en terme de *Marchand de modes*, est une

aiguillette de plusieurs doubles de rubans ou d'argent, & même de soie, à chaque bout inférieur desquels on attache des pentes, *v.* PENTES. Les autres, assemblés l'un sur l'autre, se plissent le plus près qu'il est possible, se percent d'une boutonnière, ou se cousent à l'habit" (30:425) [A shoulder knot, according to the *Marchand de modes*, is a double aiglet or double ribbons in silver or even silk, on each end of which one attaches metal tips; see "pentes." The others, assembled one on top of the other, fold as close as possible, and can be pierced in a buttonhole, or sewn on the suit].

3. The junction of the Red River and the Mississippi is in Avoyelles Parish, slightly north of a small town named Simmesport. "Historically, the Red River joined the Mississippi here [fifty miles south of Natchez] while the Atchafalaya flowed out of the system as a distributary to the Gulf of Mexico. In the 1830s, Louisianans, in the interest of navigation, manipulated this hydrology by excavating shortcuts, clearing logjams and dredging shoals. In doing so, they inadvertently allowed a steadily increasing flow of the Mississippi in the 1870s," notes Campanella's *Bienville's Dilemma*, 87.

Chapter Eleven: A Fire

1. All the editions of the original in our possession indicate Madame Launay is asking a question here. We are convinced that this is, in fact, a statement because she doesn't say "wouldn't she." The original text is as follows: "Mon Dieu, non! répondit madame Launay. Autrement, aurait-elle soupçonné Maurice à qui elle reproche, non sans raison, d'encourager le marronnage en protégeant les déserteurs, d'avoir donné asile aux deux noirs que je viens de nommer?" (245).

2. Here as earlier with a child speaking in chapter 2 (see endnote 12) and with the two runaways, Lebrun depicts these characters speaking a French patois in which they do not conjugate their verbs, although she spells the words themselves in standard French. The translation here means only to convey a similar feeling in English.

3. As with the "Cotonnerie," Lebrun here uses the name of the plantation's major agricultural product as its name. We could translate "*Sucrerie*" as "Sugarhouse" but also as "Sugar Plantation."

4. In the 1780s and 1790s, most of New Orleans, which consisted almost entirely of what we now know as the French Quarter, burned. According to Ned Hémard's "Up on the *Azotea*," the fire "destroyed much of the original French architecture. The colony's new Spanish overlords required strict new fire codes." Colonial Spanish building codes included using fireproof roofing such as slate or tile, but most probably these codes were not enforceable in the entire colony and on far-flung plantations. Even throughout the twentieth century and thus far in the twenty-first, various antebellum plantation homes have suffered serious fires, such as the extraordinary Le Petit Versailles built by Valcour Aimé in 1839

in St. James Parish, of which nothing remains from a 1920 fire. Tezcuco, built in 1855 by the prominent Jewish planter Benjamin Tureaud, burned to the ground in Ascension Parish in 2002. The Laura Plantation (built in 1805 in St. James Parish) suffered a fire that destroyed its back wings in 2004. The LeBeau Plantation (1855), just south of New Orleans, was consumed by fire in 2013.

Chapter Twelve: The Departure

1. In *White by Definition: Social Classification in Creole Louisiana* (1986), sociologist Virginia Domínguez documents instances of Louisianans attempting to "pass" as white and disavowing their African heritage. Some families kept it a secret that they had African heritage and were, therefore, "of color" or "black" according to legal documents, such as birth certificates. In *Doe v. State*, Department of Health and Human Resources (1985), a family sought to change its family members' birth certificates' racial designation from "colored" to "white." The plaintiffs lost, and the court states: "Accordingly, we hold that the defendant state officers have no legal duty to alter the birth certificates [from 'colored' to 'white']"; see https://www.leagle.com/decision/1985848479s02d3692774. Conversely, many Creoles of color who did pass as white chose to fight for racial equality. The most famous instance is that of the case of Homer Plessy (1862–1925), who staged a civil rights fight with the backing of the Citizens' Committee (also known as the *Comité des Citoyens*). In 1892, the Citizens' Committee told the train company that Plessy, a fair-skinned Black man, would be sitting in the white section of a train car, and Plessy was arrested. The case went to the Supreme Court in 1896, and *Plessy v. Ferguson* upheld the doctrine of "separate but equal" for more than a half-century in the US.

2. *Les Sœurs de la Miséricorde* or Misericordia Sisters still operate in Québec. They were founded in Montreal on January 16, 1848, by Bishop Ignace Bourget and Rosalie Cadron-Jetté. Their mission is to care for unwed mothers and children. Lebrun may have confused the Quebec *Sœurs de la Miséricorde* with the sisters in Louisiana who were called the *Sœurs* or *Filles de la Charité* [Sisters or Daughters of Charity]. Vincent de Paul founded the Louisiana order in the seventeenth century to serve the sick and poor. Charity Hospital, *L'Hôpital des Pauvres de la Charité*, was founded in 1736 in New Orleans, and the *Sœurs de la Charité* [Charity Sisters] took over its administration in the early nineteenth century. *Miséricorde* means "mercy" in English, and there is an order of religious women in New Orleans called Sisters of Mercy; however, they are not related to the Misericordia Sisters of Québec. Founded in Ireland, the order of the Sisters of Mercy ministered to the Irish in New Orleans. See http://www.centrerosaliecadronjette.org/wp/?portfolio=misericordia-sisters-2&lang=en and chapter 4, note 1 of this volume for more on the Daughters of Charity.

3. Sisters of Charity take nonreligious vows, "which are distinct from the vows of religious" (5). They devote their lives to God and to charity, understood

as serving the poor. See https://via.library.depaul.edu/cgi/viewcontent.cgi?referer=https://www.google.com/&httpsredir=1&article=2900&context=vincentiana.

4. Born in France in 1782 and consecrated as the fourth bishop of New Orleans on November 22, 1835, Bishop Antoine Blanc died in office in 1860. The Archdiocese of New Orleans did not have a native-born American archbishop until 1918, with the ordination of John William Shaw (1863–1934). See https://www.stlouiscathedral.org/about/our-history/bishops-of-archdiocese.

ABOUT THE AUTHOR

Camille Lebrun (1805–1886), the preferred *nom de plume* of Pauline Guyot, was a French writer of novels, short stories, educational books, translated works, and numerous articles. Some of her works ran to multiple editions and appeared in publication until the end of the nineteenth century.

ABOUT THE TRANSLATORS

A native of north-central Florida, **E. Joe Johnson** is professor of foreign languages at Clayton State University in metropolitan Atlanta and is the general editor of *XVIII New Perspectives on the Eighteenth Century*, the annual journal of the Southeastern American Society for Eighteenth-Century Studies. Along with many translations of French comic books and graphic novels including *Asterix* and *The Smurfs*, he has produced classroom editions of eighteenth-century French classics, coedited two volumes of essays, published on the matter of idealized friendship in *ancien régime* French literature, and is presently working on a monograph concerning the depiction of friendship in French children's literature prior to the Great War.

Robin Anita White has lived since 1996 in Louisiana, where she is associate professor of French and English at Nicholls State University in Thibodaux and resides in New Orleans. Early in her scholarly pursuits, Robin White focused on travelogues and exoticism in French colonial contexts, which led to her research on Francophone literature relating to Louisiana. The editor of a classroom edition of Chateaubriand's classic novella *Atala*, she is currently researching Louisiana literature and race in nineteenth-century Louisiana.

CPSIA information can be obtained
at www.ICGtesting.com
Printed in the USA
BVHW031752290721
612364BV00006B/13